PRAISE FOR
AT THE
SPEED of LIES

"With a sharp, compelling main character and an equally compelling mystery, *At the Speed of Lies* is a perfect—and timely—thriller."
—KIERSTEN WHITE, #1 *New York Times* **bestselling author of** *Hide*

"*At the Speed of Lies* takes readers on a gripping, suspenseful ride through the fever swamp of online conspiracies and their real-life consequences. It is truly a book for our time."
—SARAH DARER LITTMAN, author of *Some Kind of Hate*

"Starring a fierce wheelchair user who uncovers conspiracy theories and takes down ableist bullies, *At the Speed of Lies* is a page-turning thriller of a debut novel."
—LILLIE LAINOFF, author of *One for All*

"Timely and gripping, Cindy L. Otis's fiction debut is a thought-provoking commentary on the far-reaching consequences of conspiracy theories. Readers are sure to devour this smart and captivating thriller."
—EMILY LLOYD-JONES, international bestselling author of *The Drowned Woods*

"*At the Speed of Lies* is an intense read, giving a chilling glimpse into the world of how conspiracies and disinformation spread. A compelling and timely debut."
—CINDY PON, author of *Want*

"Cindy L. Otis weaves a disturbing cautionary tale with expert precision. This book should be required reading for everyone."
—JENNIFER MOFFETT, author of *Those Who Prey*

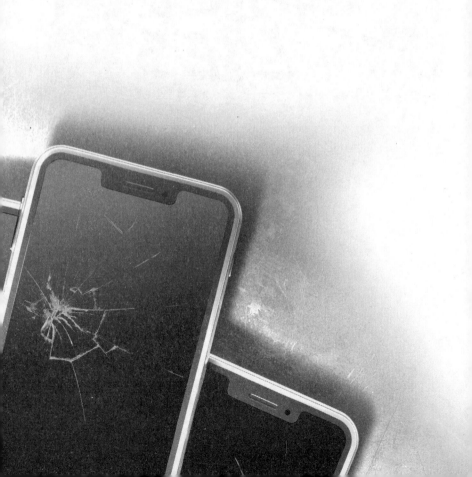

CINDY L. OTIS

Scholastic Press / New York

Library of Congress Cataloging-in-Publication Data

Names: Otis, Cindy L., author.
Title: At the speed of lies / Cindy L. Otis.
Description: First edition. | New York : Scholastic Press, 2023. | Audience: Ages 12 and up. | Audience: Grades 10-12. | Summary: High school junior Quinn Calvet gets caught up in the disappearance of kids in a nearby town, soon beginning to suspect more to the story than anyone understands, and it is up to her to figure out what's going on.
Identifiers: LCCN 2022048697 | ISBN 9781338806762 (hardback) | ISBN 9781338806779 (ebook)
Subjects: LCSH: Teenagers with disabilities—Juvenile fiction. | Missing children—Juvenile fiction. | Conspiracies—Juvenile fiction. | Fake news—Juvenile fiction. | Social media—Juvenile fiction. | High school student activities—Juvenile fiction. | High schools—New York (State)—Juvenile fiction. | New York (State)—Juvenile fiction. | Detective and mystery stories. | CYAC: Mystery and detective stories. | People with disabilities—Fiction. | Missing children—Fiction. | Conspiracies—Fiction. | Social media—Fiction. | High schools—Fiction. | Schools—Fiction. | BISAC: YOUNG ADULT FICTION / Thrillers & Suspense / General | YOUNG ADULT FICTION / Disabilities & Special Needs | LCGFT: Thrillers (Fiction) | Detective and mystery fiction.
Classification: LCC PZ7.1.O876 At 2023 | DDC 813.6 [Fic]—dc23/eng/20221114

10 9 8 7 6 5 4 3 2 1   23 24 25 26 27

Printed in Italy   183
First edition, June 2023
Book design by Cassy Price
Stock photo © Shutterstock.com

To those feeling left behind: There's no one destination, path, or timeline. This is for you.

chapter one

At least a dozen times a day, social media presents me with the chance to be a really terrible person, if I want to be. That's the thought that hits me at the boys' cross-country tryouts as I scroll through the pictures I just took and discover a series capturing the exact moment Michael Lai's shoelaces came undone, tripping him. Followed by the brutal few seconds after, when the four runners around him all collided and then landed in a giant tangled heap of arms and legs in the middle of the track.

As one of the fallen runners limps off the track, I flip through the pictures again before opening my Instagram account, The Whine. I could post the one of Michael Lai's humiliation that enabled junior Asher King's distant, *distant* third-place finish simply because he managed to avoid the pileup. Like, the-winner-and-the-runner-up-were-already-at-the-water-stand-when-he-finished distant third.

I finally settle on a few less dramatic ones of runners crossing the finish line from the accident-free previous heats, even though the pictures of the collision are pretty epic.

I stare at my screen for a minute before the right caption comes to me. Then my fingers fly as I tag the new boys' cross-country team. I look up from my phone to find Asher collapsed near me, guzzling water from a silver bottle and trying to ignore the argument two runners tripped by the errant shoelaces are having with Coach

1

Swensen, who's making notes on his clipboard with a frown. It's obvious to anyone watching that the results from the last heat were not what he wanted for his new team.

Even though Asher and I have chemistry together and are in the same grade, we've never spoken before, but somehow I find myself saying "Congrats" to him after I've hit post.

Maybe it's the embarrassed hunching of his shoulders or my love for a good underdog story that makes me say it. But Asher really is only an underdog when it comes to cross-country, because his parents own King Country Vineyards, a massive empire of vineyards, wineries, and tasting rooms across half of western New York. At least a third of the kids at school's parents work for the Kings in some way.

Asher turns toward me, looking a little dazed, his normally pale skin flushed red. "Thanks. I can't believe I'm on the team." He grins more widely than I would expect from a guy who only made the team because of an accident.

Coach Swensen blows his whistle in three long blasts to try to clear the field, but the runners who fell won't budge. Asher gets to his feet, suddenly becoming double my height, and sways a little.

"How long have you been running?" I ask.

Because of The Whine and my 3,272 followers (and counting), I make it my business to know everything, and I'm almost completely sure Asher wasn't on the team last year. Plus, his performance today screams *newbie.*

By the watercooler, one of the assistant coaches has joined in the argument over the fall and their voices get uncomfortably loud. If it turns into an actual fight, I may have to rethink my plan to take the high road for my post on The Whine, but I kind of can't tear my gaze away from Asher King.

Asher's brown eyes flick to the scene and then back at me. "As long as I can remember. I mean, if you're not running, what are you even doing with your life?"

He chuckles like we're sharing some kind of inside joke, but then he looks down at me, in my wheelchair, and his smile crumbles.

His face was already red from the race, but it goes positively scarlet. "Uh, crap, I mean . . . there are plenty of other things people can do with their lives that I'm sure are, uh, very satisfying and . . . Oh god, I didn't mean it . . ."

I can feel my jaw tighten and my shoulders rise defensively. "No worries. I'll see you later."

When I turn around, my best friend, Ximena, is on the other side of the chain-link fence waiting for me. Thank god.

"Quuuu," Ximena calls through cupped hands like an announcer yelling "goaaaaaal" during one of those soccer games her brothers always have loudly playing in the living room at her house.

"Be honest," I say when I'm near enough. "Are you here for me or just trying to scope out all the guys in itty-bitty shorts?"

"Duh, the guys in the shorts, *obviously.*" She grins.

"Creeper."

"Don't tell Max. That's something my boyfriend should have to learn on his own."

"It's adorable that you think he isn't already fully aware of that fact."

She laughs and opens the fence gate wide for me so I can come through. "Not gonna lie. When you texted you were coming to tryouts before the fair, I thought someone had hacked into your phone and was playing a prank," she says, assuming my nearness to anything sports-related is the reason for my sour mood. And normally it'd be a good guess. I'm out of place among people who think running until you can't feel your legs anymore is a fun way to spend time.

I shrug. "One of my followers kept complaining that I never covered sports stuff. They had a point, I guess. The Whine is supposed to be about all the happenings in the area. And in Canandaigua, this is basically the only thing that's happening right now."

"That may be the most depressing thing you've ever said to me. Thank god we'll be living in New York City soon." Ximena's whole face brightens at the mention of our after-graduation plans.

"Soon? We're only a month into our junior year, so we've got another—" My face scrunches as my brain tries unsuccessfully to do the math. "I don't know, many hundreds of days, and we still have to actually convince a school to let us in."

"Now, Quinnifred," Ximena says in a dramatic voice, using her nickname for me when she thinks I'm being overly pessimistic about something. "Okay, true or false: Are track uniforms the most awkward sports attire of any sport played ever?"

"Definitely true. There was far too much dude leg hair on display back there. And I practically broke my neck talking to Asher King to avoid looking at those tiny shorts."

Ximena howls with laughter. After five years of being in a wheelchair full-time, I've learned to look down a lot. Otherwise, my life would be full of nothing but butts and crotches, which is tricky when people are standing right in front of me. That's why I have bangs.

They're not just normal bangs. When deployed properly, the mahogany fringe of hair across my forehead acts as magical blinders against potentially permanent mentally scarring images.

The parking lot is still mostly packed with cars as we cross it. It looks like most of the school stayed behind to go to the annual club fair, where the school's clubs try to attract new members.

"So, what's Asher like?" Ximena asks.

"I don't know. Sweaty."

"Sure, but also kind of cute, right? He's so quiet at school, I don't think I've ever heard him say more than a sentence or two."

"He said plenty back there. Trust me."

His words are still circling in my head like a swarm of angry hornets and Ximena is eyeing me curiously, so I tell her what he said.

"Oh my god." Ximena's lips pucker in annoyance. "I have my answer. The prince of the FLX is cute, sweaty, *and* a total idiot."

"I mean, he seemed appropriately horrified when he realized what he'd said and everything. So . . . there's that, I guess."

"But it was a completely clueless thing for him to say. I hope you're not letting it get to you. Like, clearly running is ridiculous and he's in denial."

5

I crack a smile. Ximena and I have been best friends since fourth grade, so I know she's been running with Max at least three days a week since they got together.

I can feel her brown eyes staring at me, waiting for me to respond, so I shrug. "I'm fine."

It's not that I haven't gotten those kinds of comments and worse before. In fact, I get them all the time. People tell me on the regular that their life would be over if they had to use a wheelchair like I do, or that they don't know how I get up in the morning. They don't ever seem to realize they're basically telling me to kill myself.

Sometimes I imagine I'm encased in bulletproof glass. Somehow just picturing a protective box around me makes all those thoughtless comments sting less.

But I can feel Asher's words chipping away at my box, spreading cracks across it like a spiderweb because in those few words he basically said my life has no value because I live it sitting down. The sound of Ximena's phone announcing a text interrupts my thoughts.

"Max says the fair's already started."

Ximena and I take the long, circuitous route to the gym with the one accessible entrance to our ancient two-story brick school—around the back, next to the dumpster, and about a million miles away from the accessible parking spaces in the front. It annoys me more than usual today, the whole making-accessibility-as-inconvenient-as-possible-for-the-disabled-person thing, when I'm still stinging from Asher King's words. But the feelings get sucked up by the noise of the gym that hits us as soon as Ximena opens the heavy door.

A sea of students move up and down rows of tables, each one hosted by a different school club, under the bright fluorescent lights. Ximena's eyes immediately scan the room, hunting for Max. She stands on her tiptoes to see over the crowd and squeals, like she didn't just see him at lunch.

"Max is at the student council table helping Adrian. Let's go say hi."

Even though Max is a linebacker on the Tigers football team and therefore approximately three times my size, I still can't see him or Adrian's much smaller frame in the thick crowd. I shudder inside at the thought of trying to push my way through so many bodies. Even magic bangs are no match for a packed high school gym.

"Go ahead. I'll be there in a minute. I want to take some pictures for my next post first."

I pull out my phone and make like I'm going to snap some pictures, but stow it back under my leg once Ximena jogs away in the direction of Max. I push lazily against my wheels, angling myself along the edge of the worst of the crowd, letting my eyes skim over the colorful posters each club has taped to their tables.

I spot my sister's rainbow Love Is Love patch on the back of her purple backpack, almost as bright as the purple streaks in her hair, as she lingers at the Model UN table, where she's the lone visitor at the farthest end of the gym. As I near, she bends over a clipboard and signs her name in her looping scrawl.

"See you Tuesday, Ava," Bryce Marks, a senior, says. She smiles widely at my sister from under a black beret, behind the table. "We're going to have so much fun."

"What's a future biochemist need Model UN for?" I ask.

"It can only help to show colleges I'm well-rounded." Ava hands the clipboard back to Bryce and tucks her shoulder-length hair behind her ear.

"Oh, I see." I pick up a blue bound booklet from the table with the title "Model UN: A Guide to Parliamentary Procedure and Negotiation." "Well, maybe I can grab a few pictures for The Whine of you and Bryce discussing this fascinating tome."

Ava rolls her eyes. "That's a no."

"There's really nothing to it," Bryce says. "Parliamentary procedure is actually a blast once you get the hang of it."

"I'm sure." I struggle to hold back a laugh. Even though I don't actually know what parliamentary procedure is exactly, I feel pretty confident that it's not a blast.

"See you Tuesday," Ava says.

Ava and I turn toward the crowd. "I think the only club left you haven't officially joined is Chess Club," I say.

"Ooh, Chess Club."

Ava doesn't just have wide interests. She's naturally good at anything she tries. After a month of being in chorus, she got cast as Cinderella in last year's production of *Into the Woods*.

She glances around the gym but then nods at the empty space beside me. "Where's Ximena?"

"One guess."

"They're really cute together," Ava says in that pushy-big-sister tone she gets from thinking the eleven-and-a-half-month lead she has on me in age means she always knows best.

"I'm not saying they're not."

It's not that I don't like Max. He's actually really cool. But it's like Ximena grew an internal compass when they started officially going out at the end of last year, and it's forever pointing to him. So when we're together, it's like she's killing time until she's with him again. I mean, she spent all of our free period in the library today texting him under the table and stifling giggles at his replies.

At least Ava's never disappeared into a relationship. Whether she's gone out with boys or girls, her relationships have always been reliably short.

We start slowly wandering among the tables, and I stop to take a few pictures. I have to be stealthy about it because people start posing as soon as they see me with my phone. It makes it almost impossible to ever get candid shots for The Whine.

"What are you signing up for this year? You could always rejoin the newspaper," she says.

I shrug. "Between The Whine, working at the store, and homework, I'm not sure I've got time for anything else."

"You really need to step it up this year, Quinn, if you want to stand out to colleges."

"My only Bs have been in math classes, and I accepted the fact long ago that I'll never go into a career that requires numbers. As long as I keep the rest of my grades up, I'm not worried."

I could lie to myself and pretend that my confident tone comes from Ximena's unshakable belief in our post-high school plans or that I really do think I'm a shoo-in for NYU, my dream school, but it's definitely because Ava has been on this relentless college kick with me lately and I'm over it.

My sister is in the running for valedictorian or salutatorian. So next to her almost 5.0 of basically all AP classes, participation in every school club, and volunteer work at the food bank in Geneva, I, the mostly all-As student who works part-time at her family's gift shop and runs a moderately successful social media account with three paying sponsors, come off looking like a slacker. I keep my eyes focused ahead so I don't accidentally plow into someone, but I can feel Ava's disappointment.

"Ladies," Principal Stewart says to us as he passes. He's wearing a short-sleeved blue button-up shirt and a tie printed with text slang, like *LOL* and *TTYL*. I'm sure he thinks it makes him look cool and approachable, but it doesn't because he's neither. He glances disapprovingly at my phone, which I just picked up to take a picture of the Drama Club, who started posing as soon as they saw me lift my phone.

"I wonder if Principal Stewart finds it as funny as I do that his favorite student and his least favorite student are sisters," I say as I snap a few more pictures after he's disappeared into the crowd.

"You're not his least favorite student." Ava doesn't bother to argue that she secured the favorite spot as a freshman.

"Oh, she is," Ximena says, suddenly appearing behind us with a trailing Max.

"It's because he hates free speech," I say. "He can't stand The Whine because it's not an official school social media account he can control."

Even though my name isn't in the profile, it's no secret I run The Whine. I've been doing it since seventh grade.

"Or it's because he may or may not have heard you call him a dictator under your breath last year after he told you that you couldn't post anything from inside classrooms," Ximena says.

"He definitely heard you," Max confirms. "I was there to witness that blue vein in his forehead popping out more than normal." He draws an invisible line straight across the light brown skin of his forehead with his finger.

"But where was the lie? When I did newspaper freshman year, every issue of the *Daily Stripe* read like one long advertisement for him and the school."

"Like any benevolent dictator, you know Little Stewie can't have anyone questioning his authority." Ximena's voice rises into a high-pitched chirp when she says her nickname for Principal Stewart.

When we turn a corner to head up the next row of tables, a large hand shoots out in front of my face, displaying a chocolate chip cookie wrapped in gold cellophane. I grip my wheels hard to stop before I slam into the set of legs in front of me. I look up sharply.

"Cookie?" Cade Bird asks, looking back down at me with unnervingly friendly gray eyes and a smile stretched across his pale white face.

"Uh—" The last time Cade spoke to me directly was in seventh grade, when he called me Skeletor after my rheumatoid arthritis had been raging, killing all the good parts inside me, like bone marrow and cartilage, and leaving me with swollen, knob-like joints and persistent pain. He then promptly shoved my chair, and therefore me, into the nearest wall.

He drops the cookie into my hands before pulling more out of a canvas tote bag and passing them to Ximena, Ava, and Max. "My friends and I started a new school club called Defend Kids. We're having a bake sale to raise money to help find two kids from Rochester who went missing a couple weeks ago. We're going to have a table outside the cafeteria this week during lunch selling baked goods, but this one's on the house."

Behind him, Brayden Masterson is also passing out cookies, and Lily di Agostino corrals anyone passing into adding their name to their clipboard. The signs at every other club table are nothing fancier than butcher paper or poster board, but Cade's table is draped in an expensive-looking black vinyl banner that says *Defend Kids* in gold lettering.

"You should come by. If you like the cookies, you'll love my cupcakes." Cade's smile widens, and it occurs to me that this may be the first time I've seen his mouth move into any shape other than a snarl.

Still, I hold the cookie out in front of me, trying to keep a little distance from it in case it's poisoned or something.

"Thanks," Ava says. "We'll check it out."

Cade smiles again and weaves through the crowd, handing out cookies to people looking as startled as we are.

"Okay, what just happened?" Max blinks dazedly at the cookie in his hand.

"Careful. He and his minions probably mixed dog poop into the batter and are going to announce what they've done as soon as everyone's eaten them." Ximena brings the cookie up to her nose and cautiously sniffs it. "It's not worth the risk." She collects our cookies and dumps them in the nearest trash can.

Ava eyes the table.

"You're not actually going to check out a club run by Cade Bird, are you?" I ask Ava. "I know you're on a join-everything kick, but you've got to have *some* standards."

"Maybe he's changed?" she offers.

I don't even try to hold back a snort. "Cade Bird doesn't do organized school activities, unless you count bullying classmates in a group. It's probably some new punishment Principal Stewart came up with because detention wasn't working. Like mandatory community service or something."

"I don't know. He actually seemed legitimately into it." Max wraps his massive arms around Ximena from behind her and she leans into him.

"A club about *kids*? I don't buy it," Ximena says, and I nod in agreement.

I'm pretty sure Cade Bird was born a jerk and he'll die a jerk. But here he is volunteering his time, participating in an actual school activity, and . . . baking apparently?

"I'm going to do another lap before it's over," Ava says, like circling the gym one more time will magically produce a new row of clubs she can join. "I'll catch you guys later."

Max reluctantly pulls away from Ximena. "I better get back to help Adrian start packing up the booth."

"Okay, but please remind him that *he's* the junior class secretary, not you," she says, and Max laughs.

"Got it." But a second later, Max starts packing up the booth while Adrian stares down at his phone.

Ximena and I visit a few more tables, and as the crowd thins, I take more pictures for my post.

"Okay, I've officially had enough school for one day. Think Ava wants a ride home, too?" Ximena asks.

I see Ava at the Chess Club table, with a clipboard and pen in her hands. I shake my head. "She's probably going to be here awhile."

chapter two

"Hi, sweetheart," Dad calls from his usual spot on the couch when I open the front door. His legs are propped up on the arm and his fingers are flying on his laptop keyboard even as he talks. "Have a nice day?"

"Yup," I say.

"Great." Dad doesn't look up from his computer. He's in the writing zone.

Our house is the walk-out lower level of my parents' gift shop on Main Street—Vine and Things. When things are slow upstairs, Dad comes downstairs to work on freelance editing jobs or his own writing projects. He takes on whatever freelance work he can: editing restaurant menus, website copy, people's terrible five-hundred-page memoirs, and manuals for electronics no one actually buys. He's always wanted to be a full-time writer and he's got at least five trunked manuscripts sitting in the back of the coat closet. "At least I still get to work with words," he always says.

I kick off my tennis shoes and drop them on the storage bench we keep next to the door, with Mom and Dad's comforter and pillows for the foldout couch that is their bed tucked inside. I head for my bedroom, my fingers itching to get started on my new posts. I need to post something from the fair and then go through the pictures I took at the Wutzkes' bakery last weekend for my next sponsored post so I can get paid. I'm through the kitchen and halfway to my room when Dad finally looks up.

"Oh, Mom and I have that dinner at the Elk Club tonight," he says, the lack of excitement obvious in his voice.

Dad hates these dinners. But Mom and Dad say if a mostly seasonal small business that sells mainly knickknacks for tourists obsessively into cork and reclaimed wood has a hope of surviving the winter lull here that starts promptly after Labor Day, they have to keep the support of their local customers.

"Okay," I say.

I slip into my room and immediately switch on all the lights. Ava calls our house the Cave because only the front has windows. I move to my desk and open Instagram to check the notifications for my post on cross-country tryouts.

Seven new likes, one new follow, and only a handful of interactions on posts from earlier in the week.

I slump back in my chair from the disappointment that always hits when my posts generate just mediocre interest from my followers. It's like having a parent, or in this case, 3,272 virtual parents, tell you that you could have done better if you'd tried harder. I'd probably have gone viral if I'd posted the pictures of the colossal accident on the track and Asher King's surprise finish. Regret gnaws at me, and I flip over to my pictures and swipe through them until I land on the one I'm looking for. The one showing Michael Lai underneath the pile of runners, seconds after they hit the track.

I could still post the picture. It's practically begging to become a meme.

But I set my phone down on my desk and let the screen go black. It's not Michael's fault his shoelaces came undone at the worst possible moment. He'll probably spend the whole season kicking himself for not making sure he tied a sturdier knot. He's a senior this year, so this was his last chance to run in high school. Not to mention the guys he tripped will probably make sure he remembers, even if he tries to forget it.

A little while later, I hear Mom's hurried steps coming downstairs and my parents leaving. I know when they get home late tonight, Mom will appear at my door, exhausted but full of apologies for being out another night. I can't help but wonder what it will be like next year when Ava's gone.

Before the quiet of the house sinks me into too much of a depression, the door opens and closes again and Ava announces, "I'm home."

I poke my head into the living room, feeling more relieved than normal that she's back. "Mom and Dad are at the Elk Club thing. You just missed them."

She drops her bag onto the sofa and heads for the kitchen. "What do you want to do for dinner? I'm starving." She opens a cupboard and starts sifting through cans and boxes.

"Ooh, want to get takeout from Simply Crepes?"

Ava smirks and closes the cupboard. "Do you have any money?"

"Well, no." Somehow the money I make from doing two shifts a week at Vine and Things and the seventy-five dollars a month I make between my three Instagram sponsors disappears before it's even had a chance to sit in my bank account.

"Whatever We Can Cobble Together Out of the Fridge Night it is again, then!" Ava tugs on the handle and studies the contents of our fridge with a dissatisfied *hmmm.* "Greek omelet? There's feta and tomatoes. It's kind of like crepes."

I shrug. "It's not at all like crepes, but sure."

She pulls out the eggs, cheese, and milk and turns on a single burner on the stove. "I can't wait to live in a dorm next year so someone can cook for me for a change."

"I know, I know. You can't wait to get out of this miserable place." I roll my eyes.

Ava laughs. She's always making little comments about all the stuff she's going to do after high school. The understanding side of me knows she doesn't mean for her words to sting. The rest of me feels like she's counting down the days until she gets out of this town.

But I don't say anything. Instead, I get to work cracking the eggs into a bowl and beating them with a whisk. Ava intervenes right before I've whisked them into a milkshake and dumps them into the sizzling pan.

"So, I was thinking we should make a list of all the things we need to do in your last year at home," I say. "Like, I thought we could start a marathon of terrible Christmas movies tonight."

She prods at the eggs. "It's September."

"Yeah, but there are fifty really terrible Christmas movies, roughly, so we'd have to start now."

"Sounds fun, but I have a mountain of homework to do. And you probably do, too."

"I thought seniors got to slack off their last year. You always say junior year is the most important, so shouldn't you be able to skate now?"

Ava shrugs a shoulder and expertly folds the omelet over in the pan. "That's a myth. Maybe we can watch one of the movies this weekend."

"We'll never make it through the list at that rate."

She laughs. "You're acting like I've got weeks to live. If all goes right, I'll be an hour and a half away in Syracuse. I'll come home all the time. Except during midterms and finals, of course. And not, like, right after I get there."

She's already coming up with reasons not to come home and she hasn't even left yet.

"You say that, but I hardly see you now and we live in the same house."

"I'm pretty sure we're seeing each other right now." Ava cuts through the fluffy omelet with a spatula and puts a half on each of our plates.

When we were little, people used to think Ava and I were twins because we looked so much alike. But now, we couldn't be more different. I got sick and stopped growing, while Ava had a growth spurt. I became short, straight lines and sharp angles, a flat-chested stick compared to Ava's curves and height. Her outfits are always so put together, it looks like she walks around with an iron in her hand, while I'm most comfortable in oversized sweatshirts.

"Listen," Ava says, "I really think you should try to sign up for a few more extracurriculars this year. And maybe start thinking about summer internships. Since you didn't end up doing one this year, after all."

And just like that, her pushy-big-sister tone is back.

"It's not like I slacked off this summer," I reply defensively. "You know I worked almost every day upstairs. And I didn't commit a crime using the couple hours of freedom I had each day to hang out with my friends." Bitterness washes over me, and not just because of the pressure from Ava. Most of my free time this summer was spent being the third wheel to Ximena and Max, so it wasn't exactly the best summer ever.

Plus, running The Whine is much more time-consuming than most think. TikTok and Snapchat practically hand out followers like candy to anyone who can hold a phone, but Instagram makes you work to gain every single follower and then to keep their interest. It took me two whole years just to get my first thousand.

"Oh my gosh, that's not what I'm saying."

"Do you know something I don't?"

Ava stares down at her plate. "No. What do you mean?"

"Well, you've always been obsessive about school, but last year you went into overdrive." In fact, it felt like someone flipped a switch one day. Ava went from a normal level of obsessed to being on a never-ending academic rampage in which anything but perfection was unacceptable.

"I know how much you want to go to school in New York City with Ximena, and schools there are really expensive. I think you need to be realistic about how much Mom and Dad are going to be able to help financially."

I watch the steam curl above the omelet. Mom and Dad have always said they would help pay for as much as they could, but I guess we've never really talked about what that means in dollars and cents. Still, it feels like Ava's choosing her words carefully, that they're skimming the top of something that goes much deeper. But before I have a chance to ask, she picks up her plate and fork.

"I'm going to eat in my room so I can get started on my homework," she says. "If I can get it all done fast enough, maybe there will be time to start one of the Christmas movies, okay?"

"Sure." But I know from experience that her bedroom is a black hole. Once Ava disappears into it, she won't reemerge until she's getting ready for bed or needs the bathroom.

I push my plate aside, suddenly not hungry. This is what it's going to be like next year. Me, alone.

Ava says that she'll come home all the time from Syracuse. But what's going to happen when we've got an almost two-hour drive between us, rather than the thin DIY wall Dad put up to make our rooms with just some Sheetrock and paint?

She's never done a good job of hiding the fact that she's been embarrassed about where we live since we were in middle school. After a time or two of finding Mom's and Dad's pajamas, and worse, slung over the arm of the foldout in the living room when her friends came over, she stopped having people over at all. It's not that it isn't awkward for me when anyone other than Ximena is here and the foldout hasn't been put away yet, but Mom and Dad took the living room so that Ava and I could each have our own rooms. Now their bedroom is the living room, Dad's office, and Mom's workshop. And, anyway, it's silly to hide that we live in basically the equivalent of a cellar with two bedrooms. It's not like anyone's particularly rich here, except the people who live right on the water, and they're mostly seasonal residents with retirement houses in Florida they live in during the winters.

That's when the truth hits me. Maybe it's not that Ava is trying to get *to* college. Maybe she's trying to get away from *us*.

Eventually, I abandon my plate altogether and go back to my room. Ava's right. I do have a mountain of homework. I rub my eyes, a headache starting to prickle above them. If I start my homework now, I might get done before I need to go to bed right around when Mom and Dad usually get back.

But instead, I grab my phone and slide onto my bed. I collapse back into my pile of pillows to check my texts and notifications, but the only text I get the rest of the night is from Ximena, who sends me a picture of Bruno, her horse-sized Rottweiler that fell asleep with his head in his food bowl. In the background, I spot Max's scuffed-up Nikes.

I stare at the wall between my room and Ava's, wishing she'd open her door so we could steal one of the cold-brew coffees Dad hoards at the back of the fridge and talk. I could ask her if she felt this adrift her junior year and admit that sometimes it feels like I'm losing my best friend. I'd tell her about the thoughtless comment Asher King made at the track earlier today and she'd no doubt give a brilliant speech about how ableism is so rooted into our culture and our language that society has conditioned people into wrongly thinking that running around a track like a hamster on a wheel means a person's life is valuable and it'd make me feel a million times better.

But Ava's door stays closed.

A few weeks in, and junior year feels like being stuck somewhere between an ending and a beginning.

TheWhine: More than 30 different clubs filled the P. J. Dalton High School gym for the annual club fair today, offering a wide and unique array of after-school activities that will satisfy even the biggest overachievers trying to pad their college applications. Link in bio to see a list of all this year's clubs and sign-up details.

✔ Drama Club
✔ Photography Club
✔ Robotics Club
✔ Model United Nations
✔ And more!

chapter three

The next morning, I flip through the pages of my chemistry textbook, wishing I could somehow borrow Ava's near-photographic memory for second period.

"Cramming?" my friend Sulome says, slipping into the desk next to me. She shoves her backpack under her seat.

"I got started so late on my homework last night and then I never made it through the reading. I slept through my alarm this morning, too," I whisper back to her in case Mrs. Duncan is lurking nearby and decides to punish me with a pop quiz.

I blink hard just in time to watch Asher King stroll into class. I hadn't thought about how awkward chemistry was going to be after our conversation at the track until now. Behind Asher, there's a woman with brown hair and an armful of books. I recognize her as a substitute teacher I've had before.

"Good morning, everyone," she says. "I'm Ms. Segui. I'll be filling in for Mrs. Duncan, who is out sick today."

Sulome and I exchange matching celebratory grins, and I fall back against my chair, suppressing a cheer. As if he can read my mind, Asher turns in his desk and gives me a tentative smile. I purposely look away, but I can feel him still watching me.

It's weird, especially since he seemed to be hovering near where Ximena normally parks Bula when we got to school this morning and I made her park on the other side of the lot. But it's also making me wish I'd had more time to get ready this morning. Not that I should care what I look like in front of Asher.

Ms. Segui moves to the computer on Mrs. Duncan's desk at the front of the room. "You're supposed to be talking about the chemical processes of climate change, but since she's out, Mrs. Duncan wants you to watch this movie about"—she skims a piece of paper on Mrs. Duncan's desk—"the polar ice melt."

Two desks from me in the last row in his camouflage jacket, Dillon McRae grunts and pushes back his chair like he's about to flip over his desk. Instead, he crosses his arms over his chest and scowls. One of the many downsides of not being able to maneuver the narrow aisles of desks is that I have to sit in the last row near him.

Just like everyone knows Cade Bird and his group, everyone also knows Dillon. With all the active shooter drills we run each year, in what is the most morbid game ever, people can't help but speculate about who the person on the other side of that gun might be someday. Dillon McRae tops most people's list.

It takes Ms. Segui a minute to pull the video up on the SMART Board.

"Our world is rapidly changing," a male voice says in a British accent that sounds like he must have been recorded in front of a fireplace in a cozy wingback chair with a cup of tea in his hand.

"This is so stupid," Dillon mutters.

"According to NASA scientists, Antarctica is losing more than a

26

hundred and fifty-two billion metric tons of land-based ice per year. The topography of this land is literally changing . . ."

"It's nothin' new," Dillon says a little louder.

On the other side of me, Phoenix Nelson, a sophomore, and I trade awkward glances.

"Coastal communities and island nations are experiencing unprecedented flooding. Scientists are warning that if Greenland's ice sheet melts, sea levels could rise enough to wipe out coastal communities. Climate change is a man-made—"

Dillon throws up his hands, and I find myself automatically shrinking in my seat.

"Is something wrong?" Ms. Segui says over the video, standing.

The entire class turn in their seats.

"This is garbage," Dillon says. "It's all government propaganda. There's no such thing as global warming."

"This is science," Ms. Segui replies in a measured voice.

"Okay, if this is science, then why isn't this movie mentioning the three hundred scientists around the world who signed a letter saying climate change is a myth? Or explaining why it still snows?"

One of the things that's always been so scary about Dillon is how silently he stalks around school. But now that he's saying exactly what he thinks, he's actually even scarier.

"Dude, the polar ice caps are literally melting. It's a fact," Sulome suddenly says beside me. "Google it."

Dillon swivels in his chair to glare at her. "And it's also a fact that ice melts and the polar ice caps have been melting for centuries!"

"Let's just get back to watching the movie, please." But Ms. Segui's voice is drowned out by the shouting.

Sulome's cheeks practically match her pink hijab, but she doesn't shrink back and it's impressive. I'm not sure I'd have the guts to stand up to Dillon, even though she's totally right about climate change. "My brother works for the Environmental Protection Agency—"

"Then congrats. Your brother is a stooge following orders," Dillon says.

Ms. Segui asks, "What is your name?"

His eyes narrow into slits. "Dillon."

"I'm writing you a pass, Dillon. Please go to Principal Stewart's office." Ms. Segui signs a form and crosses to the back of the room.

It's like all of us are collectively holding our breath to see if he's really about to lose it. But Dillon just stands, takes the pass from her, and walks out the door.

"But, like, I have to take notes and stuff." I can barely hear Adrian's sullen voice over the noise of the cafeteria.

Sulome snorts. "Didn't you know that was kind of a main part of being junior class secretary?" It took Sulome the rest of chemistry and then the two of us reenacting the whole Dillion thing for our friends before she calmed down.

"I mean, I didn't think it'd be, like, the *main* thing I'd do. Why can't they just record our meetings?"

Ximena shakes her head at him. "Seriously. Explain to us again why you turned our lives upside down to help you campaign last year if you didn't actually know what job you were running for?"

"Come on now. We already know it's because he wanted to get one of those cool student council sweaters," Max teases.

Adrian's cheeks redden, and he pushes his round glasses up higher on his nose.

That's when I notice Asher sitting facing us at the next table over with Justin Vallorani and Ty Henry from the cross-country team, and he's definitely watching me again.

"Why is Asher King staring obsessively over here?" Ximena turns to me while Adrian tries to casually peel off his black-and-orange student council sweater and stuff it into his backpack. "Do I need to have words with him?"

I shake my head and stare down at the remains of my hamburger. "Please don't. Ignore him, like I am."

"Mena, want the rest of my fries?" Max asks, nudging his tray at us. "I saved you all the burned ones."

"Dude, how many times do I have to tell you, they're crispy, not burned," she says, feigning irritation and shoving the tray back at him.

He pokes her in the side where she's most ticklish, and Ximena erupts into the giggle at a pitch I had never heard come from her mouth until she started dating Max. I'm not sure I can spend the rest of lunch watching another one of their cute-fests.

"I'm going to go to my locker before next period," I announce, I guess to the rest of our table because Ximena and Max have their foreheads together, already completely lost in each other.

Ximena used to make fun of couples who were always touching each other, calling them "codependent barnacles." I wonder what she would do if I reminded her of that fact right now.

I push back from the table, take my tray to the counter, and head for the double doors. I don't notice Asher is leaning against the wall just outside until I've already crossed the threshold and it's too late to turn back.

I tip my head down, letting my bangs do their magic blinder work to make him disappear long enough for me to turn sharply toward a table next to the doors. I bump into the metal folding legs with my knees.

"Whoa, be careful," my sister's voice says above me.

When I look up, I blink at the sight of Ava behind a table full of cookies, cupcakes, and Rice Krispies treats, taking a dollar bill from a redheaded freshman. The black-and-gold vinyl sign I saw at Cade Bird's club table is tacked onto the wall behind her.

"What are you doing?" I ask.

"Helping out," Ava says as she transfers more individually wrapped cookies from a bag onto the table.

"Wait. Did you actually *join* Cade's club thing?"

"You should hear him out. Child trafficking is a serious problem, Quinn. We're organizing a rally about it."

"We?"

Ava knows better than anyone what Cade used to call me, so the fact that she's here and even expects me to speak to him feels like a betrayal.

"We're almost out of cupcakes," Cade says, scratching the back of his head. "My mom texted that she's two minutes away with more." A line has started to form down the hall in just the last minute.

"I can go out front and get them, if you want," Ava says.

"Cool. She drives a white SUV."

"Be right back." Ava gives me a half smile. Part of me is sure she's trying to escape having to explain herself.

Cade smirks. "I always forget you guys are sisters." The way he says it as Ava hurries off, it kind of sounds like an insult.

A girl I think is a sophomore picks up a sugar cookie and passes Cade a five. Her hand shakes a little awaiting change.

"C'mon, dude. Buy two. It's for a good cause," Cade says, dropping the money in the cashbox. It's definitely a statement, not a suggestion. He hands her another cookie, her change, and a gold flyer. The sophomore wordlessly hurries away. "You going to buy something?" he asks me.

I glance behind me. Asher is still there, looking like he's trying to decide something.

As much as I don't want to, I turn back to Cade. "I don't know. What is the cause, exactly?"

He picks up one of the gold flyers and hands it to me. *Missing* is stamped across the top in big block letters and below it are school pictures of a young white girl and boy, the girl smiling widely. The flyer lists the girl as thirteen and the boy as seven. *Last seen in their front yard in Rochester, NY, at 6:30 p.m. on September 1*, the flyer

31

reads before listing their height, weight, hair, race, and eye color, and the clothes they were last wearing. There's a QR code at the bottom, too.

"That's Jensen and Annalice Turner," Cade says. "They're from Rochester, and they've been missing for a couple of weeks."

"And a bake sale is going to bring them back?" The sarcasm spills out of my mouth before my brain remembers who I'm talking to. My whole body goes rigid, but when I glance up at Cade from under my protective bangs, his thin mouth simply curls into a smile.

"All proceeds go to Defend Kids, an organization that fights against child trafficking. Every little bit helps, my mom says."

It's weird to hear Cade talk about his mom. A part of me had kind of imagined he was so terrible because he was raised by demonic wolves. Normally his general hugeness is intimidating, but behind the bake sale table, without the typical sneer on his face, he doesn't seem quite so threatening. In fact, Cade would probably even be cute, with his broad shoulders and white-blond hair cropped short on the sides and left long on the top—if I could see past the years of awful bullying.

"You know, you should post about them on that Instagram account you run. Whatever it's called," he says casually.

I know Cade knows my account is called The Whine because everyone at school does, and I know he's followed it for years because I hate-followed him back. When The Whine started to get more of a following, Cade seemed to think it was a good time to move from me to a new target. There's something kind of delightful about Cade Bird wanting something from me now.

As much as the thought of helping him in any way turns my

stomach, it wouldn't be a bad thing to use The Whine to help spread the word about the missing kids. They can't help the fact that Cade Bird has taken up their cause. Plus, I don't have to give Cade or his club any attention to post about them.

"Yeah, maybe I will," I say, even though I've already made up my mind. Cade nods and goes back to taking people's money.

I set the flyer down and take a picture of it with my phone before typing up a caption.

"Did you already go to your locker?" Ximena says, suddenly in front of me after I hit post.

"I didn't think you even heard me." I look up. Asher's gone and the bake sale line wraps down the hall now. "Can you believe this?"

Ximena shakes her head. "Willing to forgive all these years of torture for some cupcakes he probably just bought from Wegmans."

"Not me. I'm going to hold a grudge about the Skeletor thing basically forever. But apparently my sister isn't," I add when Ava returns with a large white box of cupcakes.

Ximena's mouth drops open. "Are you kidding me?"

"Ten bucks says it's a scam and Cade is keeping all the cash for himself." I guess I should have thought about that before posting.

"Watch." Ximena points down the hall, past the cafeteria and the front office. Lily di Agostino snags a passing guy by the back of the backpack, nearly tripping him, while Brayden Masterson grabs one of his arms. He helps steady the kid and then walks him over to the line for the bake sale. Brayden is smiling the whole time. It's basically the same move they pulled at the club fair to get people to sign up. They repeat it with Phoenix Nelson, Kristen from English class, and somehow even Ollie Carter, the football team's quarterback, who's almost twice Brayden's size.

The only person they let slip past is Dillon McRae. I get Brayden and Lily's aversion. But then they snag two more freshman girls and drag them into the line.

"Looks like they've got a system," Ximena says as we watch Lily and Brayden repeat the same fishing exercise over again, "and no one has much of a choice."

When I push through the back door at the end of the day to meet Ximena in the parking lot, Asher King is standing at the bottom of the ramp by the dumpster. I freeze. No one ever intentionally uses this entrance unless they're desperate. I have to hold my breath each time I go up and down the ramp to avoid getting a vomit-inducing whiff of whatever is in the dumpster.

"Hey, Quinn. Can I talk to you for a second?"

"I'm catching a ride with my friend and she's leaving now, so—"

"I can take you home if you want. I mean, you'd have to tell me how to do the, er, wheelchair stuff, but I can drive you home."

Can't say that spending time with someone who awkwardly refers to my chair as "wheelchair stuff" is high on my priority list.

But Ximena did mention that she and Max were going to babysit his brother and sisters together after school today once she'd dropped me off. She didn't mean it to sound like some chore taking her away from who she really wanted to be with, but that's how it felt. If I go with

Asher, she'll be able to race off to find the boyfriend she apparently can't stay away from for more than five minutes anymore.

"Okay, I guess so."

Asher looks about as surprised that I agreed as I am.

I text Ximena that I have to stay late and that I'll call my parents to come pick me up, because if I tell her Asher is taking me home, she'll text me back a million different questions. She sends me back a ??? right away, but I ignore it and eventually she drives off.

"Okay, let's go." I push hard against my wheels across the parking lot. But then I remember I don't know what Asher drives, so I slow down long enough for him to catch up.

It turns out, Asher drives a truck, a monstrous red one that looks brand-new. A minor wave of panic washes across my whole body. Bula is so low to the ground that all I have to do to get in is slide from my chair across to the front seat. Getting into Asher's truck, however, is going to take a catapult and a prayer. All I need is for my knees to give out and send me sprawling onto the asphalt in front of Asher FREAKING King and breaking something.

"Do you, um, need my help or anything?" Asher asks when he opens the passenger door and sees me frowning up at the seat.

I lock my brakes in place and take a deep breath. "Just hold on to my chair for me."

Before I move, I can feel his hands grip the back of my chair. As I heave myself to my feet and into the truck, I snatch a glance at Asher's face and find it wrinkled with focus. I know the look; I've seen it a million times. He's trying to figure out why I'm in a wheelchair since I can move my legs, because 99 percent of the population thinks that being in a wheelchair means you either have quadriplegia or are ninety-five years old.

I know how the conversation will go if he asks, which, again, that same 99 percent of the population usually does.

"So, like, are you paralyzed?"

"No. I have rheumatoid arthritis."

"Oh, the thing really old people get? Cool. My grandma had it before she died, so I totally understand."

People always want to hear the details of my disability—that RA is an autoimmune condition, that I've had it since I was little, that I'm in remission now but that it can flare up at any time, kind of like cancer—like they're owed an explanation for why I am the way I am.

I wait for him to launch into the whole awkward and predictable conversation, because let's face it, I don't know much about him, but I know the guy's not great with words. But Asher doesn't say anything, just shuts the door for me once I'm inside and pops my chair into the bed of his truck.

"I guess you better tell me where you live," he says when he gets in.

It isn't complicated to direct him to my place when it's the only pale pink building right on Main Street.

Silence settles over the truck and it's quickly becoming one of the most awkward two-minute drives of my life. I check my Instagram notifications. For a second, I stare in disbelief at the numbers: 130 likes, 27 new followers. All from my post on the missing Turner kids. I scroll through my notifications, and while I do, I get two more followers. Wow.

"You run that Instagram account, right? The Whine?" Asher eyes my phone.

My head jerks up because that's when it hits me. This is the reason he's been trying to intercept me all day.

"Look, if you're worried I'm going to post something bad about you on it, don't be. It's not that kind of account." I leave out the part where I was seriously tempted to post the pictures proving his spot on the cross-country team was definitely an accident.

"No!" he says quickly, his panicked face saying that's his worst nightmare. "I didn't think that at all."

I don't know Asher well enough to know for sure, but I think he's telling the truth.

"So, were you, like, waiting for me?" I finally say when we're a few blocks away from my place.

"Yeah. I thought it was kind of obvious." He laughs, but it's a nervous one. "I kept trying to come talk to you at school, but it kind of seemed like you were trying to avoid me."

"I was."

Asher glances up from the road, and for a second, we both look at each other like we can't believe we're both being quite so honest. He turns into the parking lot behind my house and kills the engine.

"Cool place. I didn't know anyone lived in these buildings."

"They do." But really, my family is the only one that lives on the block. Everything else on this block is stores and restaurants.

"Listen, I wanted to apologize for what I said yesterday," Asher says suddenly. "It was quite possibly the stupidest thing I've ever said in my life, which is saying a lot because I say a lot of stupid stuff. I didn't think about what I was saying and I'm really sorry." His voice is serious, but the words come out of his mouth in a burst, almost as if he's been practicing them.

He only looks at me when he's done. I let out the breath I'd been holding in my chest. My mind had taken me from zero to he's-trying-to-save-his-own-skin in about sixty seconds and now it feels like I can breathe again.

"Oh, um. It's okay." And I think I mean it. Somehow while sitting with Asher in his truck, my annoyance from yesterday has shifted. Now I just kind of feel embarrassed for running away at the track. I'm not made of glass, and anyway, I've heard way worse by people who actually mean every word.

Still, I always feel like I have this unspoken responsibility to be the perfect disabled person. Like it's my job to make people feel comfortable around me because I'm usually the only wheelchair user they've met under sixty. But if I don't watch what I say or do, they might think all disabled people are mean and terrible. I'm still trying to figure out what the right answer to that impossible choice is.

I expect Asher to get out of the truck, but instead he says, "To be honest, I don't even like doing cross-country." And something like relief passes over his face, like he's been waiting to say that out loud for a while.

"You seemed to be really into it at the tryouts yesterday. *What are you even doing with your life*, remember?" I say, trying to mimic his deep voice and the way he was still out of breath.

The look of embarrassment returns instantly to his face, and he scratches awkwardly at the back of his neck. "I heard another runner say that in a post-meet interview one time. It sounded good, so I memorized it on the chance that I ever won a race. Which, to be honest, I never thought I'd do."

"Why even try out for the team, then?"

Asher shrugs. I thought his hair was black before, but now that we're eye level, I realize it's a deep brown instead. It looks like it might even be curly if he let it grow out a little. People always look so different when they're standing over me than when we're at the same height.

"My parents were both on the cross-country team at Cornell and they both studied business. They wanted either my older brother or sister to do the same and then take over the family business someday, but it didn't go that way. So I think I'm kind of their last hope. But if I'm being honest, I'm more of an indoors kind of guy." He glances at his hands. "Sorry, I don't know why I'm telling you all this."

"It's okay." I probably shouldn't ask, since I only just officially met Asher, but he's got me curious now. "So you don't want to go to Cornell, then?"

If he's startled by my nosiness, he doesn't show it. If anything, he looks thrilled that someone has finally asked him what he wants.

"If I get in, sure." He nods. "But I'd rather go to RISD. The Rhode Island School of Design. It's got the best graphic design program in the country," he says. "There's actually a summer program there this year for high schoolers that I want to apply for. But it's really competitive. I was kind of hoping to ask you for a favor, actually."

"Really?"

"Yeah." Asher hesitates like he's hunting for the nerve to keep going. "I really need to build out my portfolio for my application. You know, websites, logos, graphics, whatever. I kind of geek out to all of it." He licks his lips. "So I was wondering if, well, you've ever thought about bringing on a partner for The Whine?"

TheWhine: Spread the word about two missing kids from Rochester, NY. Jensen and Annalice Turner, last seen in their front yard on September 1. #letsfindthem #missingkids #rochester

chapter four

Asher King sits cross-legged on the floor of my bedroom with his computer in his lap and a Pepsi in his hand. Every once in a while, I glance at him from my desk. First because I can't quite believe he's spending his Saturday here, and then because I want to see the logo he's designing for The Whine. But every time I do, he catches me and shyly tilts his screen a little bit farther away from me.

I don't really know why I said yes when he asked me if he could help with The Whine. I've always been a solo act and that's the way I like it, even when Ximena's asked if she could do a guest post once in a while for fun. Maybe it was the way his eyes glowed when he started talking about all the ideas he'd had for a logo, or the way his voice naturally sped up when he talked about how he's been learning animation. Or maybe it was the desperate look on his face when he explained how much he wanted to get into that summer program at RISD, like his whole future depended on it. Because as he was talking, a whisper planted itself in my head that maybe Asher King was the key to taking The Whine to the next level. A level that might actually look good on a college application and lead to more businesses wanting to sponsor me.

Still, I think I surprised us both when I agreed. Without thinking about it, I pick up my phone from my desk and open my Instagram. Since the post about the Turner kids has been doing so well, I've gotten kind of obsessed about watching the numbers rise. But when I open it this time, I gasp.

I'm at 100,687 new likes, 611 new comments, and 806 new followers for The Whine since yesterday. I officially have over 4,000 followers. It's the most popular thing I've ever posted, beating out the time Mrs. Cerwonka, our English teacher, gave me permission to post the picture of a wolf her game camera took one night last year.

"What?" Asher looks up from his laptop.

"Nothing." I shake my head, like it'll wake me up from a dream and I'll be back to the couple of dozen or so likes my posts usually get, but it doesn't. "This post I did the other day is doing really well."

"The one about those missing kids?" I nod and Asher grabs his phone with The Whine already pulled up. "Yeah, I saw that one. Wow. It has a couple hundred more likes than when I last looked."

I can feel my face warming with pride. But as suddenly as it comes on, I'm doused with the cold reality that I'm getting attention from an actual tragedy and the Turners are still missing. And on top of that, I got the tip about their disappearance from someone I literally hate. So it doesn't quite feel like success.

"Maybe there's some more stuff we could do to help get the word out, you know? I could make a graphic people could share about them, or I could make some videos for your Stories and you could do the voice-over." The glow is back in his eyes again.

"I don't know," I say. "It's just . . . Are you friends with Cade Bird?"

Asher snorts. "No. I have this thing about not being friends with people who are basically the spawn of Satan."

I smile and Asher matches my grin. "Okay, good."

"Why? Besides the obvious reasons, of course."

"His new club is how I learned about the Turner kids and, I don't know. I want to help them, but helping Cade is . . ."

"Complicated?" Asher finishes for me.

"Yeah."

"Hmmm," he says thoughtfully, pushing a hand across his forehead, like he's trying to get hair that doesn't actually exist out of his eyes. That's when I remember his hair was shaggy last year. I guess I've been watching Asher a little closer than I realized. "But maybe something we do could actually help find those kids."

I nod. "That's what I'm trying to tell myself, too, since I found out that Cade's running the club and my own sister joined it."

As if I summoned her, the front door opens and closes, and I hear Ava's staccato footsteps, always in a hurry, against the wood floor. Somehow when I stopped being able to walk, I gained this completely useless superpower of being able to know who is nearby simply by the sound of their footsteps.

"Hi, I'm here, but only for a second!" Ava calls. She's smiling when she appears in the doorway holding a large brown box, but her face melts into a frown at the sight of Asher. "Oh . . . I didn't realize you had someone over."

"Didn't realize I needed to run it by you." I roll my eyes. "This is Asher."

"Hey," he says from the floor.

"You might have thought about cleaning up before having company." Ava's pale cheeks redden and her eyes flick to the living room/Mom and Dad's bedroom, which currently looks like a storage closet thanks to the delivery of new inventory that showed up at our front door instead of the door for Vine and Things.

"Mom said they'll deal with the delivery tonight." I guess I should have thought about the fact that the Kings probably live in one of those massive new mansions on the lake or something. I apologized when he had to weave through a few stacks of boxes to get in, but he didn't seem to mind.

"Don't worry about me. I hardly count as company," Asher says, but Ava's cheeks stay flushed.

Irritation bubbles in my chest at her obvious embarrassment about our house. Why does she care what Asher thinks about where we live?

"What's with the box?" I ask.

Ava's hazel eyes flip back to me, full of fire. "Flyers." She shakes the box a little. "I'm going with a bunch of people to hang them all around the area. Bryce and I are doing Penn Yan and then we're picking up some T-shirts."

"That girl from Model UN? That sounds fun." The image of Bryce Marks's eager face grinning from under her cheesy beret as Ava signed up for Model UN flashes in my mind.

"Bryce is actually really cool and super smart. We've basically been in all the same classes since sixth grade."

I turn to Asher. "See how she's actually complimenting herself there?" Ava frowns. "It was a joke! You're doing all this for Model UN?" I guess recruiting didn't go so well at the fair and now they're having to branch out. But that isn't a surprise, really. The only foreign country people from the Finger Lakes ever make it to is the Canadian side of Niagara Falls a few hours away.

"No. For Defend Kids," Ava says. "Bryce joined, too. We're trying to get up as many missing persons signs as possible, and the T-shirts are for the rally."

My mouth falls open. "You're spending your Saturday helping Cade?"

"No, I'm spending my Saturday helping to find the Turner kids," she huffs in her big-sister-knows-best voice. "Tell Mom and Dad I won't be home for dinner, okay?"

"Wait, but I thought we were starting our awful Christmas movie marathon tonight."

"We can do it next weekend. This is important. I never knew how big a problem child trafficking is in America until Defend Kids." She shifts the box to rest on her other hip. "Did you know that one child is abducted every five minutes in the US? The rate for queer kids and people of color is even higher. So literally every second counts when it comes to abductions. See you later."

Before I can say anything, she heads for the door.

"And the annoying thing is that she probably now knows everything there is to know about child abductions," I say after the few seconds of awkward silence. "She basically has a photographic memory."

46

"So, do you guys get along?" Asher says.

I can't tell if he's kidding because our conversation was full of barbs and irritated glances. But his face looks so earnest.

"Yeah, we've actually always been super close. But lately it's like all she cares about is getting out of Canandaigua and as far away from us as possible. Cade's club is probably just an excuse she's giving so she doesn't have to be at home."

"My brother and sister were the exact same way when they became seniors. Suddenly hanging out with me was like a punishment," Asher says. "Maybe that will be us next year."

"Maybe," I say. The part I don't say out loud is that with Ximena and Max, and now Ava, it feels like I'm being left behind.

Asher's eyes drift across the posters and postcards of New York City, arranged by borough, plastered on the wall in front of him. Eventually, he goes back to working on the logo, and I realize how glad I am he's here. I was supposed to work all day with Mom and Dad, but they sent me home because the store was so dead. I texted my friends right away to announce my unexpected freedom, but Ximena and Max had already driven up to Rochester for the day, Renata had to help her parents clean out the garage, and Sulome's cousins were visiting. With Ava now headed for Penn Yan, I would have had to spend the whole day alone if I hadn't plucked up the courage to text Asher to ask him if he wanted to come over.

I'm lost in thought when Asher tells me he's ready to show me the draft logo.

"It's just a draft. I can change anything you don't like," he says, looking a little nervous as he turns his laptop toward me.

Somehow his design is professional but fun, colorful and eye-catching but not overwhelming. "No, it's completely perfect," I say.

"Cool."

"I'm sure the people at that summer program will be impressed."

Asher smiles wide enough that a small dimple appears on the right side of his mouth. I read once when I was doing research for a biology paper that dimples are usually the result of a shortened or weakened muscle. My weakened muscles from my RA plus my damaged joints make it difficult to walk more than a step, whereas Asher's weakened muscle gives him the single cutest cheek I think I've ever seen.

And I suddenly realize I've been staring at it. My eyes snap back to the animation.

But out of the corner of my eye, I can see Asher watching me now, and I know he's about to say one of two things: *Do you ever get tired of sitting in that thing?* ("that thing" meaning my wheelchair) or *So, what's wrong with you?* Because this is what *always* happens when I start to feel comfortable around someone.

I hold my breath, waiting for him to ruin this, because it's been starting to feel too easy between us.

"I'm going to get another Pepsi and then finish a few more tweaks. Then I'll shoot you the file," he says instead.

I grin. "You're like the worst jock ever. Shouldn't you be drinking protein shakes that taste like gravel or eating stuff with beetroot in it or something?"

"Quinn!" I hear my mom's voice calling my name as she comes down the stairs from the shop and toward my room. "Dad and I are doing inventory tonight, so can you—"

Mom stops in my doorway, where Ava was just minutes ago, and immediately spots Asher on the floor.

"Oh, um. You have a . . . friend," she says, and then adds way too enthusiastically, "That's *great!*" Between her and Ava, they make it sound as if I have never had a single friend in my life, let alone one at my house. "When I heard voices, I assumed it was Ximena." She looks hard at Asher and adds, "You're not Ximena."

"This is Asher," I say through gritted teeth. Asher raises his hand in a waveless wave. "We're working on a project."

"What kind of project?" Mom asks, leaning against the door like she plans to stay.

Get out, get out, get out, I silently chant. "He's helping me do some stuff for The Whine."

"Oh?" Mom says.

"Yeah," Asher says. "I'm doing a logo and stuff."

"You have experience making logos?" she asks Asher.

"Yeah. I mean, a bit," he says. "I made one for my parents' business. And, you know, a few others."

"What do your parents do?"

Oh my god, she's grilling him like he's interviewing for a job. Like

49

he might not be experienced enough to voluntarily help me with the Instagram account I originally started to promote *my* family's business.

"They own King Country Vineyards," Asher says like he didn't want to have to admit it.

"Oh." Mom straightens a little. If anything could save Asher from more of Mom's scary grilling, that was it. "They have a new winery opening on Keuka soon, right?" she says, suddenly focused on smoothing her hair back.

"Yeah, in the spring."

"Goodness, well, they sure must be busy people."

Her gaze shifts and I know exactly what she's thinking. She has been trying to become a supplier for the King winery gift shops for years, but they've never so much as taken a meeting with her. Getting her crafts into even one of their gift shops would be like getting a painting into the Metropolitan Museum of Art. It's not like I hadn't thought about getting King Country as sponsors—they could definitely afford more than twenty-five dollars a month, and they'd probably pay in advance—but I don't want to make it awkward with Asher, like Mom is making it now.

I wonder what Mom would do if I let it slip right now that my parents don't actually like wine.

"Well, I'll let you kids get back to your important project." She turns to leave, but then she pauses. "Please, keep the door open." Mom pulls the door open as far as it will go, the hinges giving a purposeful squeak.

Heat instantly races to my cheeks. I nod while dying on the inside at the not-at-all-subtle implication in Mom's order to keep the door open.

She doesn't head back upstairs to the shop for a minute, but instead goes into the kitchen and starts rummaging in the cabinets so loudly it can't possibly be anything other than intentional. I turn back to my computer, wishing it could swallow me as embarrassed heat practically singes the back of my neck, making my palms sweat.

"Well, now you've met most of my family and I'm so sorry," I say in a low voice when I finally hear her feet trudge back up the steps to the shop.

Asher laughs, and thank god, it's light. "You're doing me the huge favor here."

My shoulders relax a little.

"I think we should do more stuff on the Turners," Asher says after a while. "I had no idea child trafficking was such a big problem, and you've got the platform."

"You know that means I'll have to go talk to Cade so we can find out more, right? And I'm sure he'll want me to post about Defend Kids." The thought of intentionally speaking to Cade makes my stomach do nervous flip-flops.

"Would it help if I came with you?"

"Yes," I say, "because, you know, strength in numbers."

Asher nods. He tinkers with the animated logo for a little while longer before he leaves. Mom reappears downstairs a few minutes after Asher's gone.

"So I wasn't expecting to find the Kings' son in your room." She sits on the edge of my bed.

I roll my eyes. "He's helping me and you basically interrogated him like he'd murdered someone."

Mom laughs. "Well, that's a dramatic interpretation of asking a few simple questions of the boy you find in your daughter's room who is there without permission. You know you're not supposed to have people in your bedroom."

I turn around. "You guys have never told me that."

"Of course we have. We talked about it." But she doesn't look so sure.

"No. You talked about it with Ava, but you've never said it directly to me."

"Come on, Quinn. Assume any rules Ava had apply to you, too."

I swallow back a retort.

She gets up to leave, but then says, "For what it's worth, Asher seems very nice."

"He is." And it's absolutely accurate. "But again, there's nothing going on with us."

"Then it won't be a problem to ask for permission next time before he comes over."

I nod compliantly just so this conversation will end.

The fact is, my parents specifically had that talk with Ava—I know because she complained to me about how awkward it was—and they specifically haven't had that talk with me. I guess to their credit, any guys I've had over I've usually met through Ximena or Max, and we've always been in a group. But I can't help but wonder if they thought I'd never actually have a guy who wanted to be in my bedroom because of my disability.

chapter five

C ade Bird's lunch table is in the far corner of the cafeteria. Once a place from which he and his handful of equally vile friends used to launch their attacks, it's tripled in size. There's an odd assortment of kids sitting at it. I spot Phoenix Nelson, Annika Blair, and Corinne DuPaul, drama kids Ava met from being in *Into the Woods* last year, on one end of the long table. On the other side, there's Bryce Marks, a girl with navy-blue hair I don't know, and two blond girls who look like they could be twins. I recognize a bunch of kids who'd been roped into standing in the line for Cade's bake sale by Lily and Brayden, too. Some of them frequent targets of Cade's attention, they nibble on their lunches cautiously, looking a little unsettled to be there.

And in the middle of it all, Cade says something and the whole table erupts in laughter, even if some of the kids on the end look like it's a little forced. For a second, a seriously absurd thought hits me: Maybe Cade is actually trying to make friends?

But I squash the idea as quickly as it flashed in my mind. The closest thing Cade has to friends is Lily and Brayden, and they're more like minions. I just don't buy his sudden transformation.

I crunch with agitation on a carrot stick, watching Cade from the end of my own particularly empty table. Max is out with a cold, which Ximena explained was code for he ditched because he didn't study for his Spanish test. Adrian is at a student council meeting and Sulome eats lunch with her friends from musical theater on Wednesdays; that way she makes sure she's still part of the crowd before the spring musical.

I only half-heartedly listen as Renata and Ximena recite the names of the bones and muscles for the anatomy and physiology quiz they have after lunch. But I straighten a little when I see Asher come into the cafeteria with a brown paper bag in his hand. He waves to his friends and then heads straight for me.

"Can I sit here?" Asher gestures at the empty seat next to me where Sulome usually sits.

"Um, sure," I finally say.

"Cool." Asher smiles and pulls out the chair while I try to act like this is all completely normal, even as Renata and Ximena send me questioning looks. Which I get because Asher had never so much as glanced at our table until the whole thing after tryouts, and last Ximena knew, I was avoiding him.

"You know Ximena and Renata, right?"

Renata and Ximena look at Asher, then to me, then back at him, like bobbleheads.

"Yeah, hey. How's it going?" he says.

"Hey," they chorus back.

"Congratulations on making the cross-country team," Ximena says, pushing back the hood of Max's sweatshirt she always wears on quiz and test days, like it's some kind of good luck charm.

"Oh, thanks," he replies, apparently not picking up on her murderous tone.

Asher unpacks his lunch bag—two sandwiches full of so much stuff they're spilling over, chips, an apple, carrot sticks, and a brownie big enough to look like a piece of cake. It's a lunch for two people, or, I guess, one long-distance runner.

Renata stares as intensely at Asher as she was studying her anatomy notes a few minutes ago, but Asher thankfully doesn't seem to notice, otherwise this will probably be the last time he sits with us and we'll get a reputation for being the Creepy Table.

Ximena goes back to her notes, but I know she's not actually reading them because her eyes keep flicking up at Asher.

"In case your mom asks for a status report, you can tell her I'm sending you the final file for the animation tonight," Asher tells me.

"You know Quinn's mom?" Ximena sweeps her anatomy notes to the side.

Asher nods and takes an enormous bite out of his sandwich.

Ximena turns to me as Asher chews. I can practically see the questions forming in her mind.

"Yeah, uh, Asher is helping me with some stuff for The Whine, so he was at my house on Saturday."

Her eyes narrow. "He's helping you?"

"He's doing some graphics and a new logo and stuff."

"Quinn's letting me help so I have some designs to put in my application for this summer program at RISD," Asher adds.

"I see," Ximena says. Normally I can read Ximena like a map, but I can't tell if she's confused or mad that I'm letting Asher help me with The Whine when I've always said no to her.

"I'm going to grab a drink from the vending machines," Asher says, getting up.

He leaves his lunch behind, which hopefully means he plans to come back at some point, at least long enough to finish it.

As soon as he's gone, Ximena and Renata lean across the table.

"Okay," Ximena whispers, "how did we go from thinking Asher was a blathering ableist idiot a few days ago to he's now hanging out at your place and working on The Whine with you? Did we get *Doctor Who*'d and a time portal opened up to suck us into an alternate universe or something?"

I laugh. "You've never even seen *Doctor Who*!"

"Fine, but Max talks about it enough that I'm pretty sure that's the basic plot." Ximena sniffs. "What's the deal?"

After I'm done explaining, Ximena says, "So, you let him drive you home?"

"Uh-huh."

"You don't like other people touching your chair. And you especially don't like having it in the back of trucks because of, and I quote, *bug guts*."

"I mean, it was a short ride."

"And then he apologized and asked *you* to help him get into that summer thing." Ximena takes one of my celery sticks and crunches on it thoughtfully.

"I guess so, yeah."

"And you're sure he's not a jerk."

"I'm sure. He's actually pretty cool."

In an instant, Ximena's face transforms from suspicion to pure joy. "Oh *really*?"

I roll my eyes. "Geez, not like that."

"Could do worse," Ximena says, now that she's apparently convinced Asher isn't ableist. "I mean, I said so before we thought he was an idiot, and now that we don't think he's an idiot anymore, I'll say it again. He's cute."

I turn to watch Asher pull a Pepsi out of the machine. "Yeah, I guess," I say.

Ximena cheers way too loudly. "Make. It. Happen. Q!" She claps on each word.

I cover my face with my hands. Sometimes I kind of wish Ximena wouldn't tease me about guys or even encourage me, even though I suppose it's a best friend's right. As soon as she thinks a guy is into me, she immediately starts trying to make us happen.

But she and Max are in a serious relationship. They have been inching around the L-word for weeks. So when she gets excited if a guy so much as looks at me, it makes me feel like I'm a kindergartner trying to hang out with the high school kids, even though I know that's not how she means it.

When Asher comes back, the tension, thankfully, is about 100 percent lower than before, and we all fall into easy conversation about classes and our looming midterms.

Eventually, Ximena and Renata decide to go to class early to see if they can try to weasel any clues about what will be on their quiz out of Mr. Schriever. Ximena gives me a knowing look on her way out that I pretend not to see.

I glance over at Cade's table instead, which has thinned a little. "Are we sure we want to intentionally talk to Cade?"

"Having second thoughts?" Asher asks.

"More like traumatic flashbacks of him tormenting me in junior high. We could try to find out more about the Turner kids without him."

"I don't know. I did some light googling last night and didn't find much of anything about them."

"Really? The computer nerd couldn't find anything?"

"I prefer the term *guru*, if you don't mind." He smirks and drains the last of his Pepsi.

"Yeah, I'm not calling you that."

I watch the second hand on the giant wall clock over the cafeteria doors inch closer to the end of lunch. Only Lily, Brayden, and Cade are still at their table.

"I guess now's our chance," Asher says.

I drop off my tray and Asher throws away his bag before we head to Cade's table, weaving through the abandoned chairs and thinning tables just as Lily and Brayden leave Cade. I stop breathing when Cade's steely eyes look up at us and he frowns.

Thankfully, Asher speaks first. "Hey, can we talk to you about those missing kids?"

"Saw you didn't mention Defend Kids in your post," he says gruffly to me, ignoring Asher completely.

I wish Cade couldn't do this to me, but it's like I'm in seventh grade again, when I was always trying to keep his attention turned away from me.

"Yeah," I say, trying to keep my voice as steady as possible, "but I figured it's about finding the kids, not promoting your club, right?"

Cade gives us a strained smile, like it's taking every muscle in his body to keep his mouth curved upward. He gets to his feet, and my body automatically shrinks back against my chair.

"Sure, but Defend Kids isn't just a *club*," he says. "It's a nonprofit founded three years ago in Utah. Now it's got chapters all over the country. My mom's organizing the first chapter upstate, but there are already more than fifty-two chapters across the country."

"Wow," I say, and I don't even have to feign being impressed since I'd kind of been assuming this whole time that Defend Kids was something Cade was just using for attention. "So is there anything new on the Turners? I want to do an update post."

"Getting lots of likes from kidnapped kids, huh?" Cade's smile vanishes and reappears in a second. "Just messing with you. I'm glad you're helping to get the word out. Even if you don't give us credit."

Kidnapped. Ava and I once decided we were going to run away when she was nine years old and I was eight, right around Jensen's age. But it was the middle of December and we only made it to Ted's Tires two blocks away. Mr. Ambrose pulled in as we were crossing the parking lot and convinced us it wasn't worth the cold or missing out on our Christmas presents and walked us home. I don't even remember what Ava and I were mad at Mom and Dad for.

Ava had told us that every second counts in abduction cases. A cold wave washes over me at the thought that it's been weeks since the Turners disappeared from their yard, and they didn't run into anyone as nice as Mr. Ambrose. They probably want nothing more than to turn around and come home like Ava and I did, and someone is keeping them from doing that.

"Do the police have a suspect?" Asher asks. "I couldn't find much about them online."

Cade shakes his head slowly. "It's so much bigger than the Turner kids. The same night Jensen and Annalice Turner were kidnapped, there were twenty-eight other kidnappings in the northeast. Fifteen from New York state alone."

"Wh-what?" My carefully controlled voice falters. "Who would do that?" I know I should let him talk and that every time I don't, he could turn on me, like a fire just waiting for a spark to set it off.

"The police said people reported seeing identical black vans circling neighborhoods right before each kid disappeared. But it takes a lot more than one person to cover the northeast in one night. It takes a group," Cade says. "You probably didn't know that more than one hundred thousand kids are abducted each year, and child trafficking is only getting worse."

Ava told my parents and me this over dinner last night—when she was spewing off all kinds of terrifying facts she'd already memorized about missing kids. Still, the number is so startling that I can almost ignore how gleeful Cade looks to be telling us so many things he knew and we didn't. That's about ten towns the size of Canandaigua just disappearing every year. How do that many kids disappear each year and we're just now learning about it?

As if reading my mind, Cade says, "People don't care, so of course the media never reports on it. It's thanks to Defend Kids that people are finally starting to learn how bad it really is. It may not seem like a big deal to you," he says, staring directly at Asher, "but we raised more than seven hundred dollars with the bake sale."

Cade keeps going. "We have a lot more planned to build awareness, like events and stuff. We're doing a rally next weekend on Main Street. We're going to do what the media never does, which is to end child trafficking. We're working with the police, too. Because the thing is, what happened to the Turner kids could happen to anyone."

At some point, I started to lean forward in my chair as Cade was talking, but I sit straight up when Cade's eyes suddenly latch on to Dillon McRae walking across the cafeteria. If for a second my mind had accepted that Cade had somewhat changed, it disappears watching Cade observe Dillon like a hunter tracking a deer.

Dillon must think Cade's too distracted talking to us that he won't notice him slip behind him, but Cade suddenly spins and hooks an arm around Dillon's shoulder and drags him toward us.

"Hey, bro," Cade says in an unnaturally pleasant voice that makes my stomach twist. "How's it going?"

Dillon's whole body stiffens under the weight of Cade's arm as it snakes around his neck and squeezes just hard enough to notice. "Um, fine."

Dillon's eyes shift from Cade's face to the cafeteria doors, and I know exactly what's going on in his head. He's trying to decide if he can escape being the unlucky target of Cade's attention today. That's what it's been like since we were kids, trying to avoid being noticed by Cade and breathing a sigh of relief, and guilt, when his attention turns to anyone but you.

"I noticed you haven't signed up to join my club yet." Dillon tries to squirm away but Cade's arm stays fastened on his neck. "You should really check it out."

"I guess," Dillon says, his hands in fists at his sides and his green eyes darting toward the doors.

"Dude, let him go," Asher says to Cade, his voice steely in a way I've never heard it.

I stop breathing as Cade's eyes lock on to Asher, something smoldering in them.

"He knows I'm just messing with him, don't you, bro?" Cade says with a wide grin, flicking the hood of Dillon's camouflage jacket. "We're meeting after school tomorrow, but I'm not forcing anyone to join. Come if you want to."

"Sure," Dillon mutters.

But when Cade releases him, Dillon doesn't hesitate before scrambling away from under his arm and skulking out of the cafeteria as quickly as he can.

"See you later," Asher says to Cade, and this time, he's the one not making a suggestion.

The strained smile reappears on Cade's face. "Whatever."

I can't stop my mouth from falling open when Cade actually leaves without punching Asher in the face. Asher King—computer nerd, rescuer of the bullied, and all-around nice guy apparently. Can't say the thought of defending Dillon ever crossed my mind, especially not after what happened in chemistry the other day.

"Are you magic or something?" I ask when Cade is safely out of the cafeteria. "Even the teachers can't get Cade to behave."

"His dad works for my parents," Asher says. "Is it terrible of me to admit that I kind of like being able to hold that over him? I swear I don't feel that way about anyone else, but"—his face darkens—"Cade deserves it, you know? Even if he's trying to be different now."

Now it all makes sense why Asher didn't seem worried about talking to Cade. He's clearly never known what it's like to have been Cade's target.

"I don't think it's terrible. In fact, it's nice to hear that you're actually a human like the rest of us."

The first bell for fourth period rings, and when I look up, I realize most of the rest of the cafeteria emptied out while Asher and I were talking.

"I have to grab my stuff from my locker," he says. "Come with me?"

We head for his locker, even though it's on the other side of the school and my next class is back by the cafeteria. I have a set route I usually stick to at school, because my shoulder joints really can't take much more pushing than what I've budgeted for. This extra detour is going to wreck them for the next few days and probably make me late to French class, but I'm not ready to leave Asher yet.

"Do you think any of what he said was true?" I ask as the hallway fills up with students.

Asher pulls out his phone and types something on it before holding it low for me. "It seems like he was telling the truth. Look. They have a website. That's where the QR code on the flyer takes you."

I try to skim the site without slamming into people in the crowded hallway. Asher pockets his phone when we get to his locker and spins the knob to unlock it, rummages through its contents, and pulls out a spiral notebook, the back of which is completely covered in intricate patterns and elaborate geometric shapes in blue and black ink. There's a delicate but layered mandala in the center and then what looks like vines and roses wrapped around it.

His eyes follow my gaze, and he turns the notebook over. "Oh. I doodle."

"Those aren't doodles. That's art," I say. "You definitely need to go to that RISD program. Whatever it takes."

"Thanks."

"I wish we knew why Cade was doing all this," I say as the warning bell rings. "I still don't buy that he actually cares about missing kids."

"Maybe his motivation doesn't matter so much if we can do something to help," Asher says thoughtfully.

"True." My one post has gotten a lot of attention already, and more people knowing may actually help the police find the Turners.

"I was thinking we should start meeting up on Wednesdays after school or something. You know, to touch base on posts and stuff?" he asks. "We could make it like our weekly planning meeting or something for The Whine."

I'm not expecting it—I kind of thought we were done once Asher did the logo—but it makes me smile. "Wednesdays sound good."

"Cool, because I have a lot of ideas." Asher grins and I watch him disappear into the crowd of people until I can't even see the top of his head anymore.

TheWhine: Did you know that every year, more than 100,000 children in the US are abducted? On September 1, Annalice and Jensen Turner were kidnapped right in their own front yard, along with 30 other kids in the northeast that same day. Help find them and put an end to child trafficking by getting the message out! #DefendKids

allie_belle: Those poor kids 😣

harriet_the_poke: The perpetrators need to be shot on sight, no mercy.

OllietheStar: This happened like 30 minutes away from us. This is what I was telling you about @miabae6

kristen_reader: 100,000?? Omg so so scary! I live near Rochester!!!

flamineagle: What is this world coming to???

dhash55: The government has to be in on it. Their silence is an admission of guilt. That's why it's going to take ordinary citizens to do something. Otherwise we've already lost.

Tambrose7: Why isn't this on the front page of the news every single day?!? DO something!!

TheRealCadeBird: Head over to my insta to find out more!!! Their kidnapping was part of a HUGE plot. I've got all the info about it. #DefendKids

mike_lee7: I'd like to see these creeps try to come for my family! #SaveTheChildren

brycemun: Come to our rally on October 7 on Main Street and help put a stop to child trafficking!

molly_bird: This is why #DefendKids is taking action. We're taking things into our own hands to defend our families! Join us! #cabal #stopchildtrafficking #D3NY

chapter six

M om asks me to work the register while she unboxes a new shipment of Christmas cards at Vine and Things. I don't bother to stifle my yawn from another late night of being on Instagram because there's no one here to see it but Mom.

She really doesn't need me here. It's been so dead in the shop, especially for a Saturday, that I'm pretty sure cobwebs are already starting to form around the cheerful North Pole village Mom just finished setting up. Apparently Mom's strategy to attract customers is to make Christmas in October happen. I take pictures of it to post on The Whine later. But the display is kind of overshadowed by the missing persons flyer Ava taped up on the window above it all, and the fact that there's a steady, cold autumn drizzle outside.

I've got four hours to go on this shift unless Mom shows me some mercy and lets me go. Even though I could use the money, all I want to do is check my notifications, but there's a strict no-phone rule in the shop.

Ever since I started posting about the Turner kids and, as much as I hate to admit it, the Defend Kids club, I've gone viral three times, including the one I did on the grand opening of the new bank down the street. It was a picture of the ribbon cutting that all of three people came to, but by the next day, the post had more than a thousand likes. People like banks it seems. Who knew?

I'm trying to distract myself by untangling some of the new beaded necklaces we just got in when the door to the store bursts open, the bell above it clanging in protest. I straighten on habit, but it's only Ava with Bryce in tow, and I let myself slump back down in my chair.

"Hey, girls," Mom calls.

"Hey. Where are all the flyers?" Ava says as soon as she reaches the counter, pointing to the empty space next to the cash register where we've kept a stack of them.

"Oh my gosh, you *do* exist! I was beginning to think I'd dreamed up having a sister," I say.

"You're so funny," she says flatly. "Seriously, where are the flyers?"

"We ran out." I shrug despite Ava's accusatory tone, like I might have secretly thrown them in the garbage or something. "Isn't that a good thing?"

"Of course! That means we're really getting the word out," Bryce says eagerly. She's wearing a purple T-shirt that says *Member of the Oxford Comma Preservation Society.* "I have some more in my car. I'll go get them."

"Cool, thanks," I say.

Bryce smiles and jogs back out the front door. For a second, Ava looks like she's been put in a trance by the sight of Bryce's curly brass-blond hair bouncing behind her as she moves. But then she catches me watching her and busies herself straightening the necklaces I'd been unpacking. Maybe all the time she's been spending with Bryce isn't only about Defend Kids.

"It's so awful, what happened to those poor kids. I can't get over it," Mom says. "Their parents must be beside themselves."

"Yeah, they just got home from a family trip to Disney World that day," Ava says. "They were playing in their yard and when their mom looked out the window a minute later, Annalice and Jensen were gone."

"I don't know what I'd do if something like that happened to you both." Mom shakes a little, like she's trying to erase whatever horrible image her brain has latched on to.

"It's slow today, huh, Mom?" Ava says, her eyes scanning the empty store.

"It's the weather. No one wants to be out right now. It'll pick up when the rain stops."

"You're probably right." Ava turns back to me. "So, your posts on the Turners have been really good lately."

"Thanks."

"I didn't think you'd help Cade in a million years."

I shrug. "I mean, same. But it's not helping Cade. It's helping the Turners, right?"

Ava smiles. "Right."

Bryce comes back with a stack of flyers. "Hot off the presses."

"That must have cost a lot," Mom says, eyeing the stack.

"And killed a small forest," I add.

"Mr. Ambrose has a copy machine at Ted's Tires and he lets us use it for free. He's a member of Defend Kids," Ava replies. "Dad said we got a new candy shipment this morning. Can I grab some for our meeting at Cade's house today? I'll pay for it."

"Nonsense. Take whatever you want. It's all still in a box in the back," Mom says.

Bryce leans a hip against the counter while Ava heads for the storage room.

The front door jingles again and this time, a woman with a short gray bob and yellow raincoat walks in.

Mom blinks at the woman like she can't quite believe we have a real live customer.

"Welcome! Let me know if I can help you find anything," she says.

"Just browsing." The woman smiles politely and wanders toward the essential oils display.

"So, how's Model UN going?" I ask Bryce since this is the first time I've really actually been with her for more than two minutes, even though she and Ava have been practically superglued together lately.

Bryce waves a hand. "Oh, I quit Model UN."

"You did?"

"Yeah. I watch my little brother and sister most days after school because my dad works late, so I really only have time for one school activity." There's a heaviness to the way Bryce leaves out a mention of another parent, so I don't ask.

"I thought you were pretty into it."

"Defend Kids matters so much more than mock role-playing. This is real life, you know? Plus, it's like one of the most important issues we as a society are facing right now, and we're only starting to build some momentum in spreading awareness. And it just feels like it's something I have to do for my little brother and sister. Like, what if something happened to them?" She takes a deep breath, her shoulders rising, and then looks at me with a sheepish smile. "Sorry. I just feel really strongly about this, you know?"

I nod because I can absolutely see why Ava likes spending time with Bryce.

When Ava emerges from the storage room, her arms are loaded with bags of gummy worms, Sour Patch Kids, peanut butter cups, and Peppermint Patties. She dumps it on the counter, and I hand her a bag.

"Seriously, Mom. I can pay for it." She frowns once she's filled the bag like she doesn't remember grabbing so much.

"Or I can," Bryce says, opening the bag slung over her shoulder.

"Why are you being weird?" I ask Ava. One of the perks of the shop has always been the endless supply of free candy.

"Don't be silly. It's on the house. It's the least we can do to help out," Mom says. "So, there are meetings on Saturdays now, too?"

"For now. There's still a lot to do for the rally next weekend. We're planning a march up Main Street and then ending with a moment of silence for all the kids who have been kidnapped this year in the US," Bryce says. "And we're starting to talk about maybe having a 5K or something next month in Geneva."

I'll pass on the 5K, but the march sounds like the perfect thing to livestream on The Whine, though I'm already getting phantom warning pains in my shoulders and hands. It's only a couple of blocks, but the whole route to the park is up a steady but merciless incline. Not to mention the fact that I won't be able to push and stream at the same time. I'm sure Asher will want to come once he hears about it, but I'm also not sure I want him to be there to watch me struggle or to have to ask him to push me.

"I'm really proud of you girls for working so hard to raise awareness about all these children," Mom says.

"You know," I say thoughtfully. "I've only ever heard about the Turner kids, but weren't there supposed to be thirty kids kidnapped on the exact same night they disappeared? Maybe I could do some posts about them, too, or a video or something."

I don't know why I hadn't thought about it until now, but once Mom mentioned *all* the kids, I realized that Jensen and Annalice Turner are the only ones people ever talk about.

"Their families haven't come forward because they don't want all the attention," Bryce says. "Social media can be so vicious, even to victims."

"That makes sense," I say. "But if the families haven't come forward, how do you know how many kids were kidnapped?"

"The police reports," Bryce says. "It's all public, but they don't include the names of the kids because they're underage, and of course Defend Kids wants to respect the privacy of the families."

"It just seems like it'd help raise more awareness if there were other personal stories Defend Kids could tell about kids in other areas."

"That's a really good point, Quinn." Bryce nods and looks at Ava.

Ava grins. "Uh-oh, I know that look. It means you have a new idea."

Bryce laughs and tugs on Ava's arm. "Aw, you know me so well!"

A second later, the gray-haired customer pops her head around the corner of the display. "Are you all talking about the Defend Kids rally next week?"

"We are," Bryce says.

The woman smiles, her pale blue eyes brightening. "My husband and I are in the Pennsylvania chapter of D3," she says. "We drove up early from Harrisburg with some friends last night so we could make a little trip of it to see the fall colors and visit some of the wineries since we've never been to the area before."

I raise a curious eyebrow. A little tour of the New York wine region in the fall, tacked onto a march against child trafficking?

"Wow!" Bryce and Ava say at the same time, turning to each other in excitement.

"I guess we're really getting the word out," Ava says.

"You sure are. I saw a post about it on Facebook from a friend who lives in Buffalo, and then I got an email from the New York D3 chapter. You all are doing great work up here to raise awareness. We're hoping to do our own rally in Pittsburgh next month because the situation there is even worse," she replies. "Twenty kids were taken from western Pennsylvania alone the same night the Turner kids went missing. Good people have to take a stand, don't they? Lord knows the government won't do anything since they're facilitating the whole thing." The woman shakes her head somberly before turning to Mom and holding up a white T-shirt that says *I ❤ FLX* in black letters. "You don't happen to have this one in an extra-large, do you?"

"I'll go check in the back," Mom says, scurrying to the storage room.

"It's inspiring to see you young people so involved in your communities. Gives me a bit of hope," the woman says to us. "It's a shame you're inheriting such a troubled world with so many evil forces working against you. It's getting to where you can barely trust your neighbors anymore not to come murder you in your bed."

"We're in luck. We had one left," Mom says, coming back with the T-shirt.

"Wonderful!" the woman says cheerfully. She drops an armful of other assorted things she collected as she talked onto the counter, and Mom starts to ring her up.

"Thanks for coming all this way for our rally," Bryce says. "We'll see you there."

"You can count on it," the woman says once Mom has handed her the bag and receipt.

"Okay, she thinks the government is in on the kidnappings?" I say as soon as she's gone.

Ava's mouth makes a line.

"Quinn," Mom says. "Lots of different people have lots of different ideas." She starts refolding some of the T-shirts the woman rifled through. "Remember cousin Barry? Great guy who also happens to believe the earth is flat."

"The earth *isn't* flat," I say. "And I thought that's why Grandma Jo stopped inviting him for Thanksgiving."

"Anyway," Mom says pointedly.

I guess to Mom, it isn't worth arguing about a woman who just bought $233.27 worth of stuff. But I'm already crafting the text I'll send Ximena telling her what happened. The woman is exactly the kind of person she'd spend a whole day arguing with on social media. While Mom and Dad think people fighting about things on social media is toxic, Ximena believes it's her personal mission in life to save every misguided soul.

"She's not exactly wrong," Ava says. "A hundred thousand kids going missing each year means someone in the government is ignoring something."

She has a point.

"I thought she seemed nice," Bryce says, tucking her hair behind her ears, revealing a line of piercings up one ear.

"What's D3 anyway?"

"It's just shorthand for Defend Kids," Bryce replies.

I eye Ava, who hasn't moved from her spot beside the ring display since the woman started talking.

"You know her math doesn't even add up, right? Cade said thirty kids were taken the night the Turners went missing, and I'm pretty sure he said fifteen of them were from New York and the rest were from around the northeast. But that woman said twenty were from Pennsylvania. And how does that even work logistically, taking all those kids at once? They charter buses or something?"

"She's probably just confused," Ava finally says, but her forehead is still furrowed. "We better get going or we'll be late for Cade's." She and Bryce load their arms with the bags of candy.

But the woman's rant has created questions in my mind. Plus, even though it made sense at first when Bryce explained why other families hadn't come forward, it seems weird not to know anything else about the thirty other kids supposedly kidnapped the same night as the Turners. Not any of their names.

And now that I'm thinking about it, no one seems to know much about the Turners either.

Ava is nearly at the door when she turns back to me. "You'll post about the rally on The Whine, won't you?"

"Does that mean you now think The Whine is a worthwhile precollege activity?"

"I think what you're doing is really helping us," she says. "So, will you?"

Even if I have questions about Defend Kids and some of their members, I can't help but feel good about Ava needing me.

"Yeah, sure," I say.

TheWhine: Annalice and Jensen Turner are still missing after being abducted from their home on September 1. Join Defend Kids this Saturday in Canandaigua for a march down Main Street to honor them, and all the kids who have been kidnapped since. We'll be meeting in front of the Villager restaurant and marching up to Ontario County Park, ending in a moment of silence at the pavilion. Let's help find them! #100thousand #DefendKids

chapter seven

Vine and Things really looks like the North Pole after I spend my shift the next day unpacking the latest Christmas shipment even though Halloween is still weeks away. Long after I'm covered head to toe in glitter, I make the trek from the front of the store around the corner and to my house. Already there's a bite to the late-afternoon air and it sends tiny needles of pain stabbing away at each of my joints.

Mom and Dad keep offering to have a stair lift put in. But they accidentally left the contractor's estimate out on the table one night, and apparently stair lifts are made out of solid gold. Building a hydraulic-powered one is a bit beyond their DIY skills.

What I don't tell them is that having to push myself up the hill to the shop is completely shredding my shoulders. Or that, even if my RA stays in remission, I think I might need an electric wheelchair someday. But I haven't said the words out loud yet. My wheelchair feels like a part of my body. Changing it would be like putting on someone else's skin.

The house is quiet when I finally push my way inside, exhausted. But it shouldn't last long. Ava will be home soon, unless she has some new Defend Kids thing I don't know about yet. She's been out three nights this week already, getting ready for the march.

My fingers itch for my phone and I head straight to the kitchen counter, where I left it before my shift started. As I swipe to unlock it,

I see another 227 new followers and 575 new likes since this morning, and that familiar thrill shoots through my veins. The last few days, even some of my old posts from a year ago have gone viral.

There's something so incredible about going viral. The fact that thousands of people think something you said or made matters. I tap on my DMs and one at the top catches my eye. It's from Piper's Grill, a restaurant on Seneca Lake, asking me what my rates are for sponsored posts. I can't keep a grin from spreading across my face, because that's the other thing about going viral—when you have attention, other people want it, too.

Even though I fully intended to start on my homework as soon as I got home, the next time I look up, a half hour has disappeared from writing back the restaurant and scrolling through my notifications. I force myself to set my phone down and start on my work. I've barely got Google Classroom pulled up on my laptop with my assignments before my phone rings. Asher is FaceTiming me.

"Hey." The screen of Asher's view jumps around so much it makes me dizzy. "You busy?"

"Just got home from work. Wow, what is happening?"

"Sorry, I'm running." He pants between words.

"I figured that part out. So training has officially begun, huh?"

I catch a flash of a pained grin as the camera bumps along. "Training never stops when you're as bad as I am. Have you looked at the comments from today?"

"You mean the ones from Cade and his mom trying to get new followers off of my posts? I'm embarrassed for them."

"I'd take it as a compliment. Everyone's trying to benefit from you turning into an influencer."

A smile tugs at my lips. "That's the *nice* way of looking at it."

"But no, not those ones. It's kind of weird stuff, like spam or something. Can I come over?"

I can feel the disappointment hit me, but I bat it away. Of course Asher only wants to come over to talk about The Whine. On my phone, I spot the sky, what I think is a yellow tree, and a sidewalk.

"Where are you?"

"On West Lake," he puffs. "Almost to Parrish Street. I can run over to your place and show you." He says *run over* like he's just around the block rather than more than a mile away still.

"Actually, can you meet me at the Black Cat instead?" I lower my phone a little to hide the fact that I'm already in my bedroom.

"On my way." Asher ends the call, and I grab my coat.

It's obviously farther away for me since I'm already home and it's up that hill again, but probably safer for Asher given Mom's interest in our friendship. Ever since she met him, she keeps dropping bits of information about his family into every conversation we have. It's been like living with the Kings' Wikipedia page.

I quickly change out of my green work polo and throw on a yellow long-sleeved shirt cropped just above the top of my jeans. If I didn't need every bit of strength left in my arms to get to the Black Cat, I'd wrangle my hair into a topknot or something to hide the fact that I definitely should have washed it this morning and didn't. Having RA is to be constantly making trade-offs.

On Main Street, most of the store and restaurant windows are filled with posters and flyers. Defend Kids has practically papered over Canandaigua for the rally.

When I get to the Black Cat, I order a drink and position myself facing the door next to the old green couch at the back. The community bulletin board beside me is covered in the familiar gold flyer. A few minutes later, Asher comes in red-faced and noticeably panting.

He fills up a glass of water at the counter on the way and drops onto the couch. "Hey."

"Did you run all the way from your house?"

Asher nods, still breathing heavy.

"How many miles is that?"

"Seven," he wheezes.

"Impressive," I say, even though I feel like that's probably considered a warm-up for most experienced cross-country runners.

"Thanks." He drains his glass in just a few gulps.

I smile because he says it confidently, but he also kind of looks like he's going to die.

"I actually have some good news to start with." He moves to the side of the couch closest to me and pulls his phone from his pocket. "I hope you don't mind, but I signed us up for an Instagram analytics account a couple days ago. It's a way to see how the posts are doing, who is engaging with your content, and stuff like that."

"I didn't know you could do that."

"I'm the computer guru, remember?"

"We never agreed on that title."

He smirks and swipes around on his phone before opening an app. Asher angles his phone screen toward me and points at a line graph with a massive spike on a page labeled Traffic.

"Okay, so this graph shows your engagement levels—your likes and shares." He scrolls down a little and under it, there's a map of the US showing a sea of red dots fanned out all across the country. "The map shows where your engagement is coming from, so where the actual users that are clicking on your content are located. Even since I downloaded this app, engagement on the posts is up by a lot. About two thousand percent, actually."

My breath hitches and a thrill runs through me. "*Two thousand?* I mean, I knew the posts were doing well, but, whoa." I make a mental note to do another post about the store to take advantage of all the new traffic as soon as I get home.

"I know, right?" Asher says, looking pleased. "And you're not just getting attention from people in the region. At least seventy-five percent of the new followers aren't even from New York state, and two percent are from outside the US." Asher's dark eyes study me like I've conquered the world and he wants to figure out how. I can feel heat creeping into my cheeks, and it takes all my energy not to grin at him like an idiot.

"How are they even finding me, though?"

Asher blinks and taps on his phone to another page of the app.

"It says the account is getting linked a lot on other websites and social media platforms." He turns his phone toward me again and it shows a list of websites. "This is where you're getting most of your traffic from." Most of the sites I recognize, like Google, TikTok, and Reddit. But there are some I don't recognize, like D3Map. "I think it's people just sharing the information you've been posting about the Turners. You know, helping to spread the word."

"But you said you think we're getting hit with spammers?"

He swipes again until he's pulled up The Whine's notifications page. "Yeah. That's the bad news. There are a bunch of accounts that are posting all these weird-looking news articles as comments." He scrolls through slowly to show me and then hands me his phone. The comments didn't look too odd when I was in my viral bliss haze after work earlier, but now that I'm scanning them, there's definitely something off.

"Did any of these things even happen?" I say, reading the list of headlines. I point to one from a site called OMGNews saying the Pledge of Allegiance was banned from schools. It looks like a normal site for a newspaper with article headlines with the names of their authors below. "I mean, I know this is wrong because we still say the Pledge every day." I point to another on the list from the site called D3Map. "And this one saying there was an Ebola outbreak that killed thirty people in Massachusetts . . . I feel like we would have heard about it if that was true."

Asher nods in agreement.

Most of the URLs look like regular news websites, even if I'm not sure I've heard of them before and the stories sound a little out there.

"I don't know. They seem pretty harmless. Probably just trying to get clicks on their sites."

"Or followers." I sigh. "Like Cade."

I stare up thoughtfully at the yellowing tiles in the drop ceiling. It's annoying that people are trying to take advantage of my posts to get clicks. But the comments boost my engagement numbers, which means Instagram will show more people my posts, and that could lead to more followers and paid sponsors.

"We'll keep an eye on them and if they get to be too much, then we can start blocking them," I say.

I expect Asher to get up, but instead he leans back like he's planning to stay, and it dashes the last memory I had of my abandoned homework.

He turns his head to the side to look at me more closely. "You have sparkles on your cheek."

"Really?" I scrub at my face with my sleeve. "We got a bunch of holiday stuff in today and I basically got consumed by a sparkle tornado."

"I can get it, if you want."

I'm expecting his hand to be sweaty from running, but his fingers are perfectly warm and soft as they gently brush at the soft skin under my right eye. It leaves my skin prickling a little where he touched it.

Asher walks me home a while later. His idea, not mine. It takes everything not to let my face show how much my shoulders and hands are hurting from the extra pushing I hadn't counted on doing today.

I think about texting Ximena to tell her what happened with Asher so I can spend the rest of the night recounting every moment at the coffee shop that led up to him touching my cheek, the way we used to analyze every move Max made before he finally asked Ximena out. But I don't, because then I'd have to admit that I'm hoping he'll do it again.

chapter eight

Okay, I have the posters, the candles, and extra batteries just in case." My sister's normally calm and steady voice comes through our shared bedroom wall panicked and rushed. "Ugh! What am I forgetting?" Whoever is on the other end must have the answer because a second later, Ava says, "Oh my god, yes, *thank you*. Okay, I'll meet you there in two minutes."

She's been like this all morning, increasingly frantic phone calls and moving through the house like a bulldozer to gather supplies for the rally. I poke my head into the hallway just as Ava appears with a massive box.

"I'm running late to meet Bryce," she snaps, brushing past me. I follow her into the living room. Ava sets down the box and grabs her tennis shoes, fumbling as she works on tying the laces.

"What's with the candles?" I nod at the box.

"They're for the vigil."

"The vigil? I thought it was the march and then a moment of silence."

Ava finally succeeds in tying one shoe before moving to the next. "It was. Originally. But then once we realized people are actually coming from all over for this, Mrs. Bird decided it needed to be bigger and it's been a total scramble to pull together. Instead of the moment of silence, she's going to give a speech and lay some flowers, and then we're ending on a candlelight vigil right as the sun starts setting. And she wants us to run the Defend Kids merch table after, too."

"I can post an update on the changes to the rally schedule on Insta. Make sure people know where to go and stuff."

"Great, thanks," Ava says.

Ava's got that same I'm-about-to-snap look she gets right before tests when Mom, Dad, and I practically have to walk around the house like monks who've taken a vow of silence so Ava can study. It sends a surge of anger through me, the fact that Cade and his mom are clearly taking advantage of Ava when she already puts so much pressure on herself.

"You know, Mrs. Bird sure sounds demanding for someone relying entirely on free labor."

"She's"—even with Ava's head down, I can see her mouth purse as she searches for the right word—"committed." She finishes the double knot on her other shoe with a hard tug.

"It doesn't seem very fair to you and Bryce, since Cade and his mom are probably going to end up taking credit for all your work anyway. Maybe you just shouldn't show up today, let them figure it out."

"You're kidding, right?"

"I mean, I want to find the Turners as much as anybody else, but it's not right how Mrs. Bird is treating you guys. Maybe you should bail on the club altogether."

She sits back on her heels. "I can't just bail. I need this."

"You need this?"

"The shop isn't doing well. Haven't you noticed how slow it's been?" Ava stands.

I blink at the topic shift. "I . . . I mean, yeah. But, I don't know, I guess I figured we were okay—"

"And we are for now. But that's because last year Mom and Dad sat me down and asked me if they could use the money they'd been saving for my tuition. And of course I said yes. Vine and Things wouldn't have survived otherwise."

My mouth falls open. "What?"

"It's not a big deal. They haven't touched yours for now."

"Ava, that's a *huge* deal." I nudge my wheels closer to her.

"I can't obsess over it any more than I already have. But now I definitely have to pay for school on my own, which means my application has to be perfect . . ."

"Why didn't they tell me?"

"Maybe they thought they could turn things around at the store, so they wouldn't have to." Ava runs a hand through her hair and picks up her box. "Or maybe they hoped you'd grown up enough to finally start paying attention to the super obvious stuff happening around you."

I'm too stunned to think of a retort before she barrels out the door with her box. I sit in the silence of the living room for a while, my brain and my body unable to process what Ava just revealed. Suddenly so many pieces are clicking into place right now. Why Ava's love of school went into total overdrive last year. Why she's become obsessive about scholarships and pushing me to work harder. Why she's throwing herself so hard into Defend Kids. All that pressure she's been putting on herself isn't actually a choice. It's necessary.

And I just feel stupid. How did I not see this? I guess I should have realized that living in the basement of the shop isn't for fun, that an empty store on the weekends meant less money, that my family has been close to losing it all. Close enough that my parents had to raid Ava's tuition money and may have to eventually dip into mine, too, which I know for a fact they'd never do unless it was their only option.

There's got to be something I can do to help. My phone chimes, announcing a Venmo payment for six months of promotion from Piper's Grill on Seneca Lake. That makes four paying sponsors.

And that's when it hits me. The Whine is really taking off now. With more followers, I could probably convince more local businesses to become paid sponsors and even increase my monthly rates. Maybe if I get big enough, I can make enough to help Ava pay for school. Maybe I could even earn my own money so Mom and Dad won't have to help with my college and they can just concentrate on keeping the store afloat.

But all that means I'm going to need to get to work, and covering the rally is the first step. I force myself to post a quick update on The Whine and hurry to take a shower and get dressed. I miss two FaceTimes from Ximena while I'm getting ready, but I don't have time to call her back.

The sun feels weak against my face when I head out, even in the cloudless blue sky, and I hurry up the hill from the parking lot to the street. I peer through the window of Vine and Things to find it surprisingly full of shoppers. Both Mom and Dad are behind the counter checking people out with matching wide grins on their faces.

From up the street, I spot a large crowd forming in front of the Villager and I head toward it, determined. After all my worrying about whether or not I should ask Asher to go with me to the rally, it turns out he's visiting his grandparents in Buffalo anyway.

It looks like half of Canandaigua is here. There's at least forty people standing around, and another car full of people pulls up, parks, and joins in the minute it takes me to move down the street. Phoenix and Annika from Defend Kids, who sit at Cade's lunch table, pass out gold flyers wearing matching club T-shirts in black and gold. Ollie has brought about half the football team and they each have their faces painted in the same colors, like this is a game instead of a rally for missing kids. Even Dillon hovers along the edge of the crowd, his hands in the pockets of his jacket. Cade must have finally bullied him into joining the club. A bunch of the business owners from Main Street are here, too.

For Canandaigua during a weekend so early in deer hunting season, it's a huge turnout. But there's another whole part of the crowd I don't recognize at all.

A woman with brown hair about Mom's age stands with her back against the Villager's brick wall with a poster leaning against her leg that reads *Defend Kids, Rise Up!* Another woman holds tightly to a poster that says *Save the Children* with the pictures of Annalice and Jensen Turner below it. A man in hiking boots holds a poster cut in the shape of a giant ear with the words *Washington's silence is*

DEAFENING! painted in big black letters. He talks animatedly with two other men, one of whom holds a sign that says *End Child Trafficking* and the other a sign that simply says *D3.*

I stand off to the side and try to take a few pictures, but I can't get the whole crowd no matter how much I zoom out. I hope it helps the Turners' parents and the ones who haven't come forward publicly yet to know that so many people are trying to help them find their kids.

I'm lifting my phone to take another picture when I notice Dillon staring at me. He licks his lips nervously and for a second, it looks like he's about to come talk to me.

As he starts to move, the Villager's door opens and a group of people steps out in front of him, cutting him off. And Renata and Adrian are two of them. They're both holding white to-go coffee cups, steam curling above the black lids. I start to head over, but I stop mid-push. The whole thing is completely normal and innocent looking, except, I realize, for the way Adrian's hand keeps brushing against Renata's, and how she leans into him closer each time their skin connects.

I weave toward them through the crowd.

"Hey," I say. "How's it going?"

Renata springs back a whole foot and smiles a little too widely when she sees me. A small frown flashes on Adrian's face, disappearing fast enough that it makes me wonder if I'd maybe imagined it.

"Oh, hey, Q!" Renata says.

"I didn't know you guys were coming to the rally."

"We weren't planning to," she says, brushing her shoulder-length brown hair behind her ears. "Ade and I were kind of walking around when we saw Ava and her friends setting stuff up at the park, so we figured we'd grab some coffee and check it out. It's not a big deal or anything," Renata adds defensively.

Adrian frowns again and awkwardly takes a sip. Did I totally miss something changing between them the last few weeks? What will happen to our friend group if it suddenly becomes couples, plus me and Sulome? I don't think I can sit through lunches with any more PDA than we already get from Ximena and Max.

Renata's smile tightens. "Anyway. What are you doing here?"

"Ava and Bryce basically organized the whole event by themselves," I say, making my voice a little louder than normal, "so I'm here to support. I'm going to livestream it for The Whine."

"No Ximena?" Adrian eyes the Ximena-sized empty space next to me the way everyone has lately. It makes me wonder if people can see how obviously out of place I feel without her. Or maybe *felt*, past tense. Since I've been hanging out so much with Asher lately, that hole hasn't felt quite so cavernous as it did.

Renata lets out a chirpy sigh. "She and Max are in the center of their love bubble now that they've finally said *the words*."

"What?" I stiffen. "When did that happen?"

"Last night. She texted me and Sulome with all the adorable details."

That must be why she was FaceTiming me while I was getting ready. The mature side of me says that she totally intended to tell me first. But the rest of me is annoyed she waited until this morning to share major news but then couldn't wait for me to call her back before texting Renata and Sulome. On a group text I'm not on apparently.

Just then, the Birds' gleaming white SUV drives up to the curb next to the front of the crowd and a moment later, Cade slips out of the back seat in a black hoodie with *D3* written in large gold letters across it and tan army boots, followed by his whole-foot-shorter mom. She's blond and wearing skintight jeans and thick black combat boots that go up past her calves with a black bomber jacket.

"My god, it's like they think they're royalty," Renata says.

"And at war," I add. "All she's missing is one of those military berets."

"I do have coat envy, though." Renata eyes Mrs. Bird as she and Cade disappear into the crowd.

People pick up their posters and clump together a little closer. If I stay here, the video will just be a crowd of butts; I need a better view. But I'm still stinging at the news about Ximena and Max.

"I should get to the front so I can start my livestream."

"Need help?" Renata takes another completely obvious step away from Adrian.

"Actually, if you could push me once I start recording, then I won't have to pause my stream at all."

"Ooh, you never let people push you!" Renata sings. "Consider me honored and on board."

"I swear, if you're about to make some sort of racing joke, Renata—"

"Q! Never!"

"I guess I'll meet you guys at the park?" Adrian says.

"Cool, sure, whatever, see ya." Renata swoops behind me and moves us swiftly away.

"I think you kind of broke his heart, dude," I say up at Renata when we're far enough away.

"Whatever. Better to do it now than later."

Maybe my friend group isn't as at risk of coupling up as I thought. Renata pushes me twenty feet ahead of the crowd and turns my chair around so I can capture the whole thing.

There have to be a hundred people now, and from this angle a little ahead of everyone, it almost looks like an army is about to march on Canandaigua. After all their hard work, Ava and Bryce should be here to march at the front, but I don't see them anywhere. Instead, Cade, Mrs. Bird, and a white man I don't recognize are at the front. Together, they unroll the black-and-gold Defend Kids vinyl banner Cade used at the club fair a few weeks ago and hold it in front of the still-growing crowd.

I hit the button to start the livestream and a second later, my screen starts to fill with usernames joining to watch. I take a deep breath.

"Okay," I say, "so I'm here at the Defend Kids rally in Canandaigua, New York. Any minute now, the march against child trafficking will start. We're going from the Villager restaurant to the county park up Main Street. If you're in the area, come join us for a candlelight vigil in the park in about fifteen minutes." I glance up at the corner of my screen and see I already have 230 people watching the livestream. I keep going. "Now, if you're a new follow, you might not know how this all started. On September first, thirty kids were kidnapped from the northeast United States, including Jensen and Annalice Turner from Rochester, New York."

I've written the story enough times on my posts that it's easy to recite all the details about the night they and twenty-eight other kids were snatched from their homes, most of them from right here in New York. That's why it still seems so strange to me that the customer at the store could have a different set of facts. But whatever.

The low murmur among the crowd vanishes when Mrs. Bird turns her back to me to face them. The breeze muffles her voice, but when she lifts a small fist into the air, the crowd cheers and does the same. It's quiet when they start actually marching except for the shuffle of feet against concrete. The trees lining the street are full golden yellow in the early afternoon light, like torches lighting our path to the park. I don't try to fill the silence with more talking because there's an energy to the group's determined marching that seems to grow stronger with each step, quickly becoming a voice of its own.

Renata starts walking backward, pulling me with her so I can keep streaming. Turns out, we actually make a great team. I point silently where I want to go and she pushes me smoothly so I can hold my phone steady. We stay in front of the crowd for a while as they move up Main Street, and then swoop to the side to show the people marching by. I can't keep up with all the comments from the people watching and I don't even try so I can focus on making sure my angles are good. A block in and someone in the crowd starts to chant "De-fend-our-kids! De-fend-our-kids!" until the entire crowd chants it in unison, like a song. And there's something really moving about it, like you can feel the sadness but also the determination of each person here all the way into your bones.

Ava and Bryce stand at the front of the park, passing out small palm-sized electric candles as the crowd marches onto the yellowing grass. I nearly gasp as I see the number of people watching has climbed to more than three thousand. I gesture for Renata to slow down so I can zoom in on them. "And here are Bryce and Ava, the organizers of today's event. Say hi, guys!" Ava and Bryce grin at me and wave, their eyes wide as they hand out as many candles as they can to the people passing through. Cade's going to be so pissed when he hears what I said, and that makes me grin. But after everything I found out in my kind-of fight with Ava back home, I don't care.

The crowd streams toward the pavilion, where Mrs. Bird is already at the top of the steps, Cade following her. On the right side in front of the pavilion, there's a wooden easel with a blown-up version of the missing persons poster of Jensen and Annalice Turner sitting on it. On the other side of the pavilion, there's a table full of Defend Kids merch—T-shirts, mugs, water bottles, and key chains. It takes a while for the marchers to gather around the pavilion, and Renata pushes me slowly over the bumpy grass around the back of the crowd.

"As many of you know, Jensen and Annalice Turner were abducted from their front yard in broad daylight on September first," Mrs. Bird says, her voice louder than I was expecting it to be. The crowd immediately hushes. "Annalice was just starting eighth grade and loves to skateboard. Her little brother just started second grade and is a real math whiz. We're here to work together to bring these precious babies home to their family!"

There's a collective cheer from the crowd, and Renata and I edge closer to the pavilion.

"The hard truth is that our fight is not easy. We know that. One hundred thousand kids go missing each year. Even now, this very moment, our children right here in this town are under attack. Defend Kids leadership received word this morning from our sources close to law enforcement that the perpetrators struck again. Last night thirty-two more kids were kidnapped from Albany, snatched from their homes." There are gasps from the crowd, one of them my own strangled cry.

"I wish we didn't have to be here today," she says. "I wish our government wasn't corrupt. I wish our children weren't constantly under attack by evil forces. I wish a lot of things, but all of this is happening and I for one am sick of it. That's why each of us must commit today to doing whatever necessary to protect our children. This. Must. End."

The crowd cheers loudly now and Mrs. Bird smiles down on them, but my mind only races.

How were thirty-two new kids taken in a night? What are their names? And what are the police doing about it? But Mrs. Bird doesn't say anything else about them, like the whole thing is as normal as reporting the weather.

She waits for the crowd to quiet down before speaking again. "And now, I invite you all to join me in laying these flowers in honor of Jensen and Annalice Turner and all the kids who have been stolen from the loving arms of their families. Let it be a sign of your commitment to stand together and fight back against these evil forces at work."

Mrs. Bird picks up a bouquet of flowers almost as big as she is with bright yellow, red, and orange fall blooms from the steps of the pavilion and moves somberly down the stairs.

People lay candles and flowers, and some people lay their protest signs. One woman lays a teddy bear while wiping away tears.

After, Mrs. Bird climbs back up the steps. "Let's take a moment of silence to think about all of the children and families who have been targeted, and each of us take a vow now to do whatever necessary to defend our kids and bring every single one of them home."

The group is silent as people bow their heads around me, but inside, my brain whispers that something about Defend Kids is off. I tap the button to stop the livestream. My phone goes back to my main Instagram page, full of new notifications again.

"Hey! You didn't call me back, which hasn't happened since the Great Flu of Freshman Year when you were puking buckets," Ximena says later that night. Even over FaceTime, I can see a glow in her eyes, and a smile seems to have permanently tattooed itself onto her face.

I lean back against my pillows in my bed, exhausted from the day. "I went to that Defend Kids rally."

"Oh! We would have come with you if you said you were going."

Even if they get married someday, I don't know if I'll ever get used to her talking about a "we" that doesn't involve me.

"Sorry," I say, but I wish I hadn't as soon as it's out of my mouth. Ximena and Max do things without me all the time; this isn't any different. Still, it would have been nice if she'd been here after Ava dropped that big bomb about my family's finances. "I mostly went to support Ava and Bryce since they organized it." I hold my phone up a little higher. "Actually, I went with Renata and Ade. Renata helped me do the livestream, so you can watch it if you want." It comes out like it wasn't totally random that I ran into Adrian and Renata, like I purposely invited them and not Ximena, but she only smiles at me.

"Look at you being the best sister! I'm proud of you, Q."

Instantly, I feel a rush of guilt for trying to make her feel jealous.

"Max and I ended up having to go to the lake without you and you totally missed it. He got cocky and thought he could balance on the post at the end of the dock. And *of course* he fell in, exactly like I told him he would. The water's like negative a hundred degrees already, so his lips were instantly blue. It was adorable."

"Well, I'm sure telling him you love him thawed him."

Ximena squeals loudly like she can't keep it in any longer, clearly missing my tone. She throws herself onto her stomach on her bed, the screen bouncing with her. "That's what I was calling you about this morning! To tell you we finally said it! Did Renata spoil it all?"

My smile tightens. "She just said you texted her and Sulome about it this morning."

"Man, I wanted to tell you everything myself first!"

And she does seem genuinely disappointed. "But I guess you couldn't hold it in."

"Well, if you'd just answered your phone." Ximena laughs. "But it's okay. I'll tell you all about it in a sec, but also you can make it up to me by coming to the football game with me this Saturday . . ."

"I'm sorry. I must not have heard right." I pretend to twist a finger in my ear. "Did you actually ask me to go to a school sporting event of my own volition?"

"Come on. I don't want to freeze my butt off in the bleachers alone—"

"So I get to freeze my butt off with you?"

"Misery loves company. I promise to tell you all the details of who said what when, and how the whole thing went down, if you say you'll come."

"Great," I say. Even though I'm really trying to fake it, even I can hear the lack of enthusiasm in my voice. But Ximena doesn't seem to notice it.

"Okay, so this is how it happened. Oh my gosh, Q, he was so obviously nervous and—"

I let myself sink deeper into my pillows, wishing they'd swallow me so I could avoid the next few minutes of smiling and nodding and total pretending.

Livestream comments on TheWhine:

patrioteagle76: So inspiring! I want to do something like this in Chicago!

jennday4: A 5 year old boy was kidnapped last year in my town and the cops did NOTHING about it!!! The establishment is rotten to the core.

phoenixrises: I was there!

bkly_blue: Sending support from Indiana! We're having a march in November.

molly_bird: Thanks so much to everyone who came out to our march today! The website for the upstate NY chapter of Defend Kids is officially live. If you'd like to see more actions like today, please DONATE on our site! This is how we can keep fighting to defend our kids!

xoteenaxo: Thank you sooooo much for fighting for these babies. I had never even heard about any of this until I saw one of your posts. BRING THOSE CHILDREN HOME!

D3f3nd3r: Calling on all D3f3nd3rs to rally their towns and communities! The Cabal will hunt the wolves until we come together to fight back! #S2AIA #D3

raeraeday: Yeah like a march is gonna do anything when the government's in on it. 😵

miabae6: Look @OllietheStar! We're at min 2:36

dhash55: It's past time for marches and rallies. We need to make people listen! The war is on . . .

kimby_j7: There's a rally in Pittsburgh next Saturday in front of the courthouse. Come make your voice heard! #SaveTheChildren #100thousand #D3

redpilldreaming: Are people actually starting to wake up and realizing the Cabal is pulling all the strings? Won't hold my breath.

TheRealCadeBird: As the organizer of the whole thing, check out my account for exclusive pics and video of our march. We've got lots more planned, so hit that follow button!

chapter nine

The newspaper room is empty except for Asher, me, and Mrs. Newcomb, who agreed to let us use the computers here every Wednesday after school to work on The Whine. They're the only ones at school loaded with the fancy video editing software, the kind that makes Asher hum happily while he works on clips from the rally.

Mrs. Newcomb smiles up at me from her desk, where she sits wielding her infamous red editing pencil like a sword. Even from here I can see the bloodied page.

I'm almost to 17,000 followers on The Whine, which is mind-blowing, but there's a lot more to running it than there used to be. For starters, my notifications are a nonstop mess, and now there are spammers using my replies to post links to their websites. It's a universal truth that the comments section of any account is the worst part of the internet.

And Cade and his mom have become some of the worst ones, desperately commenting to tell people to follow their accounts. On his, Cade posts a new Story every day about Defend Kids or the Turners and they're all mostly the same. In at least half of them, he appears shirtless, even though it's the cold rain season that stings bone-deep. From either his bed or his couch, he tells some new fact about the Turners, like that Jensen's favorite color is blue or Annalice has a pet dog name Rex, and why he created the club at school. He brags about it like he invented Wi-Fi or something, and even worse, like somehow he's enjoying the fact that the Turners are still missing. Maybe it's because he went from 52 followers to more than 3,500 in the last week alone.

On top of the spammers and Cade, now that I know about my family's money problems, I can't escape the feeling that I need to constantly post new content to try to help the store. But there's only so much news and information about sleepy western New York, especially with tourist season long over. Soon, even a bunch of the wineries and restaurants will start to close for the winter. Too many "downtown Canandaigua at sunset" pictures posted in a row and I'll start losing followers.

With all that new pressure, now is the first time I've been able to dig into those sites that Asher showed me at the Black Cat that the spammers have been linking to.

I scan the website in front of me, OMGNews.com, the one that people have been sharing of an article about schools banning the pledge. After a few minutes of googling, I find out from a fact-checking website that not only is the article about the ban totally false, but that OMGNews is actually a joke site.

Sure enough, under the "About Us" section on OMGNews, there's a disclaimer right at the top of the page in small print: *OMGNews is part of a network of parody and satire sites. Everything on here is fiction. If you believe any of it, the joke's on you!*

"Okay, so that OMGNews site is satire. People are just joking, so we don't need to block them," I report to Asher. "Though I'm not sure what's funny, clever, or ironic about tricking people. And the creators kind of seem like jerks."

Asher frowns at his computer screen. "The people commenting don't seem to get that it's a joke."

I roll my eyes. "That's their fault for not bothering to do research on what they're reading." Plus, potential sponsors won't care what kind of attention my account gets, just that I have it at all. I click out of that tab and move onto the next site on my list.

"I have to go see Ms. Iacopelli in the library for a few minutes," Mrs. Newcomb says, her voice so soft that I barely hear it over the click of my computer mouse. "You two all right here?"

"We're good," I say.

Mrs. Newcomb smiles as she gets up. "You know, you should really think about rejoining the newspaper staff next semester, Quinn. We sure do miss you."

"Thanks," I say. "I'll think about it."

"I didn't know you were on the newspaper," Asher says once she's gone.

"Only freshman year."

He stretches his arms up over his head and stands up. I try not to stare at the sliver of his stomach that it reveals. Thankfully he turns away, making a slow circuit around the room, looking at the computers and checking out the framed copies of notable issues of the *Daily Stripe* going back to their first issue in 1964. He stops in front of the most recent framed copy—the one with my article as the front-page story above the fold.

"'P. J. Dalton Students Take to the Streets to Protest Government Inaction on Climate Change' by Quinn Calvet," he says, pointing to it. "Hey, you're famous."

"Oh yeah. Didn't you know that?" I smirk up at him over my computer screen.

"So, you weren't just on the newspaper staff, you were like the star of the whole thing."

"Hardly."

"Well, you must have been pretty good at it if your article got framed."

I shrug, but the truth is, I actually really liked working on the *Daily Stripe.* There was something addictive about the adrenaline I got from being in the middle of chaos, especially at lunchtime, as everyone circled Mrs. Newcomb for their next assignments.

"Ximena told me about the 'incident' with Stewart. That have anything to do with your leaving?" Asher asks, moving to sit on the corner of my desk.

Heat rushes to my face. "I'm going to kill her."

"He always looks like the Hulk when his vein pops out like that." Asher laughs. "It was brave of you."

"I didn't know he was standing there."

Asher is looking at me like I'm the coolest person he knows. That's why I don't admit that I nearly lost it when I realized Principal Stewart had heard me.

"That guy is always on such a power trip, like he thinks he runs a country rather than a school," Asher says.

"*Yes*, thank you!"

It's such a relief to hear Asher say so, like he's confirming all my negative thoughts about Principal Stewart. I mean, what kind of person are you if Nice Guy Asher King doesn't even like you?

Eventually Asher goes back to his chair and picks up his phone, plunging into The Whine's notifications. A minute later, the sound of dramatic music plays on Asher's phone, like the start of a news broadcast.

"What's that?" I ask.

"Some people started posting their favorite videos in the comments section of that post you did on that YouTube travel channel that featured the Finger Lakes, and a bunch of them are of this one guy."

"This is Nate Hammer," a man's voice says from Asher's phone. It's rough, like he brushed his vocal cords with sandpaper. The music gets louder and then fades. "And I'm your host of *What They Don't Want You to Know.*"

Asher clicks on the video to stop it, but the name sounds familiar.

"Wait," I say, looking at the list on my phone. "*What They Don't Want You to Know* was one of the sites that's been bringing a lot of people to The Whine. I haven't checked it out yet. Let it play."

I angle myself toward Asher's screen. He hits play again as I peer over his shoulder and, for a second, I'm distracted by the smell of something beach-like, like salt and coconut.

On the screen, there's a man with pale white skin and brown hair, poufy enough that it can't possibly be real. He adjusts a pair of wire-rimmed retro glasses on his nose that I'm more used to kids at school wearing than adults.

"Last week, there was a mudslide in India that killed twenty-two people. Three days ago, it was an earthquake in Puerto Rico. Just this morning, a tornado touched down in Bolivar, Missouri. The US government and the CIA would have you believe that these events are all natural disasters caused by climate change. But what they don't want you to know is"—he pauses dramatically as the same music from the opening thunders—"the government used military-grade weather weapons it has developed to cause every single one of these incidents."

He looks seriously at the camera and points with his pen as three pictures of each of the disasters appear behind him on the screen.

"We collected hundreds of photos from the scenes of the events and in each, we've discovered undeniable proof that the CIA deployed weather weapons to each of these locations moments before these crises began."

Each picture has a giant red arrow pointing to something the viewer is apparently supposed to notice. I squint at the screen, not really sure what I'm looking at, but the pictures disappear as quickly as they appeared.

They're replaced by an image of an official-looking document behind the man with lines of text underlined in red, connecting to other underlined words. It looks like a maze I'm supposed to be able to see my way in and out of, but all of it is too small to read. As the man talks, his voice grows louder.

"They're trying to hide it, but the CIA has been secretly working with the Cabal to develop these weapons for years, and you can see it if you know what to look for in the defense appropriations bill."

His voice is getting louder every second and he's completely red in the face now. The supposed defense appropriations bill picture disappears and is replaced by a very pixelated image of something that mostly looks like a helicopter. I cock my head to the side to study it better. Yep, definitely a helicopter.

But this Nate Hammer guy launches into a whole thing about how the obvious helicopter is actually one of those "weather weapons" the government deploys all over the world to cause havoc, and how they're being paid by wind power companies to brainwash the public into thinking climate change is real.

"Why do you think the government is so intent on pushing climate change and why we in D3 are fighting so hard to expose the truth about government corruption?" He waves his arms wildly and the pen clatters to the desk. His face shifts into a wide smile and he pulls a brown box out from under his desk with *Freedom Supply* stamped in black letters on the side. "That's also why my friends and family have Freedom Supply's four-week emergency food kit. It comes with MREs, dehydrated food, and other emergency supplies. Made in America, which means guaranteed quality. I urge every true patriot to order now so you and your family have what you need when the time comes. Use the special coupon code HAMMER to receive ten percent off your first order."

The video ends and another Nate Hammer video automatically

cues up, this time with the title "How the Cabal Is Secretly Implanting Your Citrus Fruit with Microchips to Track You."

Thankfully Asher hits stop before it starts because I can't watch another one.

"Did that guy say there are *weather weapons?*" The words make me feel like I've been sucked into an alternate universe.

"Sounded like it." Asher cringes. "And people are posting tons of links to his videos in the replies. Check it out."

Asher scrolls slowly through the comments. There aren't just *some* comments linking to this guy's site within the last few hours. There are hundreds.

My eyes widen. The posts sound a little familiar. Like some of the things Mrs. Bird said at the rally, or what the customer at Vine and Things said the other day.

"This is why people always say you shouldn't read the comments section." Mostly, I'm annoyed at myself for not having done my research on these sites as soon as Asher showed them to me.

"If it helps, that dude looks like he's wearing a Muppet on his head," Asher says. "I'm sure no one is taking him seriously. It could even be another joke site."

"Maybe," I say. But the guy looked like he was pretty serious.

Asher frowns. "Should we block all of the accounts or something?"

"We'd lose so many followers that way." I sigh because if I ever stand a chance of making any money from this, I need to grow my audience, not block them. "They're annoying, but I believe in free speech, not censorship. If they were harassing other followers, then I'd block them. But they're not doing any harm."

Still, it's kind of annoying that conspiracy weirdos are using their free speech to turn my Instagram into their own forum or message board.

"I bet they're into the whole Area 51, you know, the government is hiding aliens from me in an underground military base thing," I say.

"I've always kind of thought other life had to be out there besides us," Asher says. "If we exist, why not others on other planets, too?"

"Really?"

"You don't?"

"I mean, I know scientists have found certain molecules or something on planets that suggest there could be life. But they're talking about nonhuman life, like water. Not little green alien people."

"I didn't know you were so cynical," Asher says, smiling.

"And I didn't know you were so . . . let's call it *open-minded.* Maybe you should join this Nate Hammer conspiracy guy. I think you'd look cute in a tinfoil hat!"

I want to stuff the words back into my mouth as soon as they're out, along with the nervous laugh that follows.

That's the moment I realize how close Asher and I have been sitting. I scoot back a little in my chair and preemptively imagine my little bulletproof box around me, because Asher is definitely about to come up with a reason that he needs to leave or ask some horrifically intrusive disability question.

"Think they come standard issue?" he says. "Like a uniform they give out once you're a member of the club?"

I smile. "Probably."

Asher nods in agreement. "Hey, so I was thinking. As much as I love being at school twenty-four seven, maybe we could hang out *not* at school sometime."

I don't know if he means to work on The Whine or if he actually wants to *hang out* hang out, which is something we haven't really done before.

"Sure," I say, which seems like the most cool and normal response to give.

"Awesome. You could come over, but we've got about six stairs to get in the front," he says. "So I was wondering what the best way would be to help you get inside."

He's not asking me outright if I can climb stairs or to give him my detailed medical records. He's giving me the opportunity to share with him what I'm comfortable sharing, and it's kind of doing flip-floppy things to my heart.

One or two stairs wouldn't be a problem, but six is a lot. There's really no way around them except either a ramp or being carried. I get kind of self-conscious about people carrying me, and it's not exactly the safest thing in the world. Max has done it before, but he's also a defensive lineman on the football team and can bench press my weight. No risk there.

If Asher tried it, though, I'd probably crush him.

"I talked to my parents about building a ramp and my dad said he'd help me. He's good at that kind of stuff. But I didn't want to assume that that was the best way, or, you know, that'd you'd want to come over at all."

"I do," I say quickly.

"Never really thought about it until recently, but stairs are kind of pointless."

A smile stretches across my face and I don't try to stop it. "I, of course, agree."

"So, maybe in the meantime we could, you know, go to a movie sometime or something," he says.

It's possible he's still talking about hanging out, versus *hanging out* that looks more like a date. Going to the movies is also a friend zone activity, I remind myself. But then again, the only other person who built me my very own ramp is Ximena, which means he doesn't see me as temporary.

"I'm down for a movie. But I should warn you. My movie preferences are those of an eighty-year-old grandma. You know, slow-burn British dramas, ones with Doris Day, musicals, talking animal movies. Anything super low-stakes and predictable, basically."

Asher laughs, and the warm sound makes my skin prickle a little. "I love that you just admitted that like it's no big deal."

I smirk. "I like what I like."

"So, talking animal movies. I'm going to need you to tell me more about that."

"Yeah, you know, like the heartwarming ones where you hear the dog's thoughts and you basically cry the whole time because the dog loves their human so much. I don't cry often, but I will cry during a good talking animal movie." I sniffle and pretend to wipe away a tear.

"Okay, I definitely didn't have you pegged as a softy," he says.

"Only when it comes to movies. I save my tears for talking animals. Otherwise, I've got ice in my veins. Clearly."

"Clearly." His dimple reappears.

"What about you?"

"I don't know why, because I think I'm pretty much a pacifist, but I like war movies."

"So basically we should never watch a movie together ever because we'll never agree, is what I'm taking away from this conversation," I say.

"We'll figure something out."

Things have gotten really weird in the newspaper room really fast. We went from conspiracy theorists to movies and potential dates in a matter of minutes. I don't have much experience in this, but I think, very possibly, that Asher King and I are flirting.

Asher scrolls absently through the comments again, like his hands don't know how to function unless they're using a mouse or a phone, and I turn back to my computer.

"Cade's at it again. How about we at least block him?" He shakes his head at his phone.

"Don't tempt me. He's worse than the spammers. What's he doing now?"

"He replied to your post saying there's some news on his Insta about more missing kids."

I sigh, but curiosity gnaws at me and I pull up his account on my phone.

My heart thuds when I spot his new post with side-by-side pictures of two white people I recognize instantly: Phoenix Nelson and Lily di Agostino.

TheRealCadeBird: I've been warning you for weeks that this was coming. The Cabal has struck my own town. Phoenix Nelson, sixteen years old, and Lily di Agostino, seventeen years old, from Canandaigua, New York, are missing. Last seen by their families this morning when they left their houses for school. Anyone who's been paying attention knows what will happen if we don't find them. That's why I'll be out every day working with Defend Kids to bring them home! #DefendKids #D3 #100thousand

chapter ten

'm dizzy. Blood rushes in my ears and my heart thunders wildly in my chest.

"I-is this a joke? This has to be a joke, right?"

"I don't know," Asher says stiffly beside me, his hand clutching his phone. He scrolls up and down, and my eyes desperately search for the joke. I read the words on Asher's phone again over his shoulder, my head nearly knocking against his.

But the words don't change: Two P. J. Dalton High students are missing.

For what seems like hours, we sit frozen in silence, trapped in a new nightmare.

Even after weeks of posting about child kidnapping and the Turners, I guess it felt like more of a story happening to someone else, somewhere else. Something you hear about but haven't seen for yourself. Sad, yeah, but the distance makes it seem almost unreal. But now it's like the universe decided to prove just how big of a threat it actually is. Cade's right. He and the rest of Defend Kids had been warning us for weeks that it could happen here. And it has, to kids I know, even.

"Who would do this?" I say, finally breaking the silence. "Who is the Cabal?" There's something familiar about that word that flutters in my memory, but I can't quite remember why.

Asher pulls up Google on the computer. "It's 'the contrived schemes of a group of persons secretly united in a plot, such as to overturn a government,'" he says.

Cade had said a group of people was responsible for taking all the kids the night the Turners went missing, but I didn't know it had a name. Mrs. Bird had said it was evil forces. Is this what they meant? And if so, who is actually in the Cabal?

"You two still doing okay in here?" Mrs. Newcomb asks, suddenly in the doorway. Her voice makes me jump. Once she's back at her desk and neither Asher nor I has managed a word, Mrs. Newcomb looks at our faces and frowns. "What's wrong?"

"Cade Bird says that two students from school went missing." My voice comes out in a rasp. "Phoenix Nelson and Lily di Agostino."

"What? Has anyone called the police?"

"He doesn't say in his post."

"May I see it, please?" She crosses the room and takes Asher's phone, her brows furrowing as she reads the post. "I need to speak with Principal Stewart. I think you two should probably head home for now, okay?"

We nod and she hands Asher back his phone. My whole body shakes as we silently log off our computers and pack up our things. If Mrs. Newcomb is worried, that's not a good sign.

As Asher drives me home, Main Street looks darker than normal. Creepy, even. Like an invisible dark cloud is hanging just over it, casting shadows. Did whoever took Phoenix and Lily catch them together, or grab them one by one? Did they take them right here on

120

this street, or wait for them to come out of their houses? Is someone else next? I can't stop the thoughts from swirling in my brain, and a cold shudder runs through me.

In Asher's truck, my phone lights up with one text after another from my friend group chat, jolting me out of my thoughts. Ximena sends a screenshot of Cade's post, and Adrian, Renata, and Sulome reply with their own horrified reactions in a flurry of emojis.

"Text me later, okay?" Asher asks after we've pulled up to the front of the store and he's helped me into my chair.

"Okay."

I head through the door to the store and hear Ava say, "But everyone is going! I *have* to be there to help organize things."

Mom smooths out a crease in her Vine and Things apron from behind the counter at the register, looking upset. "Hi, honey," she says to me.

"I saw Cade's post. What happened?" I ask.

"Neither of them showed up for school today," Ava says, "so the front office called their parents and both the Nelsons and the di Agostinos said Phoenix and Lily left for school this morning. Their parents tried calling them, but their cell phones were off." Her eyes are glossy, the way she looks before she's about to burst into tears. "Defend Kids is meeting at the park at seven to organize search parties and I want to go." She turns sharply to look at Mom and leans on the counter, like she needs it to keep upright.

"I want to go, too," I say quickly, moving closer.

Now that I've said it, it hits me that I don't actually know much about either of them. Lily seems to have a permanent grimace on her face, and since she's Cade's friend, I've pretty much always avoided her. Phoenix is a sophomore, so I'd never had a class with him before. He's got to be smart if he was able to take chemistry with all juniors and seniors this year. I think the only time we've exchanged words was when I needed to borrow a pen one day the first week of class. I wouldn't even know where to begin to look for them. But it doesn't matter. Two kids from our school are missing—I've got to do *something*.

"We should probably leave this to the police, girls," Dad says, setting a box down at his feet. "I'm sure they've got everything under control."

"Yeah. I really don't want either of you going anywhere tonight," Mom says. "If two teenagers can be snatched off the streets in broad daylight in Canandaigua, then—"

"Involving locals in search efforts is helping the police. Plus, you can't expect me to stay home and do nothing!" Ava says. "The first seventy-two hours are the most crucial and we have the best chance of finding them if we start now."

Mom and Dad exchange looks before Mom finally heaves a sigh. "Okay, you can go, but on the condition that I'm coming with you."

Ava nods. "I'll go look up what supplies we'll need," she says before heading for the stairs to go home.

"Quinn, I want you to stay home with Dad."

"What?" I say. "But I can help, too!"

"Honey, it's probably going to be a long night and we're likely going to go to some less-than-accessible places," Mom says.

"Hey, we could have a Bourne Identity movie marathon," Dad says cheerfully.

"You're literally the only person who likes those movies," I snap.

"Or you could stay in your room and do your homework all night," Mom warns, frowning at my tone.

I force my lips together to keep myself from telling her how unfair she's being and pull out my phone. Great. While I was arguing with Mom, Renata texted that she and Sulome are going to help Defend Kids look for them and Adrian said he'd meet them there. Now basically everyone is going but me.

"I'll be down once we've closed, kiddo," Dad calls to me as I turn for the door.

I grumble back in response and head outside and around the corner to downstairs. Ava is ransacking the hall closet for supplies with one hand and watching a video on her phone with the other.

In my room, I check Instagram. Cade's post has already gone viral, and he updated it with the plan to meet up at the park. I share the post to my Stories. It feels so futile, but if Mom and Dad won't let me go, spreading the word is pretty much the only thing I can do to help right now.

The school parking lot is fuller than normal when Ximena and I pull in the next day, and Asher is standing next to her usual space, scrolling on his phone. We wave and he glances at two police cars parked in front of the school and frowns.

"They must be here to interview people or something. I guess they're still missing," Ximena says, staring over the steering wheel at the pair of cars.

I nod. I checked Cade's Instagram a couple of dozen times this morning to see if there'd been any updates, but he'd only posted a picture from the woods somewhere around here that he said they were searching.

"It's wild. I just saw them both the other day at the Defend Kids rally." I take a shuddering breath, the only kind I've managed since seeing Cade's post.

Ava's taking it even harder. When she and Mom got home late last night with no sign of Phoenix and Lily, Ava went straight to her room and closed the door. Defend Kids had spent last night going door-to-door in the neighborhoods where Phoenix and Lily live, combing the public dock and checking the boathouses in the area, but no one found so much as a clue about where they might be. I think Ava thinks their disappearance is some kind of personal failure, like she should have been able to stop all child abductions by now because of her work for Defend Kids.

"I know. I wish my parents would have let me join the search party last night. I mean, I was just texting with Phoenix about coordinating outfits for the game on Saturday," Ximena says.

"You were? I didn't know you really knew him."

She shrugs a shoulder. "There's a group of us dating football players, so we hang out at the games. Phoenix is going out with Jake Taylor, a running back."

"Oh." It's not very mature of me, given what's happening, but jealousy hits me. Apparently there's another *us* I'm not a part of because of Max.

"Mia, that's Ollie's girlfriend," she says, "said Phoenix was mad at his parents about something and thinks he decided to just take off for a while. But I don't know. I've texted him, like, a million times and it doesn't even show that he's reading them. Then I called and it went straight to voice mail."

Ximena sighs and twists to grab her backpack from the back seat and a bright pink poster she made for her Spanish class before popping out of the car.

Asher gets my chair out of Bula's massive trunk and brings it around for me so I can transfer over.

"Hey," Asher says. "You hear about the school assembly Principal Stewart called for this morning? We're supposed to go to the auditorium instead of first period."

"It's got to be about Lily and Phoenix, right?"

"I'm guessing, yeah."

"Let me go ditch this in Señora Perez's room," Ximena says, holding up the poster board, which is almost as tall as she is. "Save Max and me a seat." I nod and she sets off across the parking lot.

"So, how are you?" Asher asks.

"I don't know. I've felt sick to my stomach ever since we found out."

Asher nods vigorously. "Yeah. I read Cade's post about a dozen times and, I don't know, there's something smug about it. Like, he seems to be enjoying the fact that they're missing."

"Cade delighting in other people's misery? You don't say." I roll my eyes. "His posts on the Turners have been like that all along, too."

"Yeah, but Lily is his friend."

"True. I mean, he has actually been doing a lot of stuff to try to find her. Like organizing the search party last night. So maybe smug is just his resting state, but he is actually worried about her."

"Good point. There's something else, though. I dropped off some books at the library a few minutes ago and Dillon was . . ." His forehead furrows. "Actually, come on, I'll show you before the assembly starts."

I shiver against the cold October wind and push hard against my wheels when Asher sets off. There's a somber mood in the hallways that hits me square in the face. Groups huddled over their phones and talking in whispers. The kids already heading toward the auditorium move in clumps, like they don't feel safe walking alone anymore, even in the school halls. More than a few of them are crying.

My heart twists when we pass Jake, Phoenix's boyfriend, surrounded by a group of friends from the football team, tears leaving wet tracks down his dark brown cheeks. If even he hasn't heard from Phoenix, that means all of this has to be real.

I follow close beside Asher, but it's like he's forgotten his long legs take him much farther faster than I can push myself. By the time we reach the library, I'm about to pass out, but Asher doesn't notice.

"There," he whispers, pointing between an arrangement of fake autumn leaves on the window that already advertise the Sadie Hawkins dance in November.

I press my face up to the glass and spot Dillon, alone at one of the four reading tables.

"Okay, yes. Can confirm. That is in fact Dillon."

"Look at the patch on his jacket."

Dillon's got his arms up, his eyes transfixed on the screen of his phone in front of his face. Finally he lets his arms down a little, and that's when I see it.

A circular patch on Dillon's camouflage jacket in black and gold, but I can't make it out.

"D3! It says D3," Asher says impatiently.

"Bryce told me it's just shorthand for Defend Kids."

"But what's the three stand for?"

I shrug. "I don't know, but there were people at the march with D3 signs."

"Yeah, but remember that weird video we watched with Nate Hammer ranting about weather weapons and the whole government conspiracy? Some of his videos mention D3. And then a lot of those comments we've been getting lately from the spammers have, too." Asher peers through the glass again and his breath quickly fogs it up.

"We should go talk to him about it." I reach for the handle of the door, but Asher practically leaps in front of it.

"Whoa, what?"

"What? Let's just ask him what the patch really is."

"I get that you always need to know what's going on, but I don't want to talk to Dillon on an average day."

I raise an eyebrow. "You were willing to stand up for him when he was Cade's target, but you're too afraid to talk to him?"

"I'm not afraid." Asher shifts on his feet and fiddles with the straps of his backpack.

"Come on, you'll be fine. Besides, I'll be there to protect you." I shove the door open. "Hey, Dillon," I say when I get to the end of his table, Asher behind me. Dillon's sharp eyes flick between us before settling on me. "We're curious about the patch on your jacket. D3. It's really cool. It's for Defend Kids, right?"

"Yeah," Dillon says.

"I figured you wouldn't really be interested in Cade's club since, you know." I wave my hand in the universal sign for "Cade is a jerk."

"D3 matters more than he does," Dillon says, but he still glances around him like Cade might be lurking behind some shelves. It's the same thing that Bryce said about Defend Kids when she told me she had quit Model UN.

"But, like, what's it actually mean, D3?"

At first, Dillon's face goes blank and his mouth turns into a thin line. But then he says, "It's for followers of the Defender." He says it like he's giving an answer to an oral exam.

"The De-fend-er?" Asher says slowly.

It sounds like a bad superhero name. Dillon looks at Asher like he's the stupidest person on the planet. Apparently we're supposed to know who this is and we definitely don't.

"Yes, the Defender. D-3-F-3-N-D-3-R. The Es are threes. D3." He points to the letter and number in his patch individually like he's teaching us how to read.

"Right," I say, a little too enthusiastically to be a convincing lie. "I've heard of him, the Defender."

"Well, you should since you post the Defender's stuff all the time."

"I do?"

"Yeah, in your posts about the kidnappings. It's not some big secret that you run that Instagram account, right?"

My whole body goes rigid. "No, I mean—"

"The Defender was the one who uncovered the Cabal's plot to begin with." There's that word again. *Cabal,* the secret group taking kids. Dillon's green eyes narrow into sharp slits, studying me from under the bill of his hat. "I thought you were working with them."

"The Cabal?"

Dillon snorts. "Yeah, right. The Defender."

"Oh, I . . ." I realize that if I tell him I have no idea what he's talking about, he definitely won't explain it. "Yeah, totally. But Asher's new to all of this so I'm teaching him everything. Right, Asher?"

"Yeah, uh—" Asher says. "There's, like, a lot of confusing stuff about it, you know?"

Dillon nods knowingly. "The most important thing you need to know is that the Defender is a highly placed source in the US government who has access to all the top secret stuff no one knows about. It's about learning how to decode the messages, mostly. I've spent probably hundreds of hours deciphering his clues, and I get most of them right." His eyes brighten the more he speaks.

"That's, uh, cool," Asher says after a long and awkward bout of stunned silence. "What are the messages, exactly?"

"Sometimes they're clues we have to find and sometimes they're messages, but even those have to be translated sometimes. They warn us about what the Cabal is doing with the government and all over the world."

Okay, that's not at all what I was expecting.

"So, who is actually in the Cabal?" Asher asks. "Cade said they're the ones who took Lily and Phoenix."

Dillon's face goes murderous in an instant. "Cade Bird knows zero. He runs around school like he started it all, but I've been part of D3 basically since the Defender came online last year, so I know more than anyone at this stupid school about deciphering the messages. Except for you," he says to me, almost reverently. I force down a shudder. "But the Defender did warn us that there would be more and more abductions, so yeah, I'm guessing the Cabal has them. I've actually been able to figure out a bunch of the Defender's messages. Like, really hard ones."

"Cool." I try to sound and look impressed instead of how I actually feel—like I'm about to vomit. As creepy as this conversation is getting, though, this is the most I've learned about D3 since the whole thing started.

"I watch that guy's show, *What They Don't Want You to Know* with Nate Hammer. He's involved in all this stuff, too, right?"

130

It kind of feels like Asher is throwing darts at a dartboard with a blindfold on, but it's weirdly impressive. I guess he passed some test because Dillon leans back in his seat, his mouth curling up a little in what's probably the closest thing to a smile I've ever seen him give.

"He works with the Defender. He helps us figure out what the Defender wants us to know and how to understand the messages and find clues and stuff."

"So here's a question I've been trying to answer," I say. "How come none of what the Defender says is ever in the news?"

"You can't tell me you actually think the media tells the truth?" He rolls his eyes.

"No, of course not," I say as coolly as I can. "You'd just think that eventually they'd catch on."

"Not when most of the media is totally owned by big corporations and the CIA, which works with the Cabal. You can't trust anything they say. The only person who tells the truth is the Defender."

"So where does the Defender leave these messages?" Asher asks, while I work to keep my jaw from dropping.

"On different websites and forums. And obviously on your account," Dillon says. "But it changes all the time, so you always have to be looking. The Defender has their own site, too, where they leave instructions and stuff, called D3Map."

Instantly I feel sick. That's one of the sites Asher said had been sending a lot of traffic to The Whine. I hadn't made it to that site yet in my research, but I make a mental note to move it to the top of my list.

"So, how do you know the Defender is who they say they are?" I ask, and then when Dillon's face scrunches angrily, quickly add, "I mean, of course they are. I'm just curious what you know about them."

"No one knows anything about the Defender except that they're super high up in government and knows all this stuff."

"So, you think the Defender is like some kind of whistleblower or something?"

"Yeah. But they can't tell us any more than that, really. It's dangerous for them to reveal their identity because of the Cabal."

"How do you know they're telling the truth?"

"Because they get everything right. Like, the Defender warns us about a big political scandal about to happen and then it does. How would they know that kind of stuff was going to happen if they weren't who they said they were?" He looks at me shyly, like he's waiting for me to tell him he's right or wrong.

But I bite my tongue so I can't point out the obvious: that in politics, there's always a scandal, at least according to how my parents talk about it.

Dillon sits up a little in his chair, his eyes narrowing. "You're just screwing with me, right?"

"I promise I'm not," I say.

He swipes up his backpack from the floor and stalks out the door without another word.

Asher and I look at each other in the sudden silence of the library before we finally leave, too. I stop when we're safely in the hallway outside the library and slump back against my chair, feeling like all the wind has been knocked out of my lungs. Asher must feel the same way because he leans against the wall next to me.

"That's . . . I mean, what he was saying was completely . . ." I'm not sure I've ever been so lost for words in my entire life.

"Bonkers," Asher finishes for me.

I nod. "So, according to Dillon, some person called the Defender is posting secret codes on the internet?"

"Yeah, but also why does Dillon think that, A, you already knew about this, and B, you're helping this Defender person through The Whine? And that some secret group is responsible for stealing the kids? He never did answer my question about who is actually in the Cabal."

An involuntary shudder passes through me. "Apparently we've been posting the Defender's messages on The Whine. But how?" I shake my head, willing the spinning to stop. "Bryce said D3 is just short for Defend Kids, so they can't possibly be what Dillon said they are. I mean, how many people out there besides him could actually believe this stuff?"

"I don't know. I think it means some of the accounts that have been spamming The Whine aren't spammers," Asher says. "They're actual people who believe in the Defender stuff and think The Whine is one of the places the Defender leaves coded messages or something. Or that you're a mouthpiece for the Defender or whatever Dillon thinks you are."

Asher counts each person on his fingers. "Then there's all the people leaving the replies mentioning it on Instagram, and also Nate

Hammer, and Cade, maybe? He said something about a cabal in his Instagram post—" He throws his hands up once he's run out of fingers. "Those Nate Hammer videos have hundreds of thousands of views and they sound a lot like Dillon, too."

"Okay, but no one in Defend Kids besides Dillon can believe this stuff. Ava would never fall for it. She's the smartest person I know. This has to be a Dillon thing." But even as I say the words, I'm uneasy.

Maybe Asher was right and we shouldn't have talked to Dillon in the first place. We got some answers, but it doesn't feel helpful and now Asher is freaked out.

"Look, I really don't think it's anything," I say, because I want to wipe the worry off Asher's face—and reassure myself. "Dillon is just being Dillon."

The warning bell rings. My phone buzzes in my lap with a flurry of texts from Ximena asking me why I'm not in the auditorium yet.

As Asher and I head for the auditorium, the conversation with Dillon replays in my mind. I wonder how he ended up falling for such obvious lies. He wasn't always this much of a loner. I think he even had a couple of friends in middle school. That's one of the odd things about a small town, I guess. You can grow up with the same exact people and still not really know them.

But that still doesn't explain everything he revealed to us. Especially how I got sucked into being part of it without even realizing it.

Asher and I automatically slow down by the windows of the front office. On the other side of the glass, the room is full of parents talking animatedly, and at the center of it, two police officers stand in front of Principal Stewart. One of the women has the same curly ginger hair and the same pointed nose as Lily. Principal Stewart glances at his watch, wearing a heavy frown. He's about to be late to his own assembly.

He says something to the parents I can't hear before the redheaded woman and a tall white man go inside his office with the police officers.

Asher and I make it to the auditorium, and it's almost deafening as everyone talks. We split up when we get inside the already packed room. I head for the last row with the only wheelchair-accessible seat, where Ximena, Max, Sulome, and Renata are sitting, and Asher finds Justin and Ty a couple rows ahead.

All around, I hear snatches of people talking about Lily and Phoenix.

"My dad thinks he saw Phoenix at the gas station in Ithaca," I hear a black-haired freshman girl say.

"I've listened to dozens of true crime podcasts and . . ." a boy with glasses says to a clump of people around him.

"You know that old creepy guy, the one who always hangs out at the park?" a senior boy asks his two friends.

"My neighbor Ashley's brother knows Lily and he said that she told him . . ." a girl with tight ringlets starts.

I don't hear the rest because Ximena asks me, "Where you been?" as I slide into the open spot beside her.

But I don't answer because I suddenly notice that Defend Kids has taken up the whole front row. On the far end, I can see Ava's brown-and-purple hair next to Bryce's blond curls. On the side closest to the stage, Cade and some other members are holding a new banner with the same black-and-gold lettering. The banner simply says: *D3.*

chapter eleven

ad to stop at my locker," I finally mumble to Ximena after she repeats her question. She seems to believe me because she goes back to drawing letters on Max's back on her other side and making him guess what they are.

Something about the D3 banner makes me uneasy, and I can't tear my eyes away from the row of club members. What if . . . What if Dillon isn't the only one who believes in the whole Defender thing?

But I give myself a hard shake almost as soon as the thought hits me. It's like I told Asher—Dillon's just being Dillon and Defend Kids is just an organization trying to find missing kids.

And Cade Bird is just . . . well, Cade Bird. Cade leans into Brayden beside him and says something that makes Brayden laugh. But Brayden turns it into a cough when other members of the club turn to look at him, like maybe laughing at an assembly presumably about his missing friend isn't cool.

I roll my eyes at them and spot Mrs. Newcomb sitting across the aisle from the club with Mr. Schriever and Ms. Iacopelli. She's staring intently at the club, like she's trying to figure something out, when the auditorium doors open behind me and Principal Stewart stomps inside with a policewoman following. They move quickly up the aisle and onto the stage while kids continue to talk and move around their seats.

"I'll wait," Principal Stewart says into the microphone at the podium, his voice booming. His mouth is in the same pinched line that normally seems reserved for when he sees me, and the noise instantly dies down once everyone sees the police officer standing next to him. "Most of you already know, but yesterday two of our students were reported missing by their families, Lily di Agostino and Phoenix Nelson. Now, I know that this is a very scary and sad time for many of you, and I want to be able to answer any questions you may have and to hear your concerns. Especially at difficult times like these, it's critical to support and look out for one another, the way Tigers have always done."

He straightens the knot of his tie at his throat. "The safety of every P. J. Dalton student is the top priority of both me and the rest of our school staff. And so before I open things up to all of you, I've asked Officer Varadi to first go over a few personal safety tips with you this morning."

"I have a question," Cade shouts from the front.

The sound of two hundred students turning in their squeaky chairs at the same time fills the room.

"Please wait until—" Principal Stewart starts, but Cade keeps going.

"Why aren't the police doing more to find our friends?"

Murmurs spread throughout the auditorium, and even from here, I'm pretty sure I can see Principal Stewart's blue vein pulse in his forehead.

"I can assure you that the police are doing everything in their power to—"

Cade passes the D3 banner to Brayden beside him and gets to his feet. "Then how come they were nowhere to be seen last night and my club and I were in charge of the search?"

"Cade, I understand that tensions are high right now, but I won't ask you, or any of you," Principal Stewart says, his eyes roving over the chattering students, "again." Cade sits down and the auditorium falls silent. "Now. Officer Varadi, over to you."

The brown-haired police officer spends the next few minutes telling us to never walk home alone, to come up with a family safe word to signal danger, and to never go anywhere with strangers. She demonstrates different safety devices, like a whistle, and how to use the SOS button on our cell phones.

It's all basic stuff. Things most of us probably learned in kindergarten. And still I can't help but feel like this talk is all too little, too late, because Phoenix and Lily are already missing and none of these things will help find them.

Officer Varadi finishes and Principal Stewart moves back to the podium.

"Thank you for that informative presentation, Officer Varadi. Now, as promised, I'd like to open things up to you all to ask any questions or make any comments," he says a little reluctantly. "Cade, I suppose you'd like to go first."

Cade springs to his feet like a bottle of soda that's been shaken one too many times. Principal Stewart will probably kill me, but I open my

Instagram and start livestreaming. Technically the auditorium isn't a classroom.

Cade says, "Yeah. So, like I was saying, Lily di Agostino and Phoenix Nelson have been missing for more than twenty-four hours now. And so far the Canandaigua police don't seem to be worried about it. Neither does anyone at our school."

Whispering spreads among the students. At the podium, Principal Stewart grips the base of the microphone. Cade keeps going. "Last night, my club Defend Kids met up at the park to start looking for them and the police didn't even bother showing up to help us! I had to organize everything myself. I think that's just wrong." Murmurs of agreement break out across the crowd. "It's like they don't think it's a big deal that two of our fellow students were kidnapped."

I lean over to whisper at Sulome, sitting next to Max. "The police weren't there last night?"

"I mean, they were there, but definitely not a lot of them," Sulome whispers back.

"Yeah, only a few came to the park where we all met up," Max says.

"You went, too?" I ask.

"Yeah, most of the team did. Ollie pretty much got everyone to show up."

I lean back in my chair.

"Cade, both the school and the police are doing all we can," Principal Stewart says into the microphone.

I slowly move my phone to pan across the auditorium just as Officer Varadi steps back to the podium.

"That's right. We're taking this very seriously. We had several officers involved in the searches last night, but we are also pursuing a number of different leads. I can assure you that we're working around the clock to find them," she says.

"The thing is, we already know who took them. The police do, too." Cade pauses for emphasis, staring hard at Officer Varadi. "It was the Cabal. An evil group that's been snatching kids all over New York. So what are the police and the school doing to protect us? Nothing!" Cade shouts, and loud boos break out across the auditorium in reply.

"Thank you for your comment, Cade," Principal Stewart says loudly into the microphone to try to wrestle control back.

"If you want to help us, follow me on Instagram and sign up to join the club, and we'll text you updates and information on how you can help," Cade says before sitting back down.

Principal Stewart looks more than frazzled by the time he fields the rest of the questions and comments from students, mostly asking for more information about the kidnapping, which neither Stewart nor Officer Varadi have. When some sophomore kid asks if he can cancel school for the rest of the week, Principal Stewart announces the assembly is over. Cade is one of the first people to their feet, and he stalks toward the back of the auditorium, carrying the banner like he did the day of the march on Main Street. I shrink back a little in my chair, recognizing the familiar anger in his steel-gray eyes.

Ava follows him with Bryce, and I give her a small smile. She returns it weakly, and that's when I notice the dark circles under her eyes. I watch as she and the rest of the Defend Kids members follow

Cade out the door. I'm not sure when it happened, but the club seems to have doubled in size and a couple of them are wearing the same D3 patch Dillon was wearing.

"It's kind of impressive how Cade found a way to make this whole thing basically about him," Ximena says, leaning back in her seat.

"He's right, though. The police probably could have been doing more. None of them came when we went door-to-door last night passing out the flyers," Adrian says, gesturing to Renata and Sulome. "And Cade even made those."

"The team took the woods around Baker Park and there was a policeman there for a bit. He didn't stay long, though." Max bites down on his bottom lip for a second. "It was kind of creepy, actually, walking through the trees at night, not knowing what you were gonna find, so it would have been nice if they'd been there."

"Who decided who went where?" I ask.

"Your sister," Sulome replies, sounding impressed. "She had a whole map marked up and assigned everyone different spots."

"Seemed kind of weird the police weren't the ones doing it," Adrian says.

Now that I'm thinking about it, it doesn't really seem like they've done anything about the other missing kids either. It's not like Rochester, where the Turners were taken, is far away. But I haven't noticed them stepping up with more police cars around town or something.

"Maybe they had to wait, like, twenty-four hours before investigating a missing person or something?" Renata asks.

"Not for kids. Once they're reported missing, the police can start investigating," I say. It's one of the many facts Ava rattled off before she and Mom left for the park. Apparently there are hundreds of YouTube videos about how to conduct searches for missing persons and she managed to watch a bunch of them while she was getting ready to go. "I'm surprised Mrs. Bird didn't take over the whole thing, if the police didn't step up."

"Cade said she's out of town or something," Renata says. "But there were lots of other parents there."

Anger burns inside me, because as much as Ava is taking on for Defend Kids, it's not like the club has near the amount of resources the police do. "So the police are just leaving it to a bunch of high school students and their parents to find them. Why aren't they doing more? It's their literal job."

"Yeah, and it's like, thanks for the safety tips, police lady," Ximena says, nodding at the stage, "but just telling us to not get ourselves kidnapped isn't going to find Phoenix and Lily."

We all nod and wait for more people to file out of the auditorium before we join the surge of kids heading to class.

The rest of the morning is a blur as everyone whispers about what happened at the assembly. And at lunch, the cafeteria is even noisier than usual. Kids seem to have been genuinely energized by Cade's words at the assembly. People are lining up on their own to sign up on the clipboards Brayden, Bryce, and Mia are holding in front of Cade's usual table.

Sulome and Renata are the only ones at our table so far when I get there, and Sulome has a small stack of gold flyers next to her lunch tray.

She passes me one. "I offered to put them up around Pittsford when I go for my voice lesson on Saturday."

It's the same kind of missing person poster Defend Kids made for the Turners, with a QR code at the bottom. But this time, it features the pictures of Phoenix and Lily that Cade used in his Instagram post.

Ximena jogs up to the table, out of breath, with Max beside her. "Oh my god," she pants, "Cade is leading a school walkout."

I straighten. "A walkout? For Lily and Phoenix?"

She nods. "We passed them walking out the front on the way here. Adrian was with them."

I glance over at the club's table, which has suddenly emptied. Actually, most of the tables are only half-full, I realize, and more kids are leaving by the second as word of the walkout spreads.

Principal Stewart and his vein are absolutely going to lose it. He didn't like it when we held a protest freshman year and that was about climate change, not what he is or isn't doing. He might even give everyone participating detention.

I stare down at the flyer again, and the familiar faces of my classmates. If the police aren't going to do something to find the kids who literally just disappeared off the streets of Canandaigua, pretty soon our town could be wallpapered in these flyers.

"I'm going, too," I say, even though my stomach sloshes at the thought of getting in trouble.

"Same," Ximena says.

The rest of my friends agree to join, too, and we abandon our lunches. On the way out, I text Asher to let him know about the walkout. Honestly I'm not sure what a walkout is going to accomplish. The march on Main Street hasn't helped anyone find the Turners yet, but I can't help but feel like I've got to do *something*. Mom and Dad wouldn't let me go help last night, but they can't stop me from joining the walkout.

chapter twelve

W "ow," Ximena says, surveying the dozens of kids standing around in coats and hats by the front steps of the school and talking in excited voices. "Good turnout."

Ava, Mia, and Brayden have their clipboards in hand, while other club members pass out stacks of flyers to anyone who will agree to hang them up. A bunch of kids even have signs that look like they were probably made quickly between periods with supplies from the art room. I spot Cade and Bryce talking next to the row of accessible parking spaces.

"On a scale of zero to suspension, how much trouble do you think we're going to get in with Stewart for this?" Max asks, his arm over Ximena's shoulders.

"I say zero," Sulome says. "He can't suspend the whole school, and it looks like the whole school is here."

Sulome is right. The parking lot has filled with students, and more keep arriving in a constant trickle down the steps.

"I'm impressed. I didn't think most people would be willing to give up their lunch hour," Renata says.

"Are you saying your faith in humanity has been restored?" Ximena asks, raising an eyebrow.

"Not entirely." Renata smirks. "But this helps a little."

I tell my friends I'll be right back and move along the edges of the crowd to take a few pictures for The Whine. Mrs. Newcomb comes over from the picnic tables where she'd been eating her lunch in a full coat, hat, and scarf.

"What's happening here?" she asks with a half-eaten sandwich in her hand.

"A walkout," I reply. "For Phoenix and Lily."

"Oh," Mrs. Newcomb says, staring at the crowd. From the way she hesitates, I can't tell if she's considering issuing mass detention warnings or if she's wishing she had known ahead of time so she could have assigned someone on the newspaper staff to cover the event.

"You can use any of the pictures I take for the newspaper, if you want. I mean, they'll just be cell phone pictures."

"Thanks," Mrs. Newcomb says, though she frowns and walks slowly around the crowd.

"Hey," Asher says, suddenly beside me. "Anything happen yet?"

I find myself smiling up at him. "Not yet, but who knows what Cade has planned. How's it going?"

He shrugs, staring as a couple of club members carry the D3 banner Cade had during the assembly into the parking lot. "I can't stop thinking about what Dillon told us in the library. About the Defender stuff."

"I know," I say, gesturing to everyone in the parking lot. "But it's just an organization. Not what Dillon said it was."

"But what about Cade mentioning the Cabal at the assembly?"

I purse my lips, because yeah. That was weird. "I mean, someone is secretly snatching kids, and that's pretty much the definition of evil, so maybe it's not so far off from the truth." I look up at Asher, but he seems unconvinced. "Okay, absolutely worst-case scenario, D3 is like a super committed sports team fan club."

"What?" A small smile tugs at Asher's lips.

"Come on, you don't see the parallels? Obsessively following a person or group. Your mood is tied to that person or group's success or failure. Jerseys and other merch to show your loyalty. Believing that wearing the same old stinky pair of unwashed socks will somehow make your team win."

"Wow. You really don't like sports, do you?"

"I don't *hate* sports. I'm even going to the football game on Saturday with Ximena. If my parents will let me out of the house. They're so freaked about Phoenix and Lily."

"For the record, I don't have a stinky pair of unwashed socks I think is some kind of magic good luck charm. But I do have a favorite pair of running shorts. How much does that freak you out, on a scale of one to ten?"

"Hmmm." I tap my chin slowly. "I'll need to hear more about these shorts before I make a call."

I don't realize how my words sound until they're out and I cringe, but Asher laughs. "So none of the D3 stuff worries you at all?" he asks.

"Am I thrilled about the fact that Dillon believes a secret government source is leaving clues about global conspiracies and basically trolling my Insta, and that Dillion, who was already creepy before this, probably has access to multiple hunting rifles at home?" I shudder and take a breath. "I mean, no. That's definitely not great. But Defend Kids is an anti-child-trafficking organization. A *nonprofit*. Kids we actually know in real life are currently missing, and they seem to be the only ones doing much to find them."

Through the crowd, Cade, Ava, and Bryce break apart, and Cade climbs onto the hood of a nearby car I'm pretty sure belongs to the sub Ms. Segui. Brayden stands in front of him with his phone up, recording him.

"Hey! Quiet down, everyone!" Cade shouts, waving his arms. He smiles when a hush settles over the crowd and everyone is looking at him.

I wish I wasn't so far away, but I still start a livestream on The Whine, hoping everyone will be quiet enough that my phone will pick up Cade's voice.

"You heard that cop at the assembly this morning. They're not doing anything to find Phoenix and Lily or to track down the group that took them, and I think we need to start assuming the worst here. That we're on our own to find them and to protect ourselves. Phoenix and Lily are P. J. Dalton students," Cade says, earning a cheer of agreement from the crowd. "And what happened to them could happen to any of us. So Defend Kids is going to keep taking matters into our own hands. And we're not going to stop until we find them!"

The crowd breaks out into cheers as Cade raises a fist into the air, and Bryce and Ava wave the D3 banner around.

"We have to keep making noise until they're home!" Cade says, and the crowd erupts again. When it's quieted a little, Cade looks down at Brayden's camera and points. "We're planning something big to show that Defend Kids is the only one really fighting for all of us, so stay tuned."

Okay, Cade is clearly enjoying the attention. But—and I'm the last one who'd like to admit it—maybe Cade really has decided to use his powers for good.

TheRealCadeBird: The cops may be sitting on the sidelines, letting kids in my town just get snatched off the street in broad daylight. But D3 won't be silent. We're making MOVES. Come to the football game at P. J. Dalton High School on Saturday night to see what D3 has planned! #D3 #100Thousand

chapter thirteen

On Saturday night, a cold wind wriggles an icy hand down my back as I push myself up the metal ramp onto the school bleachers. The game doesn't start for another twenty minutes, but already the seats are more than half-full.

It's getting dark early now, so the sky is already black, but the floodlights around the field make it as bright as day. On the field, two police officers patrol the sidelines where the cheerleaders are stretching. We passed another four in the parking lot coming in. I'm pretty sure this kind of presence isn't normal for a game, but it's almost been seventy-two hours and Lily and Phoenix are still missing.

Like I thought, the walkout didn't get us any closer to finding Lily and Phoenix. Mostly it just made us all miss lunch and fourth period. But at least Sulome was right and Stewart hasn't given us all detention for it, and even more important—it got the whole school focused on finding them. Defend Kids organized another search last night, but Mom and Dad still wouldn't let me go. Renata told me this time it was like the entire high school turned up to help.

I shiver against the cold. I'd been planning an excuse to get out of coming to the game, but then I saw Cade's Instagram post.

When Ximena and I make it to the top of the ramp, a group of kids enthusiastically waves down at us. Not us, I realize. Ximena.

"Hey!" Ximena calls back to them, waving. They're sitting high up in the bleachers, at least ten rows back. I warily eye the tall steps I stopped being able to climb years ago. They might as well be sitting on the peak of a mountain.

"Your football friends?" I ask, lifting a hand in a stiff wave.

Ximena nods. "You know Kristen from English, right? She's dating Devon, one of the defensive linemen." She points to a girl with orange and black tiger stripes painted across her whole face. "Emma dates Oscar, Charlotte's with Noah, Mia is with Ollie. Usually Phoenix is here for Jake, too, but, you know . . ." She trails off. The terrible reality fills in the silence for her.

Mia waves down at Ximena from the group, her black hair in tight spirals with orange stripes painted across her brown skin. She blows a kiss to Ximena and the two erupt in giggles. That's when I notice the gold-and-black D3 patch on Mia's coat.

Ever since the walkout, more and more people have been wearing them, on their clothes or on their backpacks. It wouldn't be so confusing if Dillon hadn't told us a totally wild version of what he thinks D3 means.

I must be making a face because Ximena says, "I know what you're thinking, and even I'm embarrassed by us. It makes it less depressing to watch us lose all the time if you have people to sit with. But I told them I was coming with you to this one."

I know she doesn't mean it, but the way she says it sounds like she's doing me some kind of favor by hanging out with me.

The stands are half-full of nonstudents, and I spot a bunch of people who have stores or restaurants near ours on Main Street. Mr.

Yang, who owns Panda Garden, waves at me from halfway up the steps, heading toward Mr. and Mrs. Ambrose.

"Quinn, come by sometime to talk about marketing the restaurant on your Instagram account," he yells through a cupped hand.

"Okay, I will!" I call back, smiling. I guess my plan may actually be working.

"Look at you, Q!" Ximena says.

We head for the ADA section, which is just an open space at the far end of the bleachers where they ripped out one of the metal benches in the first row. In the corner, there are a couple of brown metal folding chairs propped up against the railings. Ximena grabs one and sits down.

I slide my chair into the space next to her after glancing back up at the group of Ximena's football friends. Even though she hasn't said anything, it makes me feel like I'm keeping Ximena from being where she wants to be, instead of the inaccessibility of the stands that keeps me sequestered down here or the obvious fact that her friends could have come and sat down here by us if they'd wanted to.

Ximena leans back in her chair. "It's so weird that Phoenix isn't here. He's hilarious, Q, trust me. Phoenix doesn't get football either so he'll pretend he's a commentator, but he makes up fake rules about the plays, and he does this accent that's so . . ." Her lips press together until they disappear, and she shivers. "I just hope they find them." Ximena unzips her coat a little, a D3 patch poking up from under her scarf.

She follows the line of my gaze. "Bryce was selling them for three bucks for the club at school yesterday to help raise money to find them. She said they're expanding the search parties to other towns, so the money will go to that. I honestly don't even think people care about Cade's club," Ximena says thoughtfully. "They just want to do something to help find them."

I open my mouth to tell Ximena about talking to Dillon, because it's really kind of funny when you think about it. He is so sure that D3 stands for the Defender, some secret government source who is leaving coded messages about stealing kids, and that I'm working with this person without even knowing it. But Asher doesn't seem to find it funny. Ever since the library, he's been sending me screenshots of some of the weird comments we've gotten that reference D3. His last text was a string of anxious-looking emojis—frowning, mind-blowing emoji, and then five screaming emojis with a line of exclamation points.

"So, do you want to come to my house right after school on Halloween?" Ximena asks before I can say anything. "Dad's bought like ten pounds of caramel for the candy apples and about a hundred dollars in candy."

"Oh. I didn't know if you still wanted me to come over."

She gives me a funny look. "Duh, it's tradition."

Ximena and I have been passing out candy at her house on Halloween since we stopped going trick-or-treating ourselves. Her dad always buys way too much candy, so we usually end up stuffing our faces with the leftovers until our bodies hum with sugar and we're on the verge of puking. But given how Ximena and Max are basically superglued together, I was sure she'd mess with our sacred Halloween tradition, too.

"I'll have to see. My parents are still freaking out. They didn't even want me coming here tonight," I say, because now I can just blame bailing on them when Ximena inevitably announces Max is crashing.

The stands are almost full when members of the marching band file onto the side of the field in front of us, just as the smells of hot dogs and nacho cheese start to waft toward us from the concessions booth. Altogether, it's not entirely terrible, even though my feet are already numb inside my faux-fur-lined boots. I take out my phone and snap a few pictures when the teams run onto the field, our Canandaigua Tigers in orange and black and the Victor Blue Devils in blue and white, and post some of them on The Whine.

"Forty-two!" Ximena yells through cupped hands, and Max turns and waves at us from the field. "All these games and the only thing I've actually learned about football is that each team wants to get the ball to the other side of the field, which is called the end zone." Ximena gestures with both hands at opposite sides of the field like a flight attendant.

"I could have told you that. And Max's job is to—"

"Hit as many people as possible."

"You could work for ESPN with this kind of expert knowledge."

Ximena grins. "I know, right?"

I laugh, feeling a little lighter. She hasn't gone full-on football fanatic simply because of Max. The band starts the Tiger fight song, and

Ximena and I sing along and stomp our feet with everyone else. The referee blows the whistle and the game begins.

Things move so fast, I can hardly see where the ball is most of the time as the teams move up and down the field. So when the crowd *ooooh*s, we *ooooh*, and when the crowd *awwww*s in disappointment, we *awwww*, too. By halftime, the Tigers are tied with the Blue Devils 6-6, thanks to a massive tackle by Max that has even me cheering.

When the teams run back to the locker rooms, Ximena stays standing and stamps her feet, trying to warm them a little.

"Q, you're totally a good luck charm. We haven't been close to even tying this season!" Ximena says. "It's kind of fun, right?" But she keeps glancing up at her football friends huddled together high up in the bleachers.

"You can go talk to them if you want."

"Nah, I'm not going to leave you here by yourself. Not with everything that's been going on."

"Seriously. It's not a big deal. There's a billion people around."

I think Ximena is going to insist on staying again, but she says, "I should probably just go check on them and see how they're doing with the Phoenix stuff going on. I'll be gone like two minutes, I promise." She bounds up the stairs.

Something feels like it's cracking in my chest. What did I expect was going to happen? That Ximena would never have other friends besides me? And she didn't say she wanted to stay with me, she said she didn't want to leave me, which is a completely different thing motivated entirely by not wanting to feel guilt. A part of me wonders if maybe Ximena doesn't actually want to introduce me to her other friends.

"This seat taken?" Asher's warm voice hits me from the side.

I look up, trying to keep a cool smile from turning into an overeager grin. "I didn't know you were coming."

He shrugs both shoulders. "Figured I'd come see what Cade was up to. By the way, couldn't help but notice you got pretty into it when we scored."

"Stalker," I say. "Ximena explained it's rare for us, so I figured it was worth celebrating."

Asher leans back in his chair with his arms crossed and hands stuffed under the armpits of his coat. "You see all the patches?"

"Yeah. It's a fundraiser to help buy supplies and stuff for the search parties. I guess they're going to fan out to other towns."

Asher chews on his bottom lip.

"Did you see we officially hit twenty-five thousand followers?" I ask.

"No way," Asher says, pulling out his phone to see for himself.

"Yeah, it happened as I was livestreaming the walkout." The annoying thing is that Cade isn't too far behind me in followers now. Somehow it just doesn't seem fair that someone who only ever posted gross memes and shirtless bathroom selfies until now suddenly is nearing influencer status when I've put in years of work.

"Think that will help me prove to my parents that they should let me go to that RISD program this summer?" Asher asks, gazing down at his shoes. "Because I kind of got in."

"Wow, congratulations!"

"Thanks." Suddenly Asher looks a little green. "You want to come hold my hand while I tell them?" he asks.

"Telling them is probably something you're going to have to do on your own." I'm grinning because, even if it was metaphorical, Asher King wants to hold my hand. "But I'll text you encouraging GIFs before, during, and after."

"Deal." He grips his knees.

"Hey, Asher," Ximena says from behind me. She moves in front of us and leans back into the railing.

The marching band finishes the last few notes of a vaguely familiar pop medley before the referee runs back onto the field.

"I guess Cade isn't doing whatever he planned after all," Asher says, frowning as he checks the time on his phone. "I'm gonna head out."

"You don't have to go!" Ximena says.

"Ty is having this thing at his house tonight, so I'm going to head over there. You guys should stop by after the game if you want."

"My parents barely let me come here, and I'm on strict instructions to come home right after," I say.

"Same," Ximena says, frowning.

"No worries. I'll see you guys later."

As soon as Asher is gone, Ximena spins in her seat and leans forward until our noses almost touch.

"That boy just seems to appear wherever you are. He has such a crush on you!"

I roll my eyes. "He does not," I reply.

Ximena nods like a bobblehead. "You can pretend all you want that you don't like him, but *he's* definitely into *you*. He follows you around like a puppy!"

I bite my lip. She doesn't even know about all the time we're spending together outside school. Or the maybe-flirting thing. Or that we're now going to the movies together. And this is why. Because when it comes to me and guys, she goes from zero to love in a second.

"Come on. We could all use the joy of you two getting together right now," she says.

Ximena doesn't get it. Miles Theriault flat-out told me in seventh grade that I'd make the perfect girlfriend if I wasn't in a wheelchair. Of course Miles is the actual worst and I'm pretty sure I dodged a massive bullet with that one.

But then last year, I had a momentary crush on this exchange student from Berlin in my calculus class and when Ximena went to casually poke around to see if he might be interested, too, he told her, "I'm not sure how it would work." Though I'm not sure what he meant by *it* and I was too embarrassed to send Ximena back in to find out.

And then I overheard Jackson Jordan tell his friends the first day of school this year that I was pretty for a disabled girl.

Ever since I started using a wheelchair, I've been:

Pretty, but . . .

Cool, but . . .

Fun to hang out with, but . . .

So even though there have been these moments lately where I think Asher might like me, experience tells me he'll have his own "but." Which is clearly his issue, not mine. I'm just not sure my imaginary bulletproof case could take a blow like that from Asher. This is why it's just easier to not get too excited by possible new crushes. It isn't really something that Ximena would understand, and it's definitely too much to explain to her in the second half of a school football game, especially with the dark cloud of Phoenix and Lily's disappearance hanging over us.

The teams run back onto the field. I guess Cade is bailing on the game. I pull up The Whine and start a livestream, mostly as a distraction. They line up, but before they start, a group of people in black hoodies starts walking in rows onto the field. Someone out front holds a flag on a pole in his hands.

I zoom with my camera to get a closer look for the livestream of the group marching across the field in tight rows of four.

Our school flag is black with an orange tiger in a boxing stance with two paws up, so I don't spot the difference at first. But when a strong wind flattens the flag out, it reveals the giant, gleaming gold lettering. *D3.*

The group cuts across the field and curves around the middle like a well-practiced army. There's at least twenty people, but I recognize Cade's blond hair at the front, the one holding the flag.

"I guess Cade showed up after all," Ximena says.

But it's not just Cade. There's Brayden, Bryce, Annika, Corinne, the blond twins, and Mia with her tiger ears and tail still on. Ollie and two others from the football team run to join them in full helmets and pads, marching with the group. But it's all the people in black hoodies I don't recognize that is so startling; some of them even look like adults.

The referee blows his whistle in long blasts and waves his arms at the group to clear the field, but they won't leave. By the time the whole group makes it onto the field, they take up enough of it that the football players have to move over to make room for them.

Behind me, a couple of people start cheering, and then a few more join in. Soon, the metal stands below us vibrate as almost the whole crowd gets to their feet. The group stops at the front of the field, and Cade waves the flag back and forth through the air like a band conductor, a wide grin on his face. Someone in the crowd shouts, "Defend our kids, defend our kids!" twice before everyone is chanting it in a chorus.

On the field, a girl pulls back her sweatshirt's hood, revealing purple streaks in her brown hair. Ava.

The group splits down the middle and two figures from the back move up to the front, their hoods pulled low over their heads to hide their faces. They slowly pull back their hoods, revealing the faces of Phoenix and Lily.

For a second, I feel like I'm falling, barely aware of the strangled cries of the crowd or Ximena's cursing beside me.

"Is that . . ." Ximena trails off, and we both move to the edge of the stands to get a better look.

In the corner of my phone, it shows I have "3.2K viewers" to my livestream. I grip my phone tighter, feeling like I can't breathe.

Cade waves the D3 flag higher in the air triumphantly, and the crowd cheers and applauds. Phoenix waves before stuffing his hands into his pockets, while Lily raises her hands in fists above the top of her curly hair.

I hear someone shout behind me, "Defeat the Cabal!"

I spin my chair. It's Mr. Ambrose, who owns Ted's Tires. His face is red as he shouts.

Soon, most of the crowd joins in the chant.

Principal Stewart and a few adults hurry down the bleachers and head for the field. One of the cops patrolling the sidelines earlier says something into his hand radio before he rushes toward the group, too.

Ximena grips the bar in front of us. "Oh my god, they found them?" Tears pool in her eyes. "Where have they been the last three days?"

That is a very good question.

TheRealCadeBird: FOUND! This one goes out to all the Defend Kids haters.

Phoenix Nelson and Lily di Agostino went missing in Canandaigua, New York. In less than 72 hours they were found!!! While all the losers are sitting around whining, NY chapter of Defend Kids is out there fightin and getting it done! Join or GET OUT THE WAY!!

And while I'm out here fighting for kids, I make sure I have my Freedom Hydro Water Bottle from @FreedomInc with me at all times. You gotta make sure you're well-hydrated. They come in all different sizes and colors, so get yours now. #DefendKids #100thousand #D3

chapter fourteen

My wheels crunch over the gravel parking lot by the bleachers as I struggle to navigate through the swarm of people in black hoodies, parents, and police. It's chaos, bodies pushing against one another. Half the stands must have emptied after the dramatic reveal that Phoenix and Lily had been found, and in the distance, I hear the faint sound of whistles blowing as the referees try to regain control of the field.

I don't know if Ximena is behind me, and I can't stop to check now. I don't see Phoenix or Lily anywhere, but in front of me, I spot Ava hurrying toward Cade's white SUV, her head ducked low.

"Ava!" I call, but my voice is drowned out by the excited chatter around me.

I shout her name again, and this time my sister stops and turns to me.

I'm out of breath and my shoulders ache by the time I reach her. "What happened? You guys found them?"

"I can't explain right now, okay?" Ava says. Even in the dark of the parking lot, I can see her chest rise and fall.

"But where were they?"

"Did you guys find them?" Ximena asks, out of breath and suddenly beside me. "What happened to them?"

"Ava, let's go!" Cade yells through the open passenger-side window of his car. He honks his horn for emphasis.

She shakes her head. "I'm sorry. I'll be home soon." And then my sister climbs into Cade Bird's SUV and drives away.

The next morning, I scroll through the sea of Insta notifications from my bed, buried deep under my covers. Social media has been a firestorm since the football game last night, with people celebrating Phoenix and Lily's rescue. And demanding answers about their disappearance, which no one seems to have. As a result, overnight, The Whine has gotten more than 5,000 new followers, and Cade has gotten 11,000 and counting. The chaos online is even more fueled by the fact that Cade has been silent on Instagram since his super vague post at the game.

I pull myself out of my warm cocoon and into my chair, wishing Mom and Dad hadn't let Ava sleep over at Bryce's house last night after they heard about Phoenix and Lily. Because aside from Cade, Ava is one of the only people who probably knows what happened, and she hasn't responded to any of my texts. I flex my hands in my lap, cramping from too many hours of holding my phone.

I should feel relieved, shouldn't I? Even though their reveal last night looked as planned as the cheerleaders dancing their memorized routine at halftime, and Cade had obviously set his post about finding them to land as soon as they took to the field (which means he didn't go to the police as soon as he found them), Phoenix and Lily are safe. That's what should matter most.

But I can't get that chant out of my head. *Defeat the Cabal.* Mr. Ambrose started it, but lots of people in the stands had joined in. What if it means they believe in a secret Defender, like Dillon?

I move to my desk and open my laptop. Dillon told us in the library that the so-called Defender posts all their messages on a site called D3Map, the same site people have been posting links to in my replies.

I pull it up. It's a pretty simple-looking website. Nothing more than a series of white boxes on a black background with four columns of messages. Each post has a date under it of when it was posted and a comment bubble icon with the number of all the replies it's gotten. There's a white line connecting it to the previous post, like it's a map to a maze. I start scrolling and quickly go cross-eyed from the web of connected posts until I reach the very first post. It's from October of last year. So, whoever the Defender is has been around awhile, like Dillon said.

I scroll back up through them, slower this time. They're all in a mix of lowercase letters and capitalized ones. Most of them are kind of written like a haiku. A couple of words per line. Sometimes the post is just one long list of names and dates that don't seem to correspond, and then an ominous order at the end to "Dig deep, Defender."

Abraham LINCOLN
JFK
Albert Einstein
9/11
1984
Topeka, KANSAS
DIG DEEP, DEFENDER

Other posts are longer. And I only have to read a few of them to notice a pattern. These posts have two kinds of messages—vague warnings of terrible things to come, most of them blaming the Cabal, or they link to articles about bad things that have happened in the world, like a military coup in another country or a seventy-five-car pileup on a highway somewhere. It's like a game of Defender Boggle, where the person posting shakes a container of words that fall into random places on a board that the readers then have to turn into something coherent.

I click on the replies to the Defender's post about Abraham Lincoln and it unspools a long thread of people talking to one another. But there aren't usernames. Each account is listed as "Defender" with a long number at the end of it, so they're anonymous. And their replies are almost scarier than the original post, mostly because they think the random haiku of nonsense actually means something. They fight over what they think each word means in the post. It takes me a while to piece it together, but at the end of skimming through the replies, the consensus seems to be the Defender's riddle means Albert Einstein was assassinated because he had predicted the terrorist attack on the Twin Towers on 9/11.

Albert Einstein. Who died of an aneurysm. More than forty years before 9/11. The proof people provide seems random. Just memes, pictures, some maps of New York, and a whole bunch of wild speculation.

I blink at the computer screen. A person would have to wrap their brain into a pretzel shape to believe any of this. It's like they think the internet is one giant treasure map that eventually will lead them to the truth.

I read some other posts. But soon, I start to feel like I'm Alice in Wonderland, free-falling down a hole in the ground that drops me into a land of dancing, life-sized playing cards and trying to make sense of it all. A lot of the Defender's posts, I realize with a shudder, use some of the same words Dillon had—like *Cabal*—and others he hadn't, like *Node* and *S2AIA*. Trying to decipher them all is like trying to get a straight answer from the Cheshire cat himself.

I need some kind of D3 decoder because my brain is starting to feel like sludge. I click back to Google, hoping it won't fail me as I type D3Map into the search. When I do, my eyes widen. There are Facebook pages and Instagram accounts and YouTube videos all about D3.

I click through a few and they all have the same vibe as the replies to the Defender's posts on D3Map. All anonymous posters desperately hunting for meaning in vague claims and nonsense. All connecting dots between things that seem totally random. And all scary as all get out because it means that D3 isn't Dillon's personal delusion. It's something a whole group of people believes in. Maybe even people in Defend Kids.

The biggest place they congregate seems to be a subreddit called r/D3f3nd. My hand freezes on my trackpad when I see the number of members it has: 19,351.

Nausea pools in my stomach as I scroll through the thread headlines, all of them as outrageous as the Defender's messages on D3Map. In each one, they talk about all the theories and the Defender's latest messages. The newest theory D3 is up in arms over is a message the Defender posted last week on D3Map:

LOOK for Nodes.
They're hiding in plain SIGHT.
The Cabal sends the WOLVES there
before SHIPMENT.
S2AIA

It takes me forever to dig through all the threads on the subreddit to figure out a few words. They seem to finally agree that a *Node* is a place where the Cabal is keeping the children it abducts and *Wolves* is code for "children," though I have no idea why. And I can't figure out how they decide who is part of the Cabal. It mostly seems like it's anyone the members of D3 say it is: politicians, celebrities, CEOs.

Every thread I open only leads to more of the bizarre. The next time I look at the clock on my laptop, somehow, inexplicably, two hours have passed and my stomach grumbles with hunger.

After all my investigating, this is what I think I know about D3. The group started sometime last year. No one knows who the Defender is, like Dillon said, and they don't really seem to care. Believers treat the posts from the Defender like they're some kind of all-knowing god, and they themselves dutiful soldiers in what they call the D3 Army. And there's definitely more people out there who believe in this stuff besides Dillon McRae.

I absently scroll again through the subreddit, a shiver running up my back. Some of these commenters might be people we go to school with, like Dillon. And more than likely, some of them follow The Whine, too. And an even scarier thought: What if my sister is one of them?

When I can't stand looking at my computer anymore, I pick up my phone to check my few hundred Insta notifications. I'm scrolling through new replies when one comment catches my eye. It makes my blood freeze right in my veins.

> **MonsterMythBuster:** OMG, stop posting about this!! These kids literally don't exist! This whole thing is a scam. The Turner kids. Aren't. Real. Read this article. It explains everything.

Virginia Daily Gazette

Case of Stolen Identity? Online "Missing Persons"

Conspiracy a Hoax by Sandra Blair

posted 1 week ago

CHARLOTTESVILLE, VA—Like most teens today, Madelyn Berrington, 17, must see a hundred memes and videos on her social media feeds each day. But two months ago, her friend sent her one that she says has sent her life into a tailspin. It was a missing persons poster for a brother and sister from Rochester, New York. The meme claimed that a girl, allegedly 14 and named Annalice Turner, had been kidnapped along with her little brother Jensen, 8, from their home on the evening of September 1 and showed two pictures of a girl and boy—the children alleged to be missing.

But the picture of the supposedly missing girl was actually Berrington's ninth-grade school yearbook photo.

Berrington says, "My best friend texted me right away when she saw my picture on a missing persons poster on Snapchat. She thought it was some kind of joke at first, and I did, too. It took me a while to realize that they were claiming that this girl—or me, I guess—was a missing person. It was so freaky."

Even though Berrington has two brothers, she says she has "no idea" who the little boy is that the meme claimed was her brother, but our investigation found it was the picture of a seven-year-old Massachusetts boy named Bryson who was reported missing last summer but was found just twenty hours later (we have not included his last name for privacy).

At first, Berrington and her friends tried to reply whenever they saw the posts to tell the sharers that the missing persons memes were not correct. "Sometimes people would delete their posts after," Berrington says, "but we kept finding more and more on, like, every social media platform. We couldn't keep up."

But things got even worse, she says, when complete strangers started confronting her in real life from the posts, asking if she was the kidnapped girl.

Berrington, who works as a cashier at a supermarket in Charlottesville, said the worst occurred last month when a customer she was checking out mistook her for the missing girl from Rochester and called the police.

The woman was convinced Berrington was Annalice Turner and refused to leave. "She kept yelling and eventually the police had to take her from the store. I was so scared, but I think she actually thought she was saving me or something," Berrington says, still visibly shaken from the event.

The Rochester Police Department confirmed in an official statement put out last week that they had no records of a missing persons case under the Turner name. In fact, they said they have been increasingly overwhelmed with false reports about the two children, who, as far as they can tell, do not exist.

This case of apparent stolen identity has not just affected Berrington's personal life, but also the work of Rochester PD, Police Chief Paul Giannina told us.

"We've been completely inundated with phone calls from all over the country from concerned citizens worried about these two alleged victims, and they get irate when we inform them there is not an actual case. Some people have even reported having seen these children and call us to give us tips," Chief Giannina said.

Whenever a claim or a report is made, the police are obligated to investigate it, but doing so, he said, had bogged down Rochester PD and drained valuable resources police could have spent on very real crimes. "While their hearts are undoubtedly in the right place," he said, "the calls and reports have completely overwhelmed us."

But false kidnapping reports aren't just a problem affecting Rochester PD; they have been on the rise nationally in a startling new trend since last year. Diana Lim, executive director for the National Center for Child Rescue, says that the phenomenon is occurring nationwide. "Not only has there been a sharp increase in false reports," Lim says, "but there's also been an increase in claims that one hundred thousand are kidnapped each year in the US. It's absurdly false. Only about 350 people under the age of 21 are abducted by strangers each year."

Giannina cautions the general public not to believe everything they see on social media. "We are aware of claims of a massive child kidnapping ring, but our investigations have turned up no such operation in the region. In fact," he said, "we've seen that people have been posting doctored police reports online as proof."

As for Berrington, she says she wants to be able to go back to her normal life, but the claims online haven't stopped.

"It's so weird seeing my face everywhere, and for something completely untrue," Berrington says. "I don't know why anyone would make it up. It's gross. I just want it all to stop."

chapter fifteen

My brain trips over the words the first time I read the article, refusing to accept what my eyes are seeing. And then I read it again.

For weeks, I've seen Annalice Turner's pictures everywhere right alongside her brother, Jensen. Not Annalice Turner, my brain corrects me; Madelyn Berrington of Charlottesville, Virginia. And not her brother, Jensen, but Bryson Somebody. At best it was a hoax, at worst a scam. Does Cade know? Does Mrs. Bird or Ava? What about the rest of Defend Kids, and all of its chapters around the country?

I fall more than sit back in my chair as the truth settles over me. So many people have been working to find the Turners, but it was a lie and we all fell for it.

Ordinarily I wouldn't freak out about accidentally sharing something that turns outs to be untrue. But this isn't like accidentally posting the wrong date for an event in Canandaigua. I told my followers that kids were kidnapped in Rochester who literally don't exist. On top of that, I promoted a group that is connected to a massive conspiracy theory that believes some random person is leaving coded messages for them online. Why would Defend Kids do this? And more importantly, what am I going to do about it now that I know the truth?

I spin at the sound of the front door opening and closing, followed by hurried steps headed for her room. Ava. I have to tell her.

When I get to her room, Ava's at her desk, her head in her hands. Her walls surround her like a scrapbook of her accomplishments. Academic awards, science fair ribbons, and commemorative certificates, lined up in perfect rows on the wall facing her bed. Key Club, National Honors Society, National Merit Scholar, and there are more tucked away in her desk drawers and closet. I don't know how she can stand it. I guess it's motivation for her. But to me, it looks like pressure, the kind that suffocates because it's always there staring right at you, telling you that you can't slow down.

"Hey," I say from the doorway. "Can I talk to you?"

She jumps at the sound of my voice—when did it start scaring her?—and turns in her seat, but only for a second before swiveling back around. "Can it wait?"

"Not really. It's important." I push myself deeper into her room for emphasis. She'd have to climb over me to leave.

"Well, make it quick. I only just got home and I need to leave for the food bank soon."

"How can you treat this like any old Sunday?" I take a deep breath. "I mean, can we talk about last night and what happened to Phoenix and Lily? How did you find them?"

"Cade and some other club members did. I wasn't there." She rubs at her eyes, the matching circles under both dark enough that I can see them from across the room.

"Well, where were they?"

She presses her lips together. "I can't tell you anything. Mrs. Bird said we're supposed to respect their privacy while their families deal with the police."

"But they really were abducted?" The question spills out of my mouth.

Ava frowns. "Of course they were. Why would you even ask that?"

"I know," I say. "It's just, I need to tell you something . . . Someone posted an article on my Insta about the Turner kids. It turns out it's a fake and there is no Annalice or Jensen. It's the ninth-grade yearbook photo of a girl named Madelyn Berrington, and the boy is some kid named Bryson who was missing for all of a day. Ava, the Turners are totally made up."

"What?" She frowns, deep lines appearing across her forehead. "Quinn, I've seen the police reports."

"But they're fakes."

"Fakes? Come on."

"The Rochester police put out a statement and everything! You need to read the article." I pull it up on my phone and hold it out to her.

Instead, Ava picks up her brush from her nightstand and starts combing her hair. Why is she not freaking out with me? "Quinn, it can't possibly be made up."

"Just *read* it, okay?" I shove my phone into her free hand.

Ava sighs and drops her hairbrush down on her desk. She looks warily at my phone but starts scrolling. When she gets to the end of the article, her head gives a hard shake and she passes my phone back to me.

"Maybe the pictures are wrong, but it must just be a misunderstanding."

"Wait. Didn't you read the part at the end with the police chief and the statement from Rochester police? They straight-up said the Turners don't exist and the article says the stat about one hundred thousand missing kids is way off."

"Are you trying to say child trafficking isn't a thing? Quinn, twenty-eight kids were taken the same night the Turners disappeared and dozens have gone missing since then, including two kids we go to school with." She turns back to her computer like that settles the matter.

"I know," I say. And I do. It's one of the most confusing parts about all of this. The Turners might be fake and there might be more people than I'd realized who believe everything Dillon told us, but two kids in my own town were kidnapped. I saw that for myself. I try to take a steadying breath. "But how do you know any of them are real, if the Turners aren't? Why does no one ever talk about them and who they are? Where are their parents?" Now that I'm asking the questions, I wonder why I hadn't thought of them before.

"There's something else," I say, hesitating. "I talked to Dillon and he said that D3 isn't just short for Defend Kids. It's a whole conspiracy that people believe in. They think the Cabal is a secret group of evil villains kidnapping kids and that the government is helping them."

It's the first time I'm trying to explain what I've found out loud, and from the look on Ava's face, it sounds as wild and nonsensical as I think it is. But I keep going. "He also said that Defend Kids believes that a secret government source called the Defender is leaving coded messages on the internet to warn people about what the Cabal is up to and that I'm some kind of magic translator."

"Do you hear yourself?" she says.

"I know, I know. But I looked it up online and there's a whole community of people out there who believe it, too." I suck in a deep breath, my body suddenly exhausted from trying to make sense of it all.

I don't know what I was expecting from telling her. Maybe that she'd feel as embarrassed about being duped as I feel? She's spent every spare minute she's had trying to raise awareness about the Turners in the hope that somehow it'd bring them home, like it was her personal mission in life. So at the very least, shouldn't she be relieved that the story isn't true? Maybe even angry that someone would play a hoax like this?

I guess, most of all, I didn't think I'd have to start by convincing my know-it-all sister that the facts from the article are actual facts, and I definitely didn't expect it to turn into a massive fight along the way.

"Look, Defend Kids is the only reason Phoenix and Lily were even found, no matter what this article says about the Turners or the random crap Dillon is spouting." Her words hang in the air between us, and neither of us speaks for a minute, or at least long enough for me to realize just how hard my heart is beating.

"Ava, I think I need to take down all the posts about the Turners—" I finally say.

She stands. "What? Your posts are one of the ways we've been getting so much attention for the cause."

"And you need to tell Cade and Mrs. Bird about it so they know the truth."

"But the article is wrong!" Ava says.

"I don't think it is."

Ava's eyes narrow. "Is this because I haven't been spending as much time with you this year as you wanted?"

I lurch back in my chair, her words stinging like a gust of icy air to the face. "What? That's not what this is about."

"And maybe you're just trying to blow up things a little so I'll—"

"Ava, no!"

"I'm not angry, really. But I"—she massages her temples like I'm giving her a headache and sighs—"don't have time for it."

It would almost be better if Ava were yelling at me right now. Instead, her even and slow tone makes me sound like I'm the unreasonable one, just a kid having a tantrum.

I roll my eyes to mask how much her accusation cuts me. "If you can get over yourself for two seconds, you'd see that you and the rest of Defend Kids were duped."

I hear the sounds of Mom's and Dad's footsteps on the stairs coming down from Vine and Things.

"Hello, hello, anyone home?" Dad calls from the bottom of the stairs.

"In here, Dad!" Ava calls back, her voice suddenly cheerful, though her puckered lips show it's forced.

Dad pops his head around the corner of Ava's doorway, smiling.

181

"Mom and I are playing hooky on inventory day. What are you two up to because I'm thinking, wait for it"—Dad does jazz hands on either side of his face, wiggling each of his splayed fingers—"waffle lunch!"

"I actually have to leave for the food bank." Ava smiles wide as she stands because Dad's given her the escape she was looking for.

"You gonna be my sous chef?" Dad asks, squeezing my shoulder.

"Of course she is," Ava volunteers.

Dad pumps a fist in the air and heads toward the kitchen. As Ava brushes past me, she says, "Leave it alone, Quinn."

Maybe there was a right way to explain to Ava what I found, some magical words I could have said that would convince her I'm telling the truth about the Turners. But if there was, I definitely didn't say them.

As I move down the hall to the kitchen, I can't help but wonder: Defend Kids wouldn't knowingly spread an outright lie, would they?

chapter sixteen

Ximena balances on the edge of the public dock with her arms out at her sides, humming circus music, like she's walking on a tightrope. We're the only people at the lake. That's why as much as I hate the cold, this is my favorite time of year. When it's just the two of us and the water is steel gray and a little choppy. It's the first time we've been here together since school started, but it's definitely the last time until winter is over because we're supposed to get our first snow this weekend.

We haven't even made it past the first week in November, but just the idea of snow fills me with dread. In the winter, my world suddenly shrinks down to the few places I absolutely have to go. My chair doesn't do great in snow, and since the cold makes my joints hurt more than normal, I spend most of each winter feeling trapped and in pain, craving the fleeting heat that is months away.

"Every Friday should be a teacher work day," Ximena calls, tilting her head back and closing her eyes. "That way, every weekend could be a three-day weekend. It's Saturday and I'm already totally rested. Don't you feel better with some fresh air? I feel like we haven't been here in forever."

"You know I go into a deep hibernation after Halloween," I call back. But the fact is, the frigid air has cleared my head a little from the sick haze that's coated my brain since my fight with Ava last weekend.

"It sucks you had to work and missed that ice carving competition in Dundee yesterday. We dared Adrian to lick one of the sculptures and he got his tongue stuck. He freaked out." Ximena sticks out her tongue and mimics what must be her interpretation of Adrian's panicked face, flailing her arms at her sides. "It was hilarious."

"Wish I'd seen it." But it was actually a relief that we had enough customers at the store that I had to keep my Friday shift. Maybe the shop is going to be okay.

A dull ache has settled into my joints and I'm moving stiffly already, but being here is still a nice distraction from the conspiracy spiral I've been on. Things were starting to feel a little dark. After our fight, Ava stopped speaking to me entirely. My punishment for believing the truth, I guess. It also hasn't helped that I've spent so much time in a bottomless pit of D3 research. It's like I can't look away until I figure out what it all means.

I tilt my head back and watch fluffy clouds like cotton balls slide fast across the sky. Ximena and I take a selfie at the end of the dock with our hats pulled down over our eyes so only our mouths show and another one where we let the wind whip our hair up around us until we both look like we've sustained serious electric shocks. She posts them on Instagram, and my phone beeps in my pocket when she tags me in them.

It feels nice to do something normal, because things haven't felt *normal* for days.

"So you haven't said much about how things have been since your fight with Ava," Ximena says carefully. And just like that, normal is gone again.

Even though I didn't tell Ximena what the fight was about, just that it was epic, or anything about what I've found out about the Turners, my heart speeds up at the sound of my sister's name.

"Not much to tell."

"It must be weird. You guys never fight."

I shrug and pull a loose thread from the sleeve of my coat. "It's whatever." But she's right, and it's going to be even weirder when we're both home for Thanksgiving break if we're still not speaking then.

"So what's going on with you these days?" Ximena says after we've sat in an abnormal silence for a while, like it's been years since we've seen each other instead of only a few days. She makes a swirling motion with her finger pointed at my head.

"What do you mean?"

"I feel like you've only been half here the last few weeks. And this was the first time ever that you've bailed on the annual Cordova family Halloween festivities."

She's been so busy with school and Max lately that I didn't think she'd notice or care when I told her I wasn't feeling well and couldn't come over. Especially since she said Max was in fact going to crash our tradition, like I'd guessed. But apparently she did notice.

"Is it about Phoenix and Lily?" she prompts. "I feel like nothing has been the same since it happened."

"Since they haven't come back to school yet, it still feels like they're gone, in a way. It's weird."

"I bet they'll be back after Thanksgiving break."

"Has Phoenix told you anything about what happened?" I ask.

Ximena shakes her head. "I've tried texting him just to let him know I'm here for him, but he hasn't replied. It's understandable. Mia said she saw police cars outside Lily's house the day after the football game. Whatever they went through must have been awful. They're obviously both super traumatized."

I chew on my bottom lip. Cade still hasn't posted anything new about what happened to them, which is weird. I figured he would be nonstop talking about how he'd rescued them. Maybe he's actually trying to be a decent human and respect their privacy? For a second, I think about telling Ximena everything about D3 and the Turners. But I don't. I haven't even told Asher yet or deleted my posts about them, because what if Ava was right and this was all just a big misunderstanding? Even as I have the thought, I know it's not true. The Turners aren't real. But what happened to Lily and Phoenix is real. I just don't know what this all means.

"Yeah, this year's been wild." I shrug it off. "I don't know. I guess I've had a lot more going on with school and work and stuff."

"And Asher." Ximena licks her lips the way she does when she's trying to hold something in until she can't anymore. "How committed do you think he is about going to RISD for college?"

"It's pretty much his literal dream. Why?"

"Well, since Max is looking at New York schools, we should start working on Asher, too. It'd be so fun if the four of us were all in New York together."

Wait, what? "Max wants to go to school in New York now? When did this happen?" I ask, trying to keep my voice steady.

"We've been talking about it for a while, but he may not even get in anywhere," she says quickly.

"Doesn't he have, like, a four point two GPA?"

Ximena nods. "You're not mad, are you?"

I look down at my hands because Ximena is a freaking lie detector when it comes to me, noticing every involuntary face twitch or eyebrow quirk. Where did this boyfriend-obsessed best friend of mine even come from? We have been planning to live together in New York basically our whole lives, and now she wants to change all that? It's like the football game. She'd never been to a sporting event in her life until Max. She did the same thing with our summer, too. We had a whole list of stuff planned and then Max crashed it all so that most of the time, I felt like the third wheel in my own life. And now she wants me to be excited for more of that?

That's when it hits me, why Ximena is so focused on getting me and Asher together. She feels guilty letting her relationship upend our life plans and turn her into the pod person of what used to be her nightmares. If I have a boyfriend of my own, then she won't have to worry about being a total hypocrite anymore.

I can feel her deep eyes watching me, desperately waiting for me to give any kind of sign that her and Max's decision to change everything is okay with me.

"I guess it would be fun."

"It *will* be!" Ximena squeals and throws her arms around me. "Don't worry, I'll sell Asher on the city, too. You're going to ask him to Sadie Hawkins, right?"

I roll my eyes at her. "Why would I?"

She snorts. "Um, because you guys are a thing."

If we weren't headed for the friend zone before, we sure are now. Asher texted me on Thursday to see if I wanted to go to the movies yesterday before his family left for Toronto for the weekend. Memories from the movie non-date ram themselves into the front of my brain like a semitruck. I was so annoyed at myself for obsessing over whether or not it was a date that as soon as we arrived at the theater, I made sure to beat him to the ticket booth and then paid for my ticket so we wouldn't have to deal with the awkwardness. He made a face that I still can't interpret. It wasn't a frown, but he didn't exactly look relieved either. More like sick.

Then, when our hands momentarily brushed in the bag of popcorn he got, he jerked his hand back suddenly, like mine had bitten his. It surprised me so much that a kernel got stuck in my throat on the way down and I couldn't stop coughing. Like, how do you even recover from that kind of embarrassment, let alone hope to inspire date-like vibes?

But I don't want to think about my cringey non-date or the fact that being in Canada gave Asher the perfect chance to ghost me. Sure, it'd be nice to have an actual date of my own and not be the sad-looking caboose to Ximena and Max's train for a change. Our friend group can say we'd all go as a group to the dance, but inevitably, Max and Ximena will pair off, and as much as Renata says she isn't into Adrian, they will, too. So it will end up being me and Sulome, but I'm pretty sure she has a crush on her scene partner.

But even if I asked Asher to the dance, not hearing from him since our non-date when we'd been texting every day until then can't be a good sign. I haven't texted him either, not even about D3 and the Turners. He's supposed to be back tomorrow. Somehow it seems like too much to drop over text. I also haven't figured out what to do about it all yet.

"We're friends." I stuff my hands into my coat pockets.

"Could have fooled me. I mean, there's the fact that he looks at you like this." She widens her eyes and flutters her long eyelashes with an exaggerated grin on her face that borders on creepy.

"He does not!" I can feel my cheeks reddening with instant heat.

"It's really not hard. I asked Max over pizza a couple weeks ago."

"But you guys are already an official couple; it's different. You knew what he was going to say."

"Yeah, and if I hadn't asked him, we'd probably be spending the dance on his couch doing another godawful Avengers marathon or something. Which is probably what Asher will do if you don't ask him."

"Or maybe he already has a date and this is a nonissue." I burrow my chin into my coat when another gust of freezing air whips around us.

"Come on. You guys are basically inseparable these days. You're a package deal, even if you're not *official.* I hardly see you anymore." Her voice gets more of an edge to it with each word.

"So says the one with the boyfriend sewed onto her hip." I didn't mean to say the words but they still slipped out, and I'm surprised by how good it makes me feel to say them since she's the one who just upended our lifelong plans by inviting Max. Until I see Ximena's face. "Kidding, obviously."

"Do you like him? Let's start with that."

"It's complicated."

"Well, what better place to define your relationship than at a school dance with two hundred of your closest friends watching?" Ximena grins.

It feels nice to admit it, actually—that my feelings about Asher are complicated. But maybe she would understand if I finally told her that protecting my heart the way I do is an act of self-preservation, even if most nondisabled people don't get it. Maybe she would understand that I wouldn't be able to handle it if I got another "She's cute, but . . ." from Asher because I actually care about him. The fact is, I *want* Ximena to understand, so, for the first time ever, I try my best to explain it to her.

Her mouth falls open when I'm done, but she doesn't speak right away and I can see thoughts turning in her head.

"Q, I had no idea you felt that way," she finally says, and she looks absolutely devastated when she says it. "I'm so sorry that I've been pushing the thing with Asher. It's not like I think you need a guy, or even that anyone will ever be good enough for you. It's just, you deserve to have all the best things ever and if you decide you want something, whether it's Asher King or the moon, I would literally do anything to make it happen."

The truth is, maybe I started keeping stuff from Ximena a long time ago, even before D3 and Asher.

For the first time in days, the heaviness in my chest lifts a little. "I know." I smile. Or at least, I think I do. The wind is whipping so hard now that I've lost feeling in my cheeks.

My phone chirps with a text message.

"My mom's asking what time I'll be home."

"The correct answer is only after you've come over to my house and watched *Downton Abbey*. We need a girls' night."

For a second, I'm tempted to go home because I can't help but wonder if she actually wants to hang out with me alone or Max has other plans. He has literally taken over everything, but the one thing that has stayed ours is *Downton*.

"I'm in," I say, forcing a smile.

Ximena cheers and holds her arms out one last time at the end of the dock. Leaving is basically an admission that winter will hold us indoors like prisoners for at least the next four months. Walking back to her car, I can't stop myself from thinking about Asher.

Because the fact is, despite all my efforts, I think I'm starting to like him. And perhaps almost as unbelievably, given the awkwardness at the movies, I think he's maybe starting to like me, too.

D3Map

Watch and wait, my brothers and sisters. The Cabal is making MOVES and soon we will have to make ours, too. NODES are popping up everywhere. They're hiding in PLAIN SIGHT. The Cabal sends the WOLVES there before shipment. Dig deep, look out, and be ready to act S2AIA.

Posted by D3F3ND3R
November 3

Replies:

Defender849201: Make no mistake, The Defender is giving us new orders. This is our time. #D3

Defender366629: I got a whole arsenal ready for the Cabal. How about you, D3?

Defender954721: Once you know how to read the clues, you'll realize they're everywhere. The D3F3ND3R is putting up new messages for us every day.

Defender542742: We need to eradicate every last one of the Cabal, even if that means burning everything down until we're done! We'll rebuild something better from the ashes. #S2AIA

Defender998760: This is why I'm glad I've got my survival kit with a four-month supply of food and my anti-radiation pills from Freedom Supply! You can get 10% off with your first order with the coupon code FREEDOM.

Defender022368: The world will turn into chaos once we destroy the Cabal. Governments will collapse. It will accelerate the next civil war but then we'll start again. A new world without the Cabal. S2AIA, brothers.

chapter seventeen

Asher is telling his parents about getting into the RISD program right now—or at least that was his plan when he texted me once he got back from Toronto today. Followed by the green vomiting emoji.

I should be trying to enjoy my last day of freedom before school starts again tomorrow, but I end up messing around on my phone, waiting to hear from Asher again while Mom, Dad, and Ava set up for the upcoming Thanksgiving sale upstairs.

I haven't posted a single new thing about Defend Kids since Phoenix and Lily were found and I learned the Turners don't exist. But my silence hasn't stopped the comments from coming in. A while later, I have a crick in my neck from staring down at my phone, reading a debate in my replies about whether my last picture of the fall foliage was a coded message about a Node. These people would probably find meaning in a picture of a trash can if I posted it.

There's a knock on the front door and when I open it, I find Asher on the other side.

I don't have a second to wish I were wearing something cuter than black yoga pants and one of Ximena's hoodies because he throws his arms around me in a hug I'm not expecting.

It's not a half-hearted, one-armed hug. It's not weak or awkward. It's a full-on two-armed hug, close enough I can feel his heart racing and catch a faint whiff of his shampoo. My arms tighten once I get them around his neck.

"I told them," he says into the side of my hair. "Sorry I'm smothering you. I should have asked."

Asher pulls back to come inside and I shut the door behind him, already missing the warmth of his surprisingly strong arms.

I want to tell Asher that he can wrap me up in his arms anytime he wants to, but instead I say, "It's okay. So?"

"They said I can go!" Asher shakes his head like he can't believe it and drops onto the couch. "We had this whole talk about my life and how I don't want to take over the business. I told them I want to apply at RISD and other design schools. It was so wild. Once I started talking, it all kind of spilled out. And they actually listened."

I can't help but smile. "I'm so happy for you."

"I think it's like the only time in my life I've been fully honest with them." Asher's face is practically lighting up our dark living room with excitement. He looks lighter and happier than I think I've ever seen him. Probably more the result of having years of worrying about disappointing his parents finally lifted than his vacation.

"Want to hang out for a while?"

He grins. "Sure. My mom took my phone when we got to Toronto to force family bonding or whatever, and she wouldn't give it back until we got home. So I haven't logged in to Insta for a while. I think I'm having withdrawals."

Relief hits me because it means he wasn't intentionally silent when he was in Canada.

Asher stops at the fridge to grab a soda before we head back to my bedroom. It's easier to work on my computer back here, and apparently we're working. I make a mental note to listen out for footsteps on the stairs.

Asher pulls out his phone and sets up camp on the foot of my bed. "Time to check and see how our little cult is doing." Asher says it fondly. "Wow, you hit thirty thousand followers when I was gone. Nice."

I cringe because even with so many followers, I still haven't found a way to make more money from it yet. And on top of that, it doesn't much feel like a success now that I know a lot of those follows are because I unknowingly posted a lie. Asher doesn't know about all the stuff I've found out, like the Turner kids not being real, or just how many people in Defend Kids may actually believe in a conspiracy about the Defender. And I haven't told him about my fight with Ava. I guess now is as good a time as any.

But before I can open my mouth, Asher says, "You'll never believe this. Remember that Nate Hammer guy from the videos? He's going to be in Rochester at the end of the week holding some big event." He swings himself around the bed so our knees almost touch. "He's doing a national tour and he's starting where the Turner kids were taken. Maybe we should go check it out."

"You think?" I look up at him over my phone, cringing a little at his mention of the Turners.

"You, the one who walked right up to Dillon McRae, aren't a little bit curious about this guy? Does that mean you didn't convert to D3 while I was gone? Sign up for the newsletter? Buy the fan T-shirt?"

He nudges my knee playfully with his, and it makes my brain shudder a little.

If I'm going to tell him about the Turners, he's giving me the perfect opening. But he doesn't move away and I can't stop staring at our knees touching.

"Let's go to it. For research purposes." Asher smirks at his phone. "It's at the Holiday Inn in Rochester, which seems very on brand, given what we know about them."

I snort. I'm not sure I really want to be in a room full of people who believe this Nate guy, but we could probably get a lot of answers about the group at an event. Maybe I could even find something out to prove to Ava that I'm right about the Turners, or give me some kind of idea about how to tell the rest of the club and my followers the truth.

"I'm in," I say.

"Looks like we have to register. With names and everything," Asher says, frowning down at his phone. "Okay, so Asher and Quinn won't be going. But Rupert and Penny will."

"Rupert and Penny? How very undercover of us! So, we're basically characters in a small town English crime drama, huh?" I laugh. This close, I can smell his shampoo again. It's kind of coconutty and amazing.

"I hope you're good with accents, because you're going to have to do all the talking for us."

"I don't want to brag, but I've basically been training for this moment my whole life." But then suddenly it hits me. "That's the same day as Sadie Hawkins."

Asher shrugs and looks back down at his phone. "Yeah, I guess."

My face falls a little. Because the thing is, I'd almost made up my mind to ask him to the dance. As friends. And only so I wouldn't be alone when all the couples in our friend group suddenly pair off. But then I thought about how he might stop coming over if I asked him and he said no.

I shrug as nonchalantly as I can. "Oh, I assumed you'd be, you know, going to that."

"I give off the formal-dances-are-my-thing vibe, huh?" He smirks. "No one ever asked me. And, well, I wasn't sure if everyone liked that sort of thing. Dances, I mean."

I might be imagining it, but Asher gives me a pointed look. I think.

"I mean, did you want to go to the dance?" I say.

"With *you*?"

Or maybe not?

"I mean, you know . . . generally . . ."

"Oh, generally? No. I'm awkward at dances. Can't dance to save my life. But with you? Yes."

My cheeks sting with a surge of heat. My mouth opens and immediately closes when words don't come out.

"So." Asher looks down at my comforter and then back up at me. "Want to go, then? With me?"

I grin. "Sure."

Asher grins back, his head bobbing. "Cool. Cool."

"Think we should dress up?"

He raises an eyebrow. "For the dance?"

I laugh. "For the tinfoil hat convention."

Asher shrugs. "I'm going to go out on a limb here and say jeans and a T-shirt will probably be fine. But what do I know? This will be my first conspiracy convention."

"I wonder if they call them FoilCons."

"Or ConCons."

"Sounds about right. So first we'll go check out Nate Hammer and his merry band of conspiracy theorists and then we'll go to the dance—"

"Like every other normal couple." Asher grins.

"Exactly," I say as calmly as I can when the boy I—okay, fine— officially like uses the word *couple.*

But on the inside, I'm kind of screaming in a way I never let myself do. Asher still hasn't moved away, and if I leaned forward just an inch, our arms would touch. He looks at me like he can't make up his mind about something, and I realize I'm hardly breathing.

Finally he says, "Can I kiss you?"

"What?" But I heard him just fine.

"I mean, I guess I'm feeling kind of brave after telling my parents about the RISD program, but I'm afraid I'll lose my nerve by the dance, and I would really like to kiss you."

"You would?"

"Yeah. Been wanting to for a while." Then he quickly adds, "But we don't have to if you don't want."

I grin and nod. My body automatically leans into his, and it feels so normal, like we should have done it a lot sooner. The last time I kissed a boy was on a dare, and it was so uncomfortable. I was fourteen and

199

Dayton Vazquez towered over me, so I had to crane my neck the whole time, which Dayton didn't seem to notice. But this. This is perfect. My bangs fall across my eyes and Asher raises a hand to gently push them back. I don't need them as magic blinders this time.

I want to see every second of Asher getting closer. How his dimple appears and disappears, his dark eyes seem to shimmer, or, I realize for the first time, how his top lip is a little bigger than his bottom.

When his lips meet mine, my eyes close, and it's like holding on to a colorful sparkler on the Fourth of July, tiny bits of the firework tickling your skin as it burns. For a second, my mind tries to warn me about how furious Mom and Dad would be to find us kissing alone in my bedroom. But Asher's hand slips to my waist, dashing away the thought as he pulls me closer. I feel his fingers curl a little against my back, like he doesn't want to let me go.

"Okay," he breathes when we pull apart, smiling. "So that's done."

Asher's not always great with words, that's been established. But somehow, that sounded about perfect to me.

When he leans in again, every last thought about D3 and the Turners drifts out of my brain like smoke.

chapter eighteen

Normal people go out to dinner or a movie before the Sadie Hawkins dance. Asher and I go to a convention for conspiracy theorists apparently.

From the minute I wake up on Saturday morning, it feels like grasshoppers are having a party in my stomach. It's probably because soon we're going to be in a room of people who think there's a godlike person leaving them secret messages all around the internet.

It might also have something to do with getting to kiss Asher again. Because it turns out, I really enjoy kissing him. Going back to school after a long weekend definitely sucks less when you've got someone cute to kiss between periods. Ximena has been smiling so much since I told her that I'm surprised her jaw hasn't broken.

Asher and I never did decide what exactly one wears to a convention like this, so I spend a good thirty minutes staring blankly into my closet. Eventually I manage to get dressed and choke down a bit of breakfast before he arrives.

"Hi," he says, grinning a little lopsidedly when I open the door. Behind him, lazy snowflakes drift in the air, but I'm warm all over. "Are your parents here?"

"They're at the shop. Why?"

"Good." Asher stoops down so we're the same height and kisses me.

It's light, quick, and somehow still leaves me breathless. "I almost showed up an hour early because I couldn't wait to do that."

I quietly melt on the inside. "You should have."

"Now I know for next time." His dimple appears and he kisses me again.

"Oh," he says when we get in his truck. Asher turns the key and the engine roars on the first try, unlike Bula's, which usually takes a couple of cranks and some encouraging words from Ximena. "I brought you something." He reaches across me and opens the glove compartment. Inside, there's a rose sculpted onto a cuff entirely made out of tinfoil.

"I got an actual flower for the dance, but this seemed like the right vibe for Nate Hammer." Asher turns out of the parking lot onto Main Street. "Do you think it's corny?" He takes his eyes off the road only for a second to glance at me.

"You're talking to the girl who likes talking animal movies. I'm good with corny." I put it on my wrist and hold it up. The aluminum foil flashes in the sun streaming through the windows.

"I found a YouTube tutorial on how to do it. Who knew tinfoil art was even a thing?"

"You should know by now that literally everything is on the internet."

Asher's grin slips from his face. Ever since the football game, it seems like even more kids are wearing D3 patches at school, and Asher's been freaked out about them ever since we talked to Dillon. There were so many times in the last week that I could have told him

202

about the Turners, but each time I saw him, he'd kiss me and my brain would kind of go fuzzy. Everything about us, even the fact that there is an *us*, feels fragile.

"So what's my undercover name for this thing again?" I ask. "Mildred Merryweather or something?"

"Penny Bottoms." His smile returns quickly. "And I'm Rupert Sourdough."

"Right you are, govna." I nudge him in the arm, and he catches my hand in his.

For a second, I wonder if he'll take his hand away the way other guys before him have once they realized my knuckles are swollen from my arthritis. But he doesn't.

I watch the snow-filled fields whiz by as we barrel down the freeway. Usually, New York winters look to me like what I've always pictured a post-nuclear-bomb world would—leafless trees standing like skeletons, the ground covered in stark white, and a filmy gray sky. But now, holding Asher's hand, it looks like a winter fairy tale from a picture book. It doesn't even bother me that Asher's hand is a little sweaty. He only takes it away when we reach the exit for downtown to navigate through the streets.

We park at a garage behind the hotel. There's even more snow here than in Canandaigua, and Asher has to help me through an intersection where some of it has been piled up by the snowplows right at the curb cuts on the way to the hotel.

As soon as we go through the front door, I spot a group of people with *D3* on their shirts and hats in the lobby. Two women working at the front desk cast nervous glances at the clump of D3 men hovering near the breakfast bar.

Asher and I exchange looks.

A sign that reads *Nate Hammer*, mounted on a pillar with masking tape, points down a dimly lit hallway. We follow it. I wish I could hold Asher's hand right now, but I need both of mine to push myself across the thick brown carpet. We follow the noise until we get to a room that is completely full of people already. D3 definitely isn't just a couple of guys posting trash in my mentions or on the subreddit. It's bigger than that.

There are at least ten rows of chairs with an aisle cut down the middle, and already I can tell it's going to be standing room only. In the back corner of the room, people are lined up in front of a table full of D3 and Nate Hammer T-shirts, water bottles, mugs, key chains, and flags for sale. One guy holds up a T-shirt that says *They Don't Want You to Know* on the front of it.

I scan the crowd; most of them are already seated, glancing eagerly up at the front of the room, where there's a small stage and a podium with a projector screen behind it. There are more men in the crowd than women, and I'm pretty sure every single person in here is white, including Asher and me. Most of the people here are my parents' age or older.

A bunch of people have handwritten signs I can't read because they're facing the front of the room, but the ones I can see say things like *Proud member of the D3 Army* and *S2AIA*, the phrase I've seen people use in hashtags but haven't figured out.

There are also almost more American flags in this room than the town puts out on Main Street for the Fourth of July parade, on everything from T-shirts to signs to banners.

But what is most striking is how normal everyone looks. No one's wearing tinfoil hats or even looks as sketchy as Dillon McRae. They're just average people you'd see walking down the street or at the mall.

Beside me, Asher's hands are curled into fists, and he glances down at me uneasily. I shrug and we head for the back row closest to the door, where there are still a few empty seats.

"Isn't that Mia?" Asher asks, pointing a few rows ahead.

Sure enough, Ximena's football friend Mia sits three rows ahead, with Ollie on one side and two girls I don't recognize on the other side of her. So they follow this Nate Hammer guy, too?

A woman who looks a little like my grandma smiles at us as she passes, with dyed blond hair and a round face with purple-framed glasses.

"It's so nice to see the younger generation awake and watching," she says to us before moving to sit three rows ahead of us.

I lean toward Asher. "What's that supposed to mean? Is that the D3 version of being woke?"

"I've seen some of the replies from D3 people talk about themselves as awake and the rest of the world as asleep," he whispers back. "It's kind of creepy."

"Yeah, they don't sound awake. They sound ridiculous."

Asher chuckles, and his warm breath against my ear makes my

skin prickle, which is an odd sensation when I'm in a room full of people who make my skin crawl for a different reason.

"So all these people believe in some Defender?" I ask, my eyes roaming over the rows of people.

Asher shrugs just as a group of people spills through the door behind us. When I twist in my seat to get a look, I freeze. Cade and Mrs. Bird are at the front of the group, and behind them, there's a steady stream of people from school. Lily and Phoenix walk in next to Brayden and Annika, followed by about half a dozen other kids from Cade's lunch table. It's the first time I've seen Phoenix and Lily since the football game. They still haven't come back to school yet. Lily's texting on her phone as she walks, while Phoenix looks nervously around the room. But I don't have time to wonder why because Ava and Bryce are behind him.

Asher follows my gaze. "Did you know your sister was coming?"

I shake my head numbly. Bryce spots us and heads straight over with a wide grin. But Ava stays next to Cade and the others at the back of the room, her hands in her coat pockets.

"Oh my gosh, you came! Ava said you were too busy." Bryce is in her black D3 hoodie from the game. "But I totally called it! I told her there's no way you'd miss this."

"Um, yeah. I didn't know you guys would be here, though," I say loud enough for Ava to hear me.

"Oh, of course. I'm a huge Nate Hammer fan," Bryce says. "He's seriously changed my life."

I laugh, but Bryce gives me a confused look. Oh wow, she's being serious.

"Are you going to meet up with Nate after his talk?"

I blink up at her. "I don't know—"

"I can't wait to meet him. He posted on his TikTok that he's going to take pictures with fans after the event, and I'm kind of dying inside." She bounces on the balls of her feet. "You should totally take a picture with him. The two of you together would make an awesome post."

Wait. Does Bryce believe in the Defender thing, too? I open my mouth, but no words come out.

Out of the corner of my eye, there's a flurry of movement in the front of the room.

"Looks like it's about to start," Bryce squeals, like she scored tickets to see her favorite band or something.

"Can you please tell my sister that I can't wait to talk about this later?"

Bryce nods eagerly. She rejoins the group, and they all head to the front of the room, where seats were blocked off. On the way, Cade and Ollie bump fists.

I stare at the back of Ava's head, willing her to turn around and look at me.

A side door at the front of the room opens and Nate Hammer appears. I don't get a long look at him because the crowd jumps to its feet and cheers loudly, waving their signs and blocking my view entirely.

I shift in my chair until I finally see him. In the dim hotel lights, his pale skin looks a little gray. But Nate Hammer isn't some creepy-looking guy. Okay, maybe his hair is a little awkwardly fluffed up on the top. He actually looks pretty polished, in a nice navy-blue suit with a bright red tie.

"Thank you," Hammer says over the cheers as people take their seats again. "It's great to be in the presence of so many awakened individuals. I'm here because we've reached a critical time in our country's future. Dark forces are at work trying to destroy us, but more and more people are coming to learn the truth, and we will prevail."

Some of the people in the crowd murmur in agreement.

"I decided to start my nationwide tour in Rochester, New York, for a very important reason," Hammer says. "Just a few months ago, just a couple of miles away, two innocent children, Jensen and Annalice Turner, were abducted from their front yard." He launches into retelling the whole story about the Turners and the night twenty-eight other kids supposedly went missing. "But all of us here already know that this wasn't the beginning or the end, thanks to one of the most important sources working on our behalf to expose the work of the Cabal. We know that the Defender is working very hard every day to expose the Cabal's secret plans to destroy the United States. The Defender has been quite clear about that."

Even though Dillon told us about it weeks ago, it's still shocking to hear Hammer talk about it in person.

"To help us prepare for the coming war, recent messages from the

Defender have revealed a new conspiracy by the Cabal that strikes at the very heart of America—at our children. It's *what they don't want you to know . . .*" Hammer pauses dramatically at the line he uses on his YouTube videos and the whole crowd seems to hold its breath. Even I find myself leaning forward in my chair.

Hammer takes a sip of water from the podium and keeps going. "In cities all across America, like here in Rochester, the Cabal has hired a whole network of secret agents to steal American children right off the street, holding them in prison-like facilities known as Nodes, before selling them to America's own foreign enemies."

My breath catches in my throat. Beside me, sweat beads at Asher's temples and he looks a little cross-eyed squinting up at Hammer, trying to make sense of what he's saying.

"But don't just take my word for it." Hammer gestures to the screen behind him. "Let's look at the evidence the Defender has left for us. In September, the Defender posted through a previously unknown vehicle for their messages: this Instagram account, code-named The Whine. To those of us who know how to translate their messages, it became clear right away that the Defender had been using it for quite some time to warn us of this plot by the Cabal."

I gasp. The screen behind Nate Hammer lights up with screenshots of my posts on the account, some of them from years ago. There's the one with the picture of the wolf from Mrs. Cerwonka's game camera with the word *WOLVES* under it. Then there's the picture of the new bank opening from a few weeks ago, with

NODES under it. Last, my post showing one of the delivery trucks in front of Vine and Things. Under that, it says *SHIPMENT.*

I didn't think it could get much worse than Dillon thinking I've been posting about the Defender. But they think my posts *are* the proof that the Cabal is selling American children to other countries.

This is why I've been getting so many likes on my old posts? Seriously?

Hammer flashes through screenshots of The Whine and what look like other random pictures from websites, videos, and social media posts, with words and sentences in my posts underlined in bright colors that are all apparently supposed to be connected in some way that is meaningful and prove what he says. But none of it makes any sense.

Then he moves to pictures, parts of which are circled—a bank, a gas station, a skyscraper, a church—all Nodes, he says. There's even one of the Statue of Liberty. It's exactly like how all his videos are. He never stays on one of these images long enough for the viewer to figure out what the circled part is supposed to show, almost like he's trying to distract us.

Every moment of his talk seems like a well-choreographed scam, and I can only hope that now that Ava's hearing it from Nate Hammer himself, she snaps out of the delusion she's clearly under.

Angry voices rise up around us and people lean forward in their chairs, clenching their fists. You can see it on Hammer's face—the crowd is responding exactly as he'd hoped.

It's hard to wrap my head around the idea that Nate Hammer, or anyone, actually believes a word that he's saying, but something tells me he does. He's an actor and a believer both, and somehow I feel like that makes him more dangerous than a person who's only doing it to make money. But Ava, Bryce, and even Cade have to see past his garbage by now because everyone knows I run The Whine, not the Defender.

Hammer doesn't stop at the kidnapping conspiracy. Next he starts talking about that supposed secret plot to cause natural disasters with "weather weapons"; then he makes a sharp U-turn to claim that the Cabal is poisoning imported food to depopulate the earth. He finishes with a conspiracy about how the Cabal rigged an election in France last month.

I look around at the people in the crowd, sure their faces must look as incredulous as mine almost certainly does. But they don't. In fact, they look completely mesmerized, like they're under a spell.

"Soldiers together, arm in arm!" Hammer says at the end of his speech, raising a fist into the air. Everyone around us jumps to their feet, cheering with their fists raised in response.

A cold shudder runs up my spine at the words: *Soldiers together, arm in arm*. It's the hashtag I saw.

As soon as Hammer gets off the stage, a woman goes to the podium and announces a fifteen-minute break. The room erupts in excited chatter. My brain feels swollen from all the garbage haphazardly thrown at it the last hour. I'm vaguely aware that Asher is saying something, but I don't hear him because Phoenix suddenly gets up from his chair and snakes down the aisle. Cade watches him go, brow furrowed, then takes off after him.

Before I know what I'm really doing, I shove back hard on my wheels and follow them out the door. They're already almost down the hall into the lobby.

"Phoenix!" Cade barks.

Phoenix freezes, eyes wide as he turns at the sound of his name. He was clearly headed for the front doors. I duck behind the corner so they can't see me.

"Where are you going, buddy?" Cade asks, his voice over-friendly as he jogs to catch up to him.

"I have to get out of here, man." Phoenix pushes a hand over the top of his short brown hair.

"You'll miss the group photo with Nate Hammer. Just stay for a few minutes."

My wheels are silent on the carpet as I push myself forward a little more so I can hear better, sliding my chair as close to the wall as I can get it without scraping it.

"I can't do this anymore. The cops keep showing up and asking all these questions. It's too . . . too much. We have to come clean."

"No. You have to stick to the story."

"But I don't think they believe it." Phoenix shakes his head. "I didn't know it was going to get so . . . out of control." I can hear the voices of other people in the hallway behind me now, so I lean forward a little in my chair. "You said I just had to hang out for twenty-four hours.

That we were just going to make a point. Get some publicity for the club. Help the missing kids."

"And you did. Tons of people joined the club because of you guys."

"But it was way more than twenty-four hours—"

Cade shrugs. "People got really into it."

Phoenix tugs at the bottom of his D3 sweatshirt like the fabric burns his skin. "But I didn't know about all this." He raises his arms and lowers them again.

Did Phoenix just say what I think he said? That his disappearance was staged? I can't move. Can't breathe. If they decided to go back to the room now, they'd find me still frozen. Phoenix sucks on his lower lip while my heart hammers against my chest at the revelation.

"Listen," Cade says, his voice going from friendly to vicious in an instant. "If you tell them what we did, you could get into massive trouble. Not being honest about where you were could get you arrested."

"B-but it was your idea. You're the one who told us we couldn't go home—"

"I had nothing to do with any of it except for spending every waking moment trying to find you guys after I thought you'd been kidnapped. I mean, I organized search parties. I staged a walkout, all to find you guys!" Cade says in a well-rehearsed voice. "I just happened to find you in that garage. How could I know you were lying about the whole thing?"

Phoenix sways on his feet like he's about to pass out, and I feel like I'm going to vomit right here in the hallway. The Turners aren't the only fake thing Defend Kids has been promoting. The truth settles on my chest, hard. Cade orchestrated Phoenix and Lily's disappearance for attention. Defend Kids is a total scam.

"What are you doing?" Ava's voice hits me before I realize she's here. She steps in front of me with Mia and Bryce behind her. Phoenix and Cade jump at the sound of her voice and for a second, Cade just stares at me.

"I was just . . ."

Phoenix uses the distraction to dart out the door, and Cade stalks after him.

"Oh my god, can you believe that guy?" Mia shakes her head and loops her arm through Ava's.

"You mean Nate?" Bryce asks.

"Um, yeah. What he said in there . . . he's obviously nuts or something." Mia screws up her face for emphasis.

Bryce frowns at her. "This is serious stuff, Mia."

"Um, hello. He just spent twenty minutes saying Quinn's Instagram posts have, like, secret messages in them?" Mia laughs. "You're not leaving secret messages on your posts or working with this Defender dude like some kind of prophet, are you, Quinn?" She can barely get out the words, she's giggling so much.

"I definitely am not," I reply, looking straight at Ava.

Bryce's face goes red in the seconds it takes for her to look first at me, then at Mia. "If you're not one hundred percent committed to the group, Mia, then you don't belong here! This event is only for *true* believers."

Bryce marches back into the room with a huff and Mia trails after her. I watch them go, my mouth hanging open. Bryce is much more into this than I'd realized. In the weak yellow light of the hotel hallway, Ava's face looks sickly white.

"Ava, we have to talk. I just heard Phoenix say that he and Cade faked his and Lily's disappearance," I say.

Ava puts a hand on her hip. "What are you talking about? Why are you even here?"

"Why are you? I'm serious. They just admitted the whole thing. They were trying to get attention for the club or something."

"That's impossible," she snaps, shaking her head.

"Why won't you believe me about any of this, after listening to that nonsense in there and knowing the Turners aren't even real?"

"Oh, hey, Asher," Ava says, looking over my head, and I go rigid. For a second, I'd completely forgotten about Asher and the fact that he doesn't know about the Turners hoax.

His mouth is a thin line. He heard everything.

"Quinn, get a picture of all the Canandaigua members with Nate Hammer for your Insta," Cade says, suddenly appearing again. No greeting, just a demand for more attention. And no Phoenix in sight. "You should have worn your sweatshirt," Cade says to Ava, flexing in his own, like one of his shirtless bathroom selfies.

"I forgot," Ava mumbles.

I tear my eyes away from a still-silent Asher to glare at Cade. "Actually I'm not posting about Defend Kids anymore."

"What?" Cade barks.

"And I'm deleting all my old posts about it, too." I smile as sweetly as I can. "Ava can tell you why."

"I think we should go," Asher says.

"You coming?" I ask Ava. But she just shakes her head.

The event is supposed to go on for another few hours, but I think I've seen more than enough, too.

Asher doesn't say a word the whole walk out of the hotel and to the parking garage. Back in Asher's truck, the distance and silence between us is cavernous. He pushes a little past the speed limit to get us out of the city as fast as he can. The truth screams in my ear: The Turners aren't real, and Phoenix and Lily faked their disappearance.

"So, that was . . ." I say, breaking the silence, but then trailing off.

"Yeah, that was . . ." Asher shakes his head, like somehow the movement might shake loose the right words. "It was very . . . like, militant. He kept talking about a war and calling everyone soldiers."

"And did you notice how every single thing he talked about was based on making people either angry or afraid?"

"Yeah, Nate Hammer wasn't appealing to logic, and he definitely knows how to rile people up."

"And he really didn't have actual evidence for any of it. Just some coded messages and some pictures he probably took from online. But then he strung all of it together in a way that probably sounded pretty logical if you'd already drunk the Kool-Aid."

Asher's knuckles are white from gripping the steering wheel. "How long have you known the Turner kids weren't real?"

I lick my lips and admit, "Since after the football game." I tell him about the article and then Phoenix's confession I overheard back at the hotel. By the time I'm done, anger fills every inch of me. "I'm sorry I didn't tell you about the Turners. I should have."

He's silent for a minute that feels like a year, but then shakes his head. "Who would think it's okay to fake a kidnapping?"

"Cade. Cade Bird would. You should have seen Phoenix. He was so scared of him." I cover my face with my hands and let out a muffled, angry growl. "I knew Cade hadn't changed! I knew he didn't really give a crap about missing kids. He clearly made Phoenix and Lily pretend they were kidnapped to make the club look important. The whole thing is just one big giant scam."

The worst thing I thought he would do is keep the bake sale money for himself, but this? This is so much worse.

"The biggest problem is that real people believe all this Defender stuff." Asher stares straight ahead in silence for a while. "Maybe we should tell them who you are. Like put your name up in the bio so they know The Whine definitely is not involved."

I shoot him a look. "You really want those people knowing who I am? 'Cause I don't."

He gnaws on his bottom lip before he finally shakes his head. "No, I guess not."

"Look," I say when we take the exit for home. "I'll delete every single post about Defend Kids and the random ones they think mean something as soon as I get home. If the evidence of D3's whole conspiracy hinges on a bunch of my random posts that literally mean nothing, the whole thing will be over once I delete them."

"I guess." But Asher sounds unsure.

"It'll work," I say. "It has to, because Cade Bird can't win and I'm not letting all his idiots take The Whine from me."

r/D3f3nd: *posted by u/VKalender

All the posts about the Turners and Defend Kids have been removed from @TheWhine! Anyone else see this? What is happening??? I don't want to, but I'm starting to fear the worst . . . #D3

> **InTheDark_Light:** Wake up—the Cabal is at work!! Have you noticed all the posts taken down are the ones containing the D3f3nd3r's messages to us? They don't want the truth coming out. They've infiltrated @TheWhine! #D3

> **CabalHunter7:** Keep fighting, D3. They can't silence the D3f3nd3r or their soldiers! We will be heard.

> **dhash55:** Come on, we all know what is happening here. The Cabal is on the attack. But this isn't the worst, the worst is yet to come. Time to counter. Let's stop them once and for all. #S2AIA

>> -> **Throwaway98:** That's exactly what's happening. The D3f3nd3r warned us this would come. The Cabal is making moves.

>> -> **AwOkeBro:** Wish it wasn't true, but I have to agree with you. The Cabal has taken over @TheWhine. Time to launch the D3 army! Keep strong, brothers.

S2AIA_prince: Swarm @TheWhine with your comments until we defeat The Cabal!! The D3f3nd3r is counting on us! We're a digital army!

chapter nineteen

The gym is packed by the time Asher and I get to the school that night. It smells like sweat and too many kids using perfume and cologne for the first time and going way overboard on it. We've traded in D3 and American flag shirts for our classmates in sparkly dresses and suits.

Because Principal Stewart doesn't believe in spending money on decorations for school activities, the gym looks like it vomited up our last few dances and mixed them all together. There's an arch over the doorway made of corn husks, and orange-and-black tablecloths covering the tables from our homecoming dance. But you hardly notice either because of the magical canopy of white lights from last year's winter formal that makes the whole gym glitter.

I glance up at Asher standing so rigidly next to me that I almost feel like I came with one of the inanimate decorations. He's got his bottom lip between his teeth, basically the way he's looked since we left the Nate Hammer event. He barely said a word when he came to pick me up, and he was late. Luckily, my parents were too concerned over Ava's announcement after the convention that she was exhausted and skipping the dance to notice. I'm almost glad for the booming music because at least it lets me pretend he's not speaking now because of the noise.

And I get it. After I deleted all the posts D3 thought were evidence, it took hours for my stomach to stop doing flip-flops. It felt weird to be getting ready for a formal dance after basically being in an episode of *What They Don't Want You to Know* come to life and finding out the truth about Phoenix and Lily. But for right now, I want to have one night where Asher and I don't have to deal with D3 or Cade or fake missing kids.

"It looks kind of nice in a weird way, right?" I call up to him.

"Yeah," he says, but he's frowning.

I sag a little in my chair. I'd been picturing what it would be like to dance with Asher under the lights. I slow danced with Max (Ximena's suggestion) at last year's end of the year dance and Max knelt down so we could be at roughly the same height. It was awesome, aside from the fact that I was dancing with Ximena's boyfriend rather than my own. We were mostly stationary the whole time, swaying in place, and I'm pretty sure Max's knees hurt after even though he didn't complain about it. But for the first time, I was dancing with someone eye to eye. But that can't happen with Asher when he's acting like he doesn't even want to be here with me.

A clump of people dance in the middle of the gym and I spot Ximena right in the very center of it. Everyone else is mingling around the tables surrounding the dance floor. As soon as Ximena sees us, she drags Max out of the crowd by the hand.

"Oh my god, Q, you look gorgeous!" Ximena squeals when she's near enough. She holds my hand up and I twirl my chair around. "Doesn't she look GORGEOUS, Asher?"

"She does," he says, and for a second that makes my heart speed up as his face melts a little. But the rigidness returns just as quickly.

I'm actually pretty proud of my dress. It's a deep purple with sequins on the top and solid silk on the bottom. It's open in the back, with crisscross straps all the way up. The front goes to the top of my knees, but the back is long enough that it trails behind me. It'd probably be a tripping nightmare if I were trying to dance in it standing, but it actually works sitting, as long as I keep the sides of it tucked under my legs so it doesn't get caught in my wheels. I'm a little less excited about my simple black ballet flats. I knew I'd never be able to haul myself into Asher's truck on the strappy stilettos I'd rather be wearing.

But my outfit and how happy I am to have my own date don't seem to matter, because Asher is practically ignoring me.

"Good choice going mini golfing instead of coming to the movies with us," Ximena says to Asher. "The movie totally sucked."

He blinks. "Huh?"

"You beat him, didn't you, Q?"

"You know it." I plaster on a fake grin, remembering only now that I forgot to warn Asher I told Ximena we were going indoor mini golfing instead of to the Nate Hammer convention. Hopefully Asher will play along and no one else from school who went will say anything to Ximena about it.

"That's my girl! Do you want to grab a table before they're all spoken for, or do you want to dance first? Ade, Sulome, and Renata are somewhere in there." Ximena waves at the growing group of people dancing.

"Let's get a table," I say unenthusiastically because it looks like dancing is the last thing Asher wants to do.

"You guys go ahead and get one, and I'll come find you in a minute," Asher says, eyeing the doors we just came through.

"Okay," I reply, but he's already headed out before I finish the word.

We find a table in the back and listen to the music for a while, but ten minutes later, Asher hasn't come back yet.

"Think he fell in?" Ximena says.

"He probably ran into Justin and Ty." But as soon as I say it, I spot the two of them clumped together in a corner of the gym with half the cross-country team.

"We could send Max to look for him."

Max frowns at Ximena. "Please don't send me to snoop on someone in the bathroom. It's, like, an invasion of privacy."

I stare worriedly at the gym doors.

Ximena frowns at me. "Are you guys already having issues?"

"No, we're fine." I shake my head firmly. We don't have issues between us; we have conspiracy theorists who are clearly freaking him out.

"Good, because Ximena has your couple name picked out and it's pretty adorable, to be honest." Max drapes an arm over Ximena's shoulders.

"Quisher! Cute, right? It sounds like something fuzzy you want to squeeze and cuddle."

"It's cute," I agree. I don't know a lot about dating, but having to hunt for your date five minutes into it can't be a good sign. "I'm going to go find him."

"Okay. I'm off to talk to the DJ about playing our song," Ximena says, "so make sure you're back before then."

"Sure," I say.

We used to think the "Cupid Shuffle" was the most perfect throwback song when we were in elementary school. We only considered a school dance successful if we could convince the DJ to play it at least twice. But the last thing I want to do is dance in a synchronized line in the middle of the gym right now.

Ximena tows Max behind her toward the DJ while I head for the doors.

I'm more than a little relieved when I find Asher in the hallway just outside the gym, leaning against a row of lockers with his hands in his pockets. It takes a second for my eyes to adjust to the yellow light.

My wheels squeak against the freshly polished floor. But he doesn't say anything, or even look at me, until I'm right in front of him and nudge his foot with my toe, and then it's only a glance.

"You okay?" My words seem deafening in the silence of the hallway. It's been so awkward tonight that I haven't even gotten the chance to tell him how he's so cute in his suit that it makes my skin prickle every time I look at him.

"Needed some air." Asher hunches over a little. Every inch of him looks like a guitar string, tight enough to snap. "So, mini golf?"

"I had to give some reason why we couldn't go with everyone to the movies instead of telling her we were infiltrating the D3 convention. But trust me, I totally would have beaten you. I'm a pro."

Asher doesn't laugh. The relief I felt a second ago at finding him so close disappears instantly.

"So are you going to tell me what's wrong, or . . ." I trail off, hoping Asher will chime in. But he doesn't. "I know it got really weird at that Nate Hammer thing and the stuff with Phoenix and Lily . . . I mean, I was freaked out, too."

He looks up. "Was?"

"*Am.*"

"Okay, good. So you'll get it, then, when I say I'm having a hard time getting into the dance vibe." His voice is steelier than I've ever heard it.

"Of course I do," I say. "My brain is still trying to process everything."

"Okay." His one-word response sounds like it's got a bunch of question marks after it.

"But now we know what Cade is really up to and that means we can fight back."

"How could we possibly fight against people who believe in secret messages and weather weapons?"

"W-well, I don't know yet." It's harder to get the words out when Asher looks so angry, so . . . very not like Asher. "But I'm going to come up with something. I deleted all those posts, so that's a start. And we'll tell everyone that Phoenix and Lily weren't really kidnapped and about the Turners being fake. But we can't just let Cade and his D3 idiots win."

Asher shakes his head. "D3 is so much worse than we thought it was. When I got home today, I spent a couple hours looking online for anything I could find. And it's beyond freaky. They have this subreddit where they debate all of the Defender's messages . . ."

"I know."

His head jerks up. "Wait, you know about the subreddit?"

I bite my lip. "Well, I saw it when I was doing research on D3 earlier."

"You didn't say anything about it. Just like you didn't tell me about finding out the Turners weren't real either. Has lying become that easy to you?"

"No! I said I was sorry about that."

"I think we have an obvious answer here about what to do." He pauses, I guess for me to offer up the conclusion he's already come to, but I have no idea what he's thinking, so I wait. "You need to deactivate The Whine."

"You want me to shut it down?"

"You don't?" His eyes narrow. "How can you want to keep it going after today? It has messed people up. I think they're dangerous. You heard them at the event. People think a war is coming and that they're soldiers."

"They're not dangerous," I say, because no matter how far Ava has gotten into this, she would never hurt anyone. "And I think most of those people were messed up long before I started posting about Defend Kids. I mean, the Defender person has been posting since last year. These aren't people who suddenly started believing in a secret group of evildoers because of me and The Whine."

"No, but because of us, more people think that a secret group is kidnapping kids and selling them to other countries. Our whole town basically does. Even your own sister believes it!"

At the mention of Ava, my whole body tightens. "She's not one of them, okay?" But Ava did stay at the Nate Hammer convention after everything she heard and even though I told her what Cade had done. The horrifying fact is, my sister may very well be lost to D3. "Look, I never posted about the conspiracy."

"But they still believe that's what your posts are telling them. And we posted a million times about missing kids who literally don't exist."

"And I feel really stupid for falling for it. But these people probably believe there are secret messages from John F. Kennedy on the back of cereal boxes, too! They see what they want to see. We could post about toilets and they'd only think it was more evidence of the Cabal spying on them from the bathroom or something. We can't stop them from doing that!" At some point, I started yelling, and yelling at Asher is like kicking a puppy. I take a breath to bring my voice back down.

"I don't get why you even want to do this anymore. They've basically taken over your account." Asher runs a frustrated hand over the top of his hair.

"I'd lose all my sponsors, and just when things were starting to take off!"

"So?"

"Well, not all of us can just trip our way onto the cross-country team or never think about money because we're a King. Some of us have to work hard for what we want; it's not just given to us." The words come out before I can stop them, and the second they do, I feel like I can't breathe.

Asher's face hardens. "I wish I'd never even gotten involved. Then none of this would have happened."

His words burn against my skin. "Hey, I was doing fine with The Whine before you came along asking for a favor."

"I can't do it anymore."

"Do what?"

"The Whine. Helping you. We need to end all of it."

"End it?" He's not talking only about The Whine. He means us, too. We're over before we even really got started, and it feels like someone is strangling my heart.

Asher doesn't answer, just looks down at the floor. From here, I can hear the music shift. Ximena finally convinced the DJ to play the "Cupid Shuffle," so she's probably scouring the gym for me. I take a breath, hoping it'll steady the thumping in my chest.

"Look, I'll admit that what we saw today was scary. But we can find a way to block all the D3 believers from commenting or something. I can even do some posts about how the Turners aren't real. We can tell Principal Stewart about Cade. Eventually, all of this will die off."

But I'm definitely making that up. I don't have any evidence or even a plan. The people we saw today didn't look like the kind of folks who eventually lose interest in something. They seem more like people who latch on to something, turn it into something even worse, and then don't let it go.

"Nate Hammer said it himself: They think a war is about to start,"

Asher says. " If you're not going to fully shut it down, then I don't want to be a part of anything that encourages them."

My eyes sting. "Why did you even stick around once you'd gotten enough for your RISD application?"

"For you!" he says, pushing off from the wall. "I stayed around for you."

"And that's not enough now? We're not even friends, or whatever, anymore?" I gesture at the empty space between us that feels more like opposite sides of the planet.

Asher stares at the floor like I'm not even here. "You kept so much stuff from me. And now that we know how bad it is, it sounds like you're pretty determined to keep going. I can't be with someone who would do this for followers, so . . ."

He doesn't get it, what my family is going through with the store. How close we could be to losing everything. How much I need The Whine to work. "I can't just let it go."

Asher's head drops. Today hasn't exactly gone how I thought it would. I imagined more dancing. Not this. Standing on different sides of the hallway fighting.

"Look, I don't want to leave you here, but—"

"Just go," I cut in.

"How can you think that of me?"

"Well, you're the one ditching me at the dance." I ignore the look of pain on his face. "Seriously. Leave. I'll get a ride with Ximena." This time, I really do mean every inch of the iciness in my voice because if he's going to abandon me, he's not the guy I thought he was and I don't want anything to do with him.

I turn away and push numbly against my wheels, my head swimming as it unhelpfully replays the last few seconds over again. I push through one side of the gym's double doors, cheeks burning at the idea that I'm going to have to admit to everyone Asher just dumped me. I'm grateful it's dark enough in here that no one will notice as I search the crowd for Ximena and Max.

The music stops suddenly. The gym lights flick on and there's a collective groan as we all shield our eyes from the sudden brightness.

I hear Principal Stewart's muffled voice. "I need everyone's attention immediately, please." It takes saying it at least two more times before the crowd quiets down. I can just see him above the heads of the crowd. "We were just informed by the Canandaigua police that a bomb threat was made against the school. I need everyone to follow the same process as our fire drills and evacuate quickly and quietly to the football field. Thank you."

And there is quiet. Until the fire alarm goes off and everything around me erupts at once.

chapter twenty

lashes of brightly colored dresses and people in black suits hit me as everyone in the gym runs toward where I'm sitting in front of the doors. My heart thunders in my ears, and I can't make sense of the noise of so many people yelling or the bodies pushing past me.

The crowd starts moving faster. Someone stumbles into me, and I put my arms up defensively, panic tearing through me.

"Sorry," a guy says, his face full of fear as he rights himself. He disappears into the mass of tightly packed people, swallowed up by the rustle of silk and tulle.

I can't see more than a few inches in front of me and people keep bumping into me, not bothering to look down as they head for the door. I have to move because I know it's about to get so much worse. I angle myself through bodies, looking for gaps between them that I can slip through so I can find the edge and figure out what to do. But it's like trying to push through a strong wave.

I try to turn my chair so at least I'm moving in the same direction as everyone else out the doors when an elbow slams hard against my head. I clutch the side of my face, pain pulsing. I want to shrink down into a ball, tuck my head under my arms, and hide until it's all over. But I have to get out of here. Voices get louder and bounce around the hallway until it's deafening, like being underwater.

"Quinn!" Ximena's voice pierces through the noise, and suddenly she and Max are by my side. Relief hits me. She hugs me tightly while Max stands in front of us—to block us from what has quickly become a stampede, I realize—and I take the first breath I've managed since Principal Stewart made the announcement. "Are you okay?" she asks.

I nod even though every inch of me is shaking.

"Where's Asher?" I can hardly hear Ximena's voice over the shouting.

"H-he's gone."

Ximena gives me a questioning look, but there's no time to explain.

"Where did the others go? They were right behind us." Max turns and cranes his neck to look over the crowd, and a second later, Sulome appears with Adrian and Renata, gripping each other's hands.

"You guys okay?" Sulome asks.

"Come on, we have to go," Ade says.

Ximena doesn't ask before grabbing the handles on the back of my chair and I don't stop her. We let the stream of bodies pull us toward the front doors, but Renata and Sulome move ahead of us to clear a path and Max and Adrian trail behind to make sure no one runs into us. In this chaos, when they could be running like everyone else, my friends are protecting me. When we reach the front doors, Sulome and Renata stop.

"Crap, the stairs," Renata says, spinning wildly to look for another route. A girl bumps into Renata, and she shoves the girl, growling, "Watch it!"

"Should we go back through the gym?" I ask.

Now having the only ramp at the back of the school behind the

233

dumpster isn't just an accessibility annoyance, it's potentially an issue of life or death.

"I'll carry you." Max is already scooping his hands under my arms and legs. "Ade, got her chair?"

"I'll help," Ximena says.

Max holds me tightly against his broad chest so I don't bounce in his arms as he moves quickly down the steps, the cold hitting us as soon as we're out the doors. I curl my toes so my ballet flats don't fly off my feet.

"Don't worry. I've got you, Q."

Somehow, Max's words do make me feel a little less like screaming. Over his shoulder, I watch as Sulome and Renata form a barrier around Ade and Ximena, who each take a side of my chair and lift it down the steps, as carefully as if they were carrying me—instead of ditching my chair and running from a potential blast zone.

In the distance, there's a peal of sirens getting louder. Police cars race into the parking lot, bathing everything in a red-and-blue glow. Max doesn't stop at the bottom of the stairs. He carries me into the parking lot to put some distance between us and the building, and the rest of our friends push my chair after us toward the football field where we're supposed to gather.

Max is breathing hard by the time he sets me in my chair.

"Thank you," I say, but the words aren't nearly enough.

"Just wanted an excuse to spend some quality time with you." Max winks at me.

What if Max and Ximena hadn't found me in the crowd?

What if Max hadn't been here to carry me?

What if I'd been using an electric wheelchair, about two hundred pounds heavier than my manual one?

What if, what if, what if . . .

My hands automatically move to smooth out my dress as Ximena pushes me onto the grass. We huddle together, turning back to look at the school.

"So much for evacuating calmly, huh?" Renata rubs her hands up and down her bare arms quickly, visibly shaking in her long black dress.

My hand trembles as it reaches for my phone to text Asher about what happened, but he made it pretty clear we were done back in the hallway and I don't think an emergency evacuation changes that. Instead, I text Mom to tell her that we had to evacuate, that I'm fine, and that I'll be home as soon as they let us leave.

A line of police cars is parked in front of the school, and at least three officers are directing students still coming down the steps to the field. All around us, people in brightly colored dresses and tuxes clump together, most of them on their phones or hugging their friends. A few bright stars poke through the quilt of clouds in the sky.

"I was so freaked out when we couldn't find you," Ximena says to me. "Please tell me Asher didn't run and leave you behind."

"No. He got sick and went home before any of this happened." The lie comes so much more easily than the truth.

"Can't we just leave?" Adrian asks when two police SUVs pull up to the school.

"Aren't we supposed to wait for the teachers to do a roll call?" Max says.

Adrian shrugs. "Keeping us next to a giant brick building that may or may not explode seems like a real good idea, yeah." He slides off his black suit jacket and throws it over Renata's shoulders. Renata burrows under his arm and a small smile flickers on Adrian's face.

Max takes off his jacket, but Ximena shakes her head. "Give it to Quinn."

He offers it to me, and I take it with shaking hands while Ximena puts an arm around Sulome. His jacket is big and heavy enough that I can practically wrap myself in it like a blanket.

"How are they supposed to know who made it out and who might still be inside when, like, half the people coming to the dance are probably still at Cade's pre-party?" Renata tucks her long, pin-straight hair behind her ears.

"Cade had a pre-party?" I ask.

"Only for his club friends," Sulome says.

"Hard pass," Ximena says.

A pair of black SUVs pull up to the school and officers in black vests come out, followed by a square truck, much bigger looking than the police cars I'm used to seeing around town, and two fire trucks. For minutes that stretch like hours, we watch in silence as police officers come in and out of the school.

"You okay, Q?" Ximena's dark eyes study my face closely.

It's like my body forgot how to breathe and I force myself to inhale. "I can't believe we're waiting to see if our school is about to blow up."

"Where would a person even get a bomb in Canandaigua?" Sulome asks as a group of officers talk on the front steps of P. J. Dalton.

"Oh, you can get instructions on how to make one online. It's easy," Adrian says. We all give him a serious side-eye. "I mean, *I've* never looked it up. My brother is an explosives specialist in the army. He told me."

"You know, it's probably a prank. Remember when that one guy pulled the fire alarm during finals freshman year to get out of taking his algebra test? Maybe someone is very anti-school dance."

I can't help but feel like if Renata is being the optimistic one of our group, we're all doomed.

"But a bomb threat is way more serious than a fire alarm," Sulome says. "Like, you can go to jail for that even if it's a joke."

"Seriously. And if they don't go to jail for it, then I will, because if this is someone's idea of a joke, I'm gonna kill whoever did it." Ximena stamps her black-strappy-heeled feet against the cold, balling her hands into fists.

A woman in an emerald-green dress walks toward us, holding up a corner of the fabric to carefully pick her way across the grass with one hand and clutching a clipboard in the other. It takes me a minute to recognize Mrs. Newcomb.

"Everyone okay here?" she asks when she's close enough.

We all murmur unconvincing yeahs and Mrs. Newcomb gives us a reassuring smile in return.

"Is there really a bomb?" Max asks.

"The police are pretty confident it was a false report, but they're still checking everything out to make sure." Mrs. Newcomb writes our names down on the clipboard. Even though I'm the only one here who's taken her newspaper class, somehow she seems to know everyone.

"Won't that take a while? You can make a bomb look like anything. Ouch!" Adrian rubs his side where Renata elbowed him, frowning.

"I've got your names now, so you can head to the back of the parking lot. The police are going to start letting cars out soon, but make sure to only go where they tell you, okay? No hanging around. I'm sorry that your dance was cut short."

"I don't think anyone feels like dancing anymore anyway," Ximena says.

"Have the police said anything about who made the call?" Max asks.

"I'm afraid we don't know anything yet." Mrs. Newcomb tucks her pen under the clasp of the clipboard. "Does everyone have a ride home?"

We nod, even though my ride abandoned me, and move stiffly down the track while Mrs. Newcomb heads off toward the next clump of students huddled together along the field.

Max offers to push me, and I let him. Every bump and divot in the grass would probably feel spine-breaking if I weren't already numb from head to toe.

"I can take you guys home if you want," Adrian says to Renata and Sulome.

The three of them wave before heading for Adrian's blue pickup truck.

"I'm going to have to go ask them about getting Bula out," Ximena says, gesturing to the yellow caution tape and orange traffic cones the police have used to rope off the front end of the parking lot where Bula is parked.

"I'll come with you," Max says.

"You okay here, Q?" Ximena says.

"'Course," I say.

The last thing I needed was to end this day with some idiot playing a prank. But I guess the teeny tiny silver lining is that cutting the dance short means I didn't have to spend the whole night watching Ximena and Max dance after Asher abandoned me. It'd be a glimpse of what my life will be like in NYC after we graduate, and I don't think I could have handled that particular torture tonight.

Ximena and Max hurry to go talk to the woman officer directing cars slowly out of the parking lot, while Principal Stewart walks along the grass with another police officer. They're heading straight for me, but they both seem too distracted to notice I'm here.

". . . and they were very upset. Said people didn't understand what was really happening and that they needed to wake up," the officer says.

There's something familiar in those words that freezes every cell in my body.

"I see," Principal Stewart says.

"They mentioned the Nelson and di Agostino kids, saying we hadn't done enough to find them. Then they mentioned those missing kids in Rochester and that someone called the Defender told them they, quote, had to take action, end quote. You know who or what they're talking about?"

"The Defender? I haven't a clue what that means. Have you been able to identify the caller yet?" Principal Stewart asks, his head stooped.

"Not yet. But we will." The officer's voice is gruff. "We may need to come ask you and some of the students some more questions. About this and the Nelson and di Agostino cases. We're not quite done with our investigation there."

"Certainly. Thank you, Officer."

Principal Stewart goes back to checking in with each clump of students, and I take a deep breath, trying to steady myself. But it doesn't work because it feels like the whole world is tilting and shifting. Principal Stewart may not know what the caller meant, but I do. It was Dillon. Dillon made the threat to the school. He's the one person who believes every single line about D3 and every message posted by the Defender. The police officer said the caller did it in response to instructions from the Defender, and Dillon's the one person committed enough to actually follow through. Without thinking, my hand reaches for my phone to call Asher before I remember we're over.

I turn at the sound of a car unlocking next to me. Siobhan Clark and three other seniors are about to get into the car when Siobhan looks up.

"Think that's one of those weather weapons?" She tucks her dark brown hair behind her ears and points at two red dots blinking from a helicopter drifting slowly across the sky. She aims her phone's camera up to the sky, recording a video of its progress.

Siobhan is in my French class and I've never even seen her talk to Dillon. But somehow she's not only learned about weather weapons but believes in them, too?

The helicopter is close enough now that I can hear the distinct whoosh of its blades, but Siobhan keeps recording it.

I let out a frustrated growl. "It's a helicopter! Not a weather weapon and not some secret government plot. A *helicopter*! Just like all the other helicopters that fly over here all the time!"

The whole group turns to gape at me. Siobhan stuffs her phone into her coat pocket, and they all get into their car. What is happening to my town?

"They said we should be able to leave soon," Ximena says, suddenly beside me. "They've cleared the whole school and there's nothing there. I guess it was just a jerk after all." She moves in front of me when I don't respond. "Q?"

The cracked pleather of Bula's back seat feels especially cold through my thin dress. It's starting to snow, and the snowflakes make it look like Bula is a spaceship flying through white stars. It makes me wish we were in a time machine instead so I could go back to about two hours ago. Or maybe even two months ago.

"It had to be someone who goes here, right? Or at least lives in Canandaigua." Max's deep voice cuts through the weird silence we've been sitting in since the police directed us out of the parking lot.

"Why else would you care about some high school in the middle of nowhere?"

"I don't like the thought of having to walk the same halls as someone who thinks this kind of thing is funny." Ximena grips the wheel and shudders. "Do you want to go check on Asher?"

She wouldn't be asking if she knew that not only did he dump me, but he also totally ditched me at the dance. If she did, Ximena would probably already be plotting his demise.

"No. He said he thinks it's food poisoning or something," I say. I don't have the energy to tell the truth now. I don't know how I would possibly explain it all, anyway. Asher and I must have set some kind of record, beating everyone I know for shortest relationship ever.

Ximena shoots me anxious looks in the rearview mirror, but I avoid her eyes. My panic is probably plastered all over my face. I can't shake the feeling of dread.

"What a sucky night," Ximena says, then spends the rest of the short car ride to my house ranking the top ten dresses at the dance in an attempt to distract me from it all.

When I come through the door, Mom jumps up from the couch, wearing her flannel pajamas, and Dad jogs in from the kitchen. And suddenly the tears I've been holding back all night spill down my cheeks.

"Oh, honey, are you okay?" Mom throws her arms around me, and I bury my face in her shoulder. Dad crouches down next to me.

Mom leans back and wipes the tears from my cheeks. Through my sniffs, I tell them as much as I can, but there's so much I leave out.

About D3, and Ava, Nate Hammer, Cade's scams, and my role in unknowingly promoting all of it. How all of that got us to tonight.

I need a plan to stop D3.

"First kidnappings and now bomb threats? What is happening to this town?" Dad says, and moves to sit on the edge of the couch.

"Is Ava asleep?" I'm surprised our voices haven't already woken her up. After Nate Hammer and now tonight, she has to see that this whole thing isn't just wrong, it's dangerous. Maybe she could even help me figure out how to stop D3.

"No, she went out with some friends. But I texted her to tell her to come home as soon I got your messages."

My breath hitches in my throat. She was supposed to be home, safe and far away from D3. But if she's not here, where is she?

chapter twenty-one

I meant to stay up and wait for Ava to come home. I wanted to confront her, demand answers, shake her until I broke the hold D3 has on her. But I was so completely exhausted that by the time I slithered out of my dress, into my pajamas, and lay on my bed to wait, I immediately fell asleep.

But this morning, Ava is in the kitchen making a peanut butter and jelly sandwich on the counter, in a gray hoodie and sweats. I know everything about Ava, but it feels like looking at a stranger.

"You look awful," I say.

"Didn't get much sleep last night."

I hesitate. I've successfully cornered her, but somehow it's hard to get the questions out. Maybe because I'm afraid of the answers. I don't know this Ava and that terrifies me.

"About last night," I finally manage. "Where were you?"

She doesn't look up. "Out." She seems a little better than when I saw her in Rochester, less like she's about to vomit.

"At Cade's?"

"No. Alone. I went for a drive. I needed to clear my head." She stares down at the sandwich, like making it is the most important thing she's ever done in her life.

The thing is, I don't believe her. I can't. Not after everything that's happened. The old Ava would have never lied to me, or even really embellished the truth. She's always said she's never understood the point of lying when you could say what you think. But the new one— the one so infected by Defend Kids that it doesn't bother her to know the whole thing is *built* around a hoax—seems to be okay with maintaining a long distance from the truth.

"I heard about what happened last night. Are you okay?" She finally looks at me, like she expects to find bruises or something, but she still doesn't quite meet my eyes before looking back down at her sandwich.

"I guess. As well as I can be after having to be carried down the front steps of the school in the middle of a bomb threat, standing in the cold in a dress, and then finding out that it was all thanks to your little club." Not to mention getting dumped by my date, I think bitterly.

"What do you mean?"

My eyes narrow on their own. Does she really not know? Not only is this new Ava comfortable with lies, she is also harder to read.

"I overheard the police say that the person who made the call went off about D3 and how they were following the Defender's orders." I say it slowly, like somehow it might make her really hear me this time.

She sets down the knife on the counter with a clatter, the color draining slowly from her face. "That's not possible. I . . ." She trails off.

Anger surges inside me in an instant, hot and coursing until my hands are shaking. It's like at some point, she put up these invisible curtains over her eyes that she draws whenever D3 is involved. It hits me then that college won't be the thing taking Ava from me, because D3 already has.

"It was Dillon, wasn't it?" I say.

Ava shakes her head. "No. It can't have been him."

"Then who was it?"

Her eyes flash as the back door to the store creaks open and a second later, Mom and Dad start down the stairs.

"I haven't told them, if that's what you're worried about," I say flatly. "But maybe I should."

Ava shoots me a silent plea.

"Aww," Dad says when he comes into the kitchen, looking disappointed as Ava screws the tops back on each jar. "I was about to make us all pancakes."

"Sorry, Dad," Ava says with a forced smile on her face. "I told Bryce I'd help her watch her brother and sister this morning." She hurries off, forgetting her PB&J on the counter.

I reach for a jar of pickles sitting on a shelf inconveniently above my head on the second-highest shelf at the grocery store. It takes me longer than normal to grasp it, and then requires practically my whole body strength to pull it off the shelf *and* keep it from landing on my head on its way down. I don't know if my joints are so sore from yesterday or if my dark mood has infected them. Either way, they twinge with every movement. But the pain in my joints is nothing compared to how much it hurts replaying every single minute of last night over and over in my mind in the middle of the aisle at Tops. From my fight with Asher:

How he wished he'd never gotten involved with The Whine. Or me.

How he left me almost as soon as we got there.

How he looked at me when I wouldn't back down, like I was the worst person he'd ever known.

How he never even bothered to text me.

Then to hearing the police officer tell Principal Stewart about the caller. And then this morning talking to Ava and not knowing if I could trust her when she said she knew nothing about the call.

Replaying it all is like the moment before you fall asleep when all your most humiliating moments run through your brain in a long reel, except worse.

I wedge the jar of pickles between my knees to hold it and head back down the aisle to our grocery cart with what feels like a dark shadow trailing behind me like a cape. But it's just my mom, who made it clear that after last night, I'm not leaving her sight.

"So, last night before the . . . the . . ." Mom starts.

"The bomb threat?" I finish for her.

She nods and plucks a box of Cap'n Crunch from the shelf, dropping it into our shopping cart. "Did you at least get to enjoy the dance a little bit?"

I've spent all morning trying to dodge her questions about the dance, but there's nowhere to hide in the cereal aisle and I'm still not ready to tell her about Asher. He must have heard about what happened at the dance by now and yet he still hasn't even checked in on me. All these weeks I thought he was such a nice guy—how thoughtful and sweet he was. But last night it was like he didn't even want to understand or see where I was coming from. It's like he was just looking for an out.

I swallow back the anger so it won't show on my face. "Yeah. It was super magical," I finally say, pretending to read the nutrition label on the back of a box to avoid looking at her.

Mom pushes the cart down the aisle and I follow her. "I want to see every single one of your pictures when we get home."

I don't answer, but my mom doesn't seem to notice. While she scans the canned goods, I take my phone out and go to my account settings on The Whine.

I have to believe that as much as Defend Kids has morphed Ava into someone I hardly recognize, she wouldn't ever knowingly put me in a situation like last night. But even as I think it, my head fills with crushing doubt. Because one thing I know about D3 is that it gets into people's heads, makes them question facts and logic. Maybe the best way I can protect her would be to shut down The Whine, like Asher wanted, and then tell our parents everything that's happened so they can keep her far away from Defend Kids, on threat of grounding.

My finger hovers over the button to delete my account. But I can't bring myself to do it. Asher may just get to decide to go to college wherever he wants without factoring in the cost, but that's not my reality. I need my paying sponsors to save up for college. Plus, I've worked so hard on The Whine that it doesn't seem fair to just give it up. There has to be an easier way to stop D3, even if it means reporting Cade and the club to Principal Stewart.

Familiar voices make me look up. I see Asher coming into the grocery store with Ty and Justin, and my stomach instantly drops.

They're a blur of orange and black in their cross-country sweatshirts as they jog around the checkout counters and head for the back of the store.

He's the last person I want to see right now, and I'm sure the feeling is pretty mutual. But something makes me want to follow him.

"I saw some friends from school," I say, because if she knows it's Asher, she'll want to talk to him. "Can I meet you up front?"

"Sure," Mom replies.

I don't even know what I'm going to say as I turn around and push myself back up the aisle. Maybe I won't say anything, just make sure he sees that I'm not home crying my eyes out over him. Or maybe I'll yell at him, unleash all the anger that's been building inside me since he ditched me in the empty hallway. I pause at the end of the aisle and spot them hovering in front of the glass door refrigerators, but they don't see me.

Before I call his name, I hear Justin say, "So, what happened last night? We saw you come into the gym with Quinn and then we didn't see you anywhere after we evacuated."

Asher reaches for a bottle of Pepsi but grabs a water instead when he sees Justin and Ty do it. "I went home early. Wasn't really my thing."

Ty sucks in air sharply through his teeth and gives Justin a knowing look. "Uh-oh."

"Is that code for you guys broke up?" Justin asks.

Asher's brow furrows, but he shrugs. "I guess."

"Sounds like you should have come stag with us," Ty says, wiping his sleeve across his sweaty forehead so his blond hair sticks up in spikes.

"Or at least come to Cade's house after Stewart finally let us go. We basically moved the dance over there." Justin cracks open his water and chugs half of it.

"Pass. Cade's a jerk," Asher says. He slams the fridge door shut with a *thwack*.

"Yeah, but his place is right on the water and his parents are always out of town," Justin says.

"Dating is too much work, anyway," Ty says when Asher frowns.

Justin snorts. "You wouldn't be saying that if Arielle Fields wasn't dating Ryan Sherriff."

"You're probably right," Asher says.

"Of course I am," Ty replies. "And shut up," he adds for Justin.

Fury bubbles in my stomach because it means Asher knew about the bomb threat and still didn't text me. It's official: We're over and I'm on my own when it comes to D3. I force myself to look away. That's when I see Dillon pushing a cart full of boxes of butter past me toward the back of the store.

Dillon! My entire body inhales. I don't know if or why Ava would be covering for Dillon, but the fact is, there is no one more committed to the Defender crap in all of Canandaigua than Dillon McRae.

I have to find out for sure if he made the call, and the only way is to ask him right now. It's probably a bad idea to confront the guy most likely to have threatened to blow up our school, but this year is turning out to be one long string of bad decisions.

It's not hard catching up with Dillon.

"Hey," I say as he swings the cart around and positions it in front of the dairy section.

He turns and blinks down at me in genuine surprise. "Um, hey."

"So, you work here, huh?" I say, despite his red apron, name tag, and the lifetime supply of butter in his cart.

"What gave it away?" It takes me a second to realize he's making a joke, and when I laugh, even though it's nervously, his mouth curves up into a tentative smile. He tugs open the box on the top. "My mom's the shift manager here, so . . ." He eyes the double doors to the back of the store, like she might jump out at any moment.

I guess that explains why his hair is slightly more brushed than normal.

"Did you hear about what happened at the school dance last night?"

"About someone making a fake bomb threat? Yeah." He shrugs and turns his back to me to make room on the shelves.

If Dillon had anything to do with it, he's not letting on. I close my hands into fists like it might summon some courage.

"Did you do it?"

He turns back to me. "Why would I?"

"Well, I heard someone in D3 made the call."

"And you figured it was me?" His eyes scrunch like something stings. "I don't need to threaten the school." It's not exactly reassuring, but for some reason I think I believe him. "Violence isn't even necessary. But you can see it, can't you?"

"See what?"

"How people are starting to wake up to the truth about all of this." He gestures like the grocery store his mom manages is some kind of evil dystopia masterminded by the Cabal.

"I think so." I see that the Cabal is made up. That D3 is a dangerous lie. That it's changing my town. And that I've been profoundly naive for not seeing all the harm being done sooner. "Do you think Cade would have made the threat?"

He shakes his head quickly. "No."

"Why not?"

He frowns and scratches at a constellation of pimples on his chin before scooping up an armful of butter boxes and stacking them on a shelf. "You can get in a lot of trouble for doing something like that and Cade wouldn't risk it. He's not a true believer. It's all for show. He's not like you and me. Could have been like fifty guys I talk with online, or any of the thousands of us out there. But I'm positive it wasn't Cade."

All the air seems to have escaped my lungs. "Oh."

The last box placed, Dillon crosses his arms and looks at me seriously. "D3 is everywhere and it's much bigger than people realize."

Something about the way he says it, like he and I share some secret inside joke, like we're comrades fighting against the same enemy, twists at my heart. He doesn't deserve to be manipulated by all the lies.

"You need to know something, okay? Everyone in D3 thinks my Instagram is where the Defender leaves coded messages. But you know I'm the one who runs the account, not some secret source. The truth is . . ." I take a deep breath because I'm losing my nerve the more I go on. "I didn't know anything about D3 that day I spoke to you in the library. I have nothing to do with the Defender. I don't know who they are and I'm not some special Defender translator."

I stop short of telling him about the Turners, or Phoenix and Lily's fake disappearance, because even though Dillon didn't make the bomb threat, it seems giving him small doses of the truth at a time is the safest approach. Dillon stands in front of me silent and with his hands at his sides, like he's frozen by my words. But then his eyes narrow. They're the color of moss and the look makes me shrink back in my chair a little.

"So you've been duping everybody?" he growls.

"I didn't mean to. I didn't know what I was posting until you told me what D3 was." I lick my lips. "But don't you see what this means about D3? Everyone believes my posts were evidence for the whole D3 conspiracy, but I didn't know anything about it."

"People make all sorts of predictions and judgments about the Defender and their messages," he replies icily. "Doing our own research and analysis is a necessary part of the movement. But it also means people can be wrong sometimes."

My mouth drops open because he's talking about wild speculation and conspiracies as if they're the results of careful analysis and investigation, like scientists making some earth-shattering discovery after decades of research in a lab. Like the fact that I'm not working with the Defender like he thought I was is just a science experiment that didn't go as planned and not what my reveal really should be—proof that D3 is a giant scam. I want to scream right here in front of the dairy shelves.

Helplessness swallows me, so I tell Dillon I have to go and head to the front of the store. Dillon may be erratic and have fallen for a lot of lies, but I don't think *he's* lying about not being the caller. But if it wasn't Dillon, it has to be Cade, despite what Dillon thinks. Cade faked Phoenix and Lily's disappearance and then trotted them out onto the football field like the star of a play. So he must have done this for show, too. Just his next pathetic grab for attention.

All I want to do is go back home, slide into my bed, dive under my covers, and hide. People actually believe my Instagram account proves some secret group is kidnapping children and selling them, and it doesn't matter that none of it is true because clearly they believe in it enough that someone tried to do something about it. That's enough to make me want to stay in my bed for the rest of my life.

Even though I deleted all the posts D3 has been using as evidence for their conspiracies, it's obviously not enough. I have to start locking D3 out of The Whine. As I wait for my mom at the front of the store, I open Instagram and block as many accounts posting about D3 as I can.

D3Map

By trying to silence us, the Cabal is declaring WAR. Our work is more important than ever. They're opening NODES in every city. We must get the TRUTH out to every single person in the world. We must open their EYES. Soon, it will be time to act. S2AIA!

Posted by D3F3ND3R
November 13

Replies:

Defender113923: Red alert #D3!! The D3f3nd3r is talking about @TheWhine! The Cabal has infiltrated it!

Defender668873: The Cabal doesn't want the truth out there.

Defender045981: They're slowly taking over. D3 soldiers are going to be the last bastion of freedom!

Defender312220: it's all happening exactly the way the D3F3ND3R said it would, brothers.

Defender409822: The Cabal is closing in. But I'll blow this whole world up to stop em if I have to.

Defender889335: S2AIA

Defender690032: The cabal may not want the truth out there, but I'm going to go get it and then we'll show the world once and for all.

chapter twenty-two

A thousand percent, it was Dillon McRae," Renata says on Monday at lunch, then pops a grape into her mouth. "He'd definitely get a kick out of anonymously terrorizing the school." She chews thoughtfully before resting her chin on her open palm propped up on our lunch table. Her other hand is under the table, holding Adrian's.

"I just think he's a little *too* obvious," Ximena says.

"And the most obvious answer is usually the right one, duh," Renata says.

"I'm with Renata," Adrian says, his cheeks a little pink and his eyes glassy with a happy haze. I'm pretty sure he'd agree with Renata on just about anything right now.

I'm happy for them, if they are, but it only makes the fact that Asher is back at the table of his cross-country friends, his back to me, all the more cutting.

My friends must sense something happened at the dance because no one at my table has so much as asked me about Asher. But after thirty minutes of debating it, they do have a shortlist that Ximena typed up on her phone of ten potential suspects who have both the motivation and the guts to make the threat. From Kiersten Klein, who Ximena says she heard was angry at Paxton Mather because he went to the dance with Lindsey Rosenfeld instead of her, to James

Bennion, the kid who pulled the fire alarm our freshman year, and now Dillon.

"What do you think, Q?" Max asks.

They all stare at me expectantly. "I don't think it was Dillon," I finally say, leaving out the part about how I know. "But I also think this game is morbid."

"I'm with Quinn. Can we *please* talk about something else?" Sulome sighs. "I think I've had enough of Which of Our Classmates May Want to Murder Us for one day."

So have I, but only because I've literally spent every minute since Saturday thinking about it. I need to talk to Cade and get to the bottom of this. He's the one who organized the stunt at the football game, and this feels eerily similar. Plus he had this mysterious pre-party he conveniently kept going once Principal Stewart canceled the dance, so he very easily could have made the call himself. On the other hand, Dillon could be right. If Cade made the call, the entire school would know by now because one thing I know about Cade is that he likes to be the center of attention.

A chorus of laughs erupts over at the Defend Kids table, where Lily di Agostino seems to be reigning without Cade there. I haven't seen Phoenix yet, but this is Lily's first day back at school and she's not even pretending to be traumatized from her supposed kidnapping. No one else must know her disappearance was fake because she only seems to have gotten more popular out of it. And she's completely lapping it up.

The sight of the club makes my stomach swirl. There's at least twenty people around the table today. Maybe some of them are hoping Lily will give them a play-by-play of her abduction, but a bunch of the kids there went to the Nate Hammer event and all of them are wearing their black-and-gold D3 hoodies, like they're actual believers. It's freaky that what Hammer said didn't scare them all away. I chew on my lip in irritation because even though I've been blocking any accounts posting on The Whine that look like D3, they're still everywhere.

"Your bad mood have anything to do with Asher being MIA?" Ximena says in a lowered voice so the others, who've already switched to discussing the new Marvel movie, don't hear.

I guess I couldn't realistically think I'd avoid the topic of *him* completely, but the sound of his name still feels a little like walking straight into a wall.

"It's kind of, sort of . . . over."

It's the first time I've said the words out loud, my brain too tired to keep them locked inside anymore. Even Mom and Dad still think we're together. But I might as well admit the truth. I spotted Asher at his locker on my way to French class this morning. The sight of him made me stop in the middle of the hallway, my breath catching in my throat. Somehow, he must have known I was there because he turned around slowly and looked at me. For a second, everything around me slipped away and it was just me and Asher, like before. But then he shut his locker and walked off in the opposite direction while I sat there, too stunned to move.

Ximena sucks in air between her teeth like she's been burned.

"Noooo, Q. What happened? What did he say? Do you want me to talk to him?"

There are literally no good answers to any of those questions unless I tell Ximena the whole bonkers story, and I don't have it in me, especially here in the middle of the cafeteria.

And suddenly it's all too much.

"I'm going to go to class early," I say.

"I'll come with you," Ximena says, pushing her chair back to stand up, but I shake my head.

I drop my tray off and turn for the doors, nearly knocking into a pair of knees. "Sorry," I say breathlessly before noticing that this particular pair of knees belongs to Asher. I look up.

"Hi," he says.

"Um, hi."

He scratches the back of his head. "I heard about what happened at the dance."

The thundering in my chest turns into a full-on storm. "After you left."

Asher's cheeks are pink, the color they get when he's been running awhile. "Yeah. Um, are you okay?"

My hands are already sweaty, and they slip against my wheels. "I mean, yeah. As okay as one can be when their date ditches them and then there's a bomb threat."

"I almost texted you, but—"

"But you didn't. That's fine. You said everything you needed to say at the dance." I wish I could force my voice to sound like steel so he wouldn't know how totally wrecked I felt when he left Saturday night.

But at best, it comes out bitter. I sit a little straighter and imagine I'm back in my bulletproof box, which, frankly, I never should have left.

Asher doesn't say anything, just fidgets with the straps of his backpack.

"Well—" I start pushing backward.

"Well."

I started using a wheelchair once I realized my legs wouldn't reliably hold me up anymore. I'd be stiffly walking along and suddenly my body would give up on me. The seconds between being upright and being a heap on the floor would stretch out, and when I landed on the hard ground, it would knock all the breath out of me and leave me gasping. And that's what it feels like, watching Asher look for the exit.

Before he can be the first to leave, I push hard against my wheels and weave through the maze of tables and out the cafeteria door.

Ximena pops up and follows me. "Come with Max and me. Let's ditch next period and drive around or something," she says when she reaches me in the hall.

I snort, my eyes filling with angry tears. "Great. That's *just* what I need right now."

Ximena's mouth falls open, stunned by my words, and this time when I leave, she doesn't follow me. I'm not really sure where I'm headed with fifteen minutes left for lunch, but the idea of slipping back into the role of third wheel seems unbearable. The only good news is that soon it will be Thanksgiving break and I won't have to see Asher for a few days. But for now, I feel the familiar pull of the girls' bathroom, the tiled fortress I used to hide out in long enough to put myself back together each time Cade went after me.

But that's when I spot Cade. He's in front of his open locker, wearing his black-and-gold D3 hoodie, without his usual fan club around him. I'm trying to summon the courage to cross the hall when he slams his locker shut and heads straight for me, looking angry.

"Your Instagram broken or something?" he barks.

I feel myself shrinking back naturally at the sound of his voice, harsh like the tips of nails. "What?"

"All the posts about Defend Kids are gone and people keep saying they've been getting blocked."

I've probably blocked around five hundred accounts since I decided to try to silence the worst of D3 on my account, but it's like whenever I do, more of them appear in my notifications. It's like that game you see at old arcades, Whac-A-Mole, where as soon as you bop one more, three others pop up in its place. If I tried to remove every single trace of D3 on it, it'd be a full-time job.

"I'm sure it was an accident, right?"

The way he says it is like he already knows the answer, but I tell him anyway. "No, it wasn't an accident." I have to take a deep breath because now that I'm here, the only thing I want to do is run. "Someone from D3 made the bomb threat during the dance, and I'm guessing it was you."

He smirks. "Wasn't me."

"Are you sure you didn't do it at your little pre-dance party?"

"Jealous you didn't get invited or something?"

How Ava has spent so much time with him and not punched him in the face, I'll never understand.

"No. But I overheard the police say the caller said all sorts of stuff about D3 and the Defender."

"Well, I didn't do it."

I search his face for any sign that he's lying, but find none. If Cade is telling the truth, then what? I was sure the caller had to either be Dillon or Cade, but if it isn't, it could have been anyone, and that thought is scarier than anything else. I swallow the growing knot in my throat.

"Then someone in your club did it. How do you think that person is going to feel when they find out the club believes in a scam?"

"What's that supposed to mean?"

"I found a news article about how Annalice and Jensen Turner aren't real people. The whole thing was made up. That school picture of Annalice on the missing persons posters is a school picture of some random girl in Virginia, and Jensen is some little kid who went missing and was found like a day later." I wait for Cade to at least pretend to be surprised, but he doesn't. "And something tells me you already know all about it."

Cade shrugs a giant shoulder and smirks. It's not the careful and controlled mask I've seen all year. "Who's to say what's true or false?"

"I mean, the girl in Virginia whose identity was basically stolen is. I'm pretty sure she gets to say what's true about it and what isn't!"

He rolls his eyes.

My brain feels like it's about to explode. "So, basically, you started a school club to find two missing kids knowing they were fake?"

"I know some websites have *said* they're fake."

"Not *some* websites. Actual news articles and the police in Rochester."

"Everyone's entitled to their own opinion."

"No they're not, not when a fact is a fact." I shake my head, that familiar feeling of cloudiness filling my brain, the same one that always emerges whenever I spend too much time trying to make sense of D3. "So what about the Defender and the super evil Cabal stuff? And all the things Nate Hammer spews? Weather weapons and government conspiracies and stuff. Do you think any of that is true?"

"Who cares whether I do or don't?"

"A whole bunch of people do. They think some evil group is prowling American streets snatching kids because of you and your club . . ." I trail off at the look of boredom on Cade's face. "And you don't believe any of it, do you? You've just been doing all of this for attention and Instagram followers, haven't you?"

His icy-gray eyes narrow. "So? I want to get out of this town, and being an influencer is as good as any way to do it. Besides, you weren't complaining about it until now. You've gotten thousands of followers for your stupid account thanks to me, so don't try to act all superior."

"But I didn't know about any of it until recently." Still, guilt hits me. I should have acted faster when I found out what was happening.

Cade's nostrils flare. "Wait. Is that why Principal Stewart just told me he's suspending my club from school grounds? Did you narc?"

"He suspended Defend Kids?"

"Just now. He said it's temporary, pending some stupid investigation."

Something like hope blooms in my chest, but it's immediately crushed by Cade's death glare. "No, I didn't tell him anything."

"Good, because I didn't do anything, and if you're smart, you'll drop it." His voice says it's not a suggestion. "And while you're at it, stop blocking people."

A few years ago, I would have done anything to avoid the threatening look he's giving me. But it's different now and I won't back down. I push my bangs back and look at him square in the face. "Look, you might be okay running scams to get followers and free crap for promoting stuff or whatever reason you're doing this for, but I'm not. I'm going to do a post about the Turners so people know the truth about Defend Kids."

He purses his lips. "You're screwing yourself here, you know that, right? As soon as you post it, you're going to lose all your followers."

"I don't care about that anymore. You faked Phoenix and Lily's disappearance. I heard you talking to Phoenix at the Nate Hammer thing." The words tumble out before I can stop them.

His pale cheeks redden with instant fury. "You don't know what you heard."

"I know you told them pretending to be kidnapped would help get attention for the club. I know you pretended to find them in some garage. I know he wants to come clean and you won't let him."

"It's like I told Stewart. You can check my posts. I never actually said they were kidnapped or that Defend Kids rescued them."

"B-but . . . you implied it with that stupid stunt at the football game! And you're forcing Phoenix to lie about it."

"You should have figured out by now that people are going to believe what they're going to believe." The sound of his laughter makes the blood rush to my face. "You can't prove I did anything wrong."

And he's probably right. There's no way Lily will rat him out, and I think Phoenix is probably too afraid of what Cade would do to him to say anything.

I narrow my eyes and silence stretches between us as he holds my gaze, waiting for me to back down. But I don't. I'm going to stop Cade's stranglehold on my school.

"Like everyone already knew, you're worthless, Skeletor." The word comes out in a low hiss.

Hearing the word feels like getting punched in the gut, and in an instant, that surge of resolve I'd felt shatters and is replaced by a familiar feeling: how small and ugly and *inhuman* the word made me feel. That's the thing with past traumas, I guess. You think you've gotten over it, healed, even, like a wound that's closed up, until suddenly it's bleeding again, as fresh as the day you first got it.

He steps closer, and my heart speeds up on its own, but I force out the words anyway. "Call me whatever you want, but I'm doing it."

"Actually, you don't get to call her whatever you want." Ava's voice cuts through the anxiety spiral Cade's one word had tilted me into.

"Look, you need to talk to her," Cade says. "She's trying to spread lies about the club."

"Screw the club! I'm done with it," Ava spits. "And if you ever call my sister that vile word again or even look at her the wrong way, you'll seriously regret it." Ava's hazel eyes are practically full of flames as she glares at Cade.

"Whatever," Cade growls. "Don't need you anyway. Either of you. Delete the posts and block whoever you want. Because you know what gets people's attention more than anything? When they think someone's trying to censor them."

He storms off and I take the first breath I think I've managed in a while.

"You okay?" Ava asks.

I nod and we stand in silence as the hallway starts to get crowded. After weeks of barely speaking to me, I'm afraid that if I move or speak, D3 will snatch Ava back again. A group of kids with D3 patches wave at Ava as they walk by and she half-heartedly waves back.

"Look, I'm sorry. About all of it. Can we talk? After school?" Ava asks. "I'll tell you everything."

"Yeah." I turn to face my sister. "But I'm going to post the truth about the Turners. I have to. People need to know, even if it means I'll probably be Cade's target for the rest of high school and I lose all my followers."

I'm expecting an argument again, but to my surprise, Ava says, "I think you should, too."

Those five words spark a small flicker of something that feels like hope. And somehow, it's enough to cut through the fear I'd been submerged in by Cade and the devastation left by Asher trampling on my heart. Because maybe, just maybe, my sister is coming back to me.

chapter twenty-three

Ava seems out of place sitting cross-legged on my bed next to me, like my room got used to her not being in it much the last few months. I never thought until now about how weird it will be for *her* when she leaves for school next year and Mom, Dad, and I fill in the spaces she'll create when she's gone. After all, Mom and Dad will probably move out of the living room and into Ava's room, and slowly our house will settle into it being the three of us.

Ava nudges the mug of tea sitting on my nightstand she made for me in my direction and takes a sip from her own mug, as if showing me how to do it. I don't like tea, but Ava got into it at some point and she swears it's "calming," which is something we definitely both need.

"It's chamomile. Bryce turned me on to it," Ava says, as if reading my thoughts. She stares into the amber liquid, like she hopes it'll swallow her up.

I pick up my mug and blow lightly before taking a sip. The taste isn't entirely unpleasant, but it's not something I'd choose to drink if I weren't with Ava.

I don't say anything at first because Ava's literally spent the past few weeks basically doing whatever she could to avoid me, and a part of me worries if I say the wrong thing, she'll run off.

But eventually I say, "I have so many questions." I wait until she nods before I keep going. "I guess, first off, do you believe all that stuff about the Defender and the Cabal?" I try to keep the judgment from my voice for the same reason I'm worried about speaking at all. But I need to know how far she's in all this.

"That's not actually as easy a question to answer as it sounds." Ava's lips press together thoughtfully. "I guess not exactly. But it's hard to explain. Like, child trafficking is an actual thing, right? Bad people really do kidnap kids and do terrible things to them."

"Right."

"So the basic premise of the club wasn't wrong. But Defend Kids makes it sound like it happens all the time, that kids are being hunted down in the streets by a group of criminals." She shakes her head, like she can't find the right words. I squirm, waiting. Because my sister has always had an answer for everything until now, with the eleven months ahead of me that means she always knows so much more about life than I do.

"A hundred thousand kids go missing each year. They say it, you know, like it's a fact. Over and over again until you believe it. You start thinking that the police and the government, the people responsible for stopping it, must know how bad the problem really is and just don't want you to know about it because it makes them look bad. And then I felt like I was seeing it play out for myself when Phoenix and Lily went missing. It seemed like the police were so slow to start looking for them, and then when they did get involved, it felt like they weren't doing enough. Instead, it was Defend Kids organizing the search parties and stuff. Stuff like that made it really easy to believe what

Cade and the others were saying about the government and the cops." She picks at the hole on the knee of her pink-striped flannel pajama bottoms. "You start feeling like there's a threat around every corner and it makes you wonder, what if it happened to you? Would anyone try to find you?"

"That sounds terrifying."

Ava shakes her head again, like she's trying to erase something painful. "I never believed in a Defender, though. To me, it always seemed like it was a random person trying to take advantage of the situation and all the people trying to find Jensen and Annalice. But people in the club really seemed to believe it and it made me nervous." And suddenly she laughs, but it's hollow. "I still call them Jensen and Annalice, even though they don't exist. Isn't that funny? I don't even realize I'm doing it. They were *so* real to me until you showed me that article."

I know how I felt when I read the truth about the hoax and I got so angry at Ava when she wouldn't accept it. But I didn't think about how devastating it would be for her to learn the truth. How sucked in she'd already gotten by D3 and how confused she'd feel after.

I force myself to breathe. "Did you ever confront Cade about the Turners or the Defender?"

"Yeah. I told him about the article you found. But he said it didn't matter as long as it was drawing attention to the club, and that they were a symbol of the larger problem. And then I told him I was worried about the Defender thing, and he said the people who believed in the Defender still were against child trafficking, so as long as our goal aligned, it was okay." She shrugs. "I don't know, the way he explained it made a lot of sense at the time, but now that I'm saying it all out loud . . . And for a while, it's like my brain found a way to compartmentalize things." Ava pushes her hands up hard on her face and over the top of her hair. "It's no excuse, but by then, I'd become friends with a lot of people in the club and it got harder to speak up, too. And it seemed like for every question or doubt I had, the club had an answer for it that was really hard to disprove. Like, how do you disprove the existence of the Cabal when bad people really do exist?"

It kind of sounds like the same strategy to get a scared animal out of the place they're hiding—leaving a trail of small bites of food to get them to keep going. But instead of coaxing an animal to somewhere safe, D3 is getting people to believe the more and more extreme, little by little.

"But when you told me you'd overheard Cade admit he staged Phoenix and Lily's kidnapping and their supposed rescue, I confronted him about it. He totally denied everything."

"So you didn't know it was all planned before?"

"No." She sighs. "I feel so stupid. Cade was always so focused on doing big, showy things to get attention. I thought it was for the cause, but it was really all for him. Then I actually thought that by staying in it, I could keep people focused on the actual goal of the club. I think Cade knew I'd try to stop them if he told me the truth about everything—I was already asking a lot of questions about stuff—so he stopped telling me anything."

"Why didn't you leave with Asher and me at the Nate Hammer thing?"

"I guess I was just clinging to hope that people would realize how twisted the group was. And some did. Mia and Ollie broke up after because Mia wanted to leave the club and Ollie didn't."

"But Ollie still believes in it?" I ask.

Ava nods. "I don't know. Does any of what I said make sense at all?" She looks up at me for the first time since she started talking, and I find myself nodding back at her, because Ava needs me right now probably more than she's ever needed me before.

"Yeah, it does." I don't know what it's like to get sucked into something like that, to not believe the truth when it's right in front of me. Even when I thought the cops weren't doing anything to help find Phoenix and Lily, it never once crossed my mind that they would be in on a plot to kidnap kids, like D3 believed. But I get the confusion—trying to make sense of things totally at odds with each other. I didn't question what the article said about the Turners—it had changed everything about Defend Kids for me in an instant. It had taken Ava a lot longer to get there, though. But I was just as confused as she was about how much of the club was actually wrong when two kids we knew were missing.

"I should have seen what was happening a long time ago. You tried to warn me and I didn't listen," Ava says. "And I should have never trusted Cade when I knew exactly who he is. At some point, even when I finally saw what was really happening and I couldn't pretend anymore, I still didn't feel like I could admit it to you. I wanted to try to fix it first."

Guilt still settles itself hard on my shoulders, because I could drown in the number of warning signs I saw before I did actual research. And when Asher started getting really nervous, I brushed it off.

I lick my lips. "There's something else I need to ask you. Did you have anything to do with the bomb threat?"

"Absolutely not," she says firmly.

"Did you know it was going to happen?"

"No, I promise I didn't. I really did go for a drive that night."

Some of the anxiety wound up in my chest releases a little. "Do you know who did it?"

At this, Ava's gaze drops to her mug again.

"Ava, you have to tell someone if you know who did it. This person is obviously dangerous."

"They're not dangerous," she says quickly. "They were like me and got caught up in everything. But they took it too far. They just need more time to realize the truth. I'm going to help them—"

"You think you can fix them like you fixed the club?" Her face scrunches like she's about to break into pieces. "I'm sorry. I didn't mean it that way. At least Principal Stewart has suspended the club from school."

Ava sits upright. "He did?"

I turn on my side. "Yeah, Cade told me right before you got there. It's temporary, I guess, but it's got to help, right?"

"I don't know. I don't think a lot of the members are going to take that well. And Defend Kids isn't just a school club anymore." She chews on her bottom lip.

"Do you think we should tell Mom and Dad about everything?"

It hits me then how badly I want to tell them. The lies have been piling up for so long, and I hadn't realized how tired I am of all the secrets I've been keeping until now. There'd be something so freeing about telling Mom and Dad, even if it meant they'd ban me from social media forever.

"That'd be some fun news to break. 'Hey, Mom and Dad, I accidentally joined a group that believes a secret organization is kidnapping kids thanks to some all-knowing super spy posting coded messages through Quinn's Instagram account.'" Ava shakes her head and I suck in a long breath. It really is as bonkers as it sounds, and yet, people in our town believe it. She falls back on my pillows like her body doesn't have the strength to hold itself up anymore. "Yeah, we can't tell them about D3 now. If we did, then I'll also have to tell them that I'm probably *not* getting a scholarship because I'm failing trig."

"You're joking."

"I'm not. Oh god." She lets out a nervous laugh and blinks up at the ceiling. "That's the first time I've said that out loud to anyone."

"You're failing? Like, *failing* failing?" I have to say the words because Ava has literally never failed at anything.

"*Failing* failing."

"How?"

"I guess I took too much on this year and then everything got out of control with Defend Kids. D3. Whatever. Everything else fell by the wayside, and then suddenly I blinked and the semester was almost over and I have a big old D. I have to ace my final or else I could lose my shot at Syracuse."

The words pour out of her in one big wave, the result of holding them in for so long, I guess. I don't think Ava has ever lost more than a game of Monopoly before. She just doesn't fail. She's always been the first person to listen to my problems, and she hates talking about her own, like somehow she's admitting she isn't perfect.

"I kind of lost myself this year," Ava says now, pulling her knees up to her chest and wrapping her arms around them. "Lost track of what I was trying to do. I'm sorry for everything. I know this wasn't how you envisioned we'd spend my senior year."

"I'm sure it isn't how you thought it'd go either." I roll onto my back and for a while, we lie next to each other in complete silence.

"So, what's on that list of yours? The one of all the things we're supposed to do my last year at home."

It feels like a year since I made that list. I ignore the approximately eleven billion notifications Instagram says I have on my phone and pull up my notes before passing it to Ava.

A full-on smile breaks out on her face as she scans the list, the first one I've seen in a while.

"Let's work on getting some of these checked off. But first, if you want, I'll help you write that Instagram post, the one setting the record straight about the not-Turners," she says.

"What about Phoenix and Lily?"

"We'll figure out what to do about them. But first the post, then we're going out."

Even though the darkness feels like it could swallow me whole, there is one reason for hope that breaks through. I'm not in this alone anymore. And even better, Ava and I are on the same side again.

TheWhine: We recently learned that claims of two missing kids, Jensen and Annalice Turner, reported missing in Rochester, were actually false. According to a news article (link in bio), the picture claiming to be Annalice was stolen from someone else's social media account. The Rochester police said in a statement that the kids do not exist and they believe the whole thing was a hoax. We have deleted all our previous posts we did about them.

> **funXBob7:** You've been posting about them for weeks and they're not even real?!?

> **bitcarter:** LIAR!!! I've seen the police reports!

> **Kennwadio912:** If you needed any more evidence the Cabal has infiltrated @TheWhine . . .

> **roborn_chris:** So you don't even check to see if stuff is true before you post it??? Unfollowing.

> **thebigshark:** I don't see no apology for posting LIES all this time . . .

> **violetbookworm:** Oh wow! Thanks for telling us. Who would run a scam like that? It's not cool to mess with people like that.

> **patrioteagle76:** The Cabal doesn't want the truth out there, but we will prevail! #D3

r/D3f3nd: *posted by u/dhash55

The Cabal has a Node in my city. After the Defender's warning yesterday, I'm sure of it. It's a "bank," at least on the outside. I've spent the last few weeks keeping an eye on it. Every Tuesday at 9 p.m., an armored truck goes to the back of the building. It stays there for about thirty minutes and then leaves. We know that's one of the ways they're transporting the wolves. I think they keep the wolves in the Node for three days before moving them because the truck comes back every Friday. There's an airport twenty minutes away from the Node, so I think they're then shipped out from there. What do I do??

> **GrimReaper:** You need to get evidence so we can show the world and unmask the Cabal!!

>> -> **happerdash:** Get inside and livestream it, D3. Put it on YouTube!

> **MemeGuy:** Save our children, D3! The Cabal could come after any one of our families next. Did you see they've taken over @TheWhine and filled it with lies?

> **GodandCountr33:** You have to be smart about it D3f3nd3r. #S2AIA #D3

> **Pakman63:** DM me with the info and I'll be there. We'll raise an army to tear it down.

>> -> **OllietheStar:** Same

>> -> **GrimReaper:** bro 10/10 he's a fed.

Geej617: How do you know any of this? Sounds like you found a bank or something, D3. Whoopty doo.

> **-> GrimReaper:** 10/10 he's a fed too.

> **-> Geej617:** You literally think anyone who doesn't agree with you is a fed. Smdh. All I'm saying is it sounds like dhash55 is jumping to a whole lot of conclusions with zero evidence. The D3F3ND3R wouldn't want that.

> **-> GrimReaper:** fed

Andyboy9: Protect the wolves, D3. Record it all so we can expose the cabal. The Cabal for Prison!

dhash55: Thanks for the support. S2AIA! The Cabal is making moves to keep us from showing the world the truth, so tomorrow I'm going in. I'm going to get the wolves back and expose the truth. Watch me take the Cabal down.

> **->Tambrose7:** Don't let us down. We're with you, Defender!

chapter twenty-four

"More?" Ava says when my phone beeps announcing new Instagram notifications for the millionth time since my post went up. She frowns from the chair next to me at our kitchen table.

I bury my fork in my plate of lo mein and twist it, pulling as many noodles as it will hold as I stare at my phone in my other hand. "It was bad before the post and now it's out of control. They're so angry. And I've lost, like"—I quickly do the math—"six hundred and fifty-two followers in just the last few minutes."

Posting the truth about the Turners filled me with so much shame after that I thought I was going to throw up. It was an admission that, for weeks, not only had I been totally duped, I had also misled my followers. And I didn't even tell them about Lily and Phoenix. After everything, I can practically feel all my hard work leach away—if I lose enough followers, my sponsors won't be far behind them, and then I'll never be able to help my family.

I shove the forkful of noodles into my mouth and chew before scooping up another. I told Ava I wasn't hungry when she offered to pay for Panda Garden takeout, because it's not exactly like we can afford it. But my stomach betrayed me, growling loudly as soon as I'd said it, and she called in the order.

"Don't look at them." She dips a fried piece of chicken into the neon-red sweet-and-sour sauce. "Put it on silent for now and we'll deal with it all later."

For a few minutes, we eat quietly, and it must be having a full stomach of Panda Garden—the definition of comfort food—because eventually I start to feel a little better.

"I never heard how your big date with Asher went. Are you guys official now?"

I set my fork down. "No, definitely not." Just hearing his name out loud is painful.

Ava frowns. "Did something happen?"

She has no idea how complicated the answer to her question is, but she's not going to let this go until I answer. "We had a difference of opinion."

"Oh geez," she says. "Did you find out he was, like, secretly a homophobe or ableist or something?"

"No, nothing like that. But for the record, being ableist or homophobic wouldn't be a difference of opinion. It'd make him a terrible person."

She nods.

"We disagreed over how to handle D3."

"Oh." Her face falls, matching my own.

"You like anyone these days?" I ask to change the subject.

She gives me a hard look and laughs. "Are you kidding? Who would want to date this mess?"

"I'd kind of wondered if maybe something was happening with you and Bryce."

But Ava just sighs. She clearly doesn't want to talk about it, so I don't push her. We've had enough confessions and guts-spilling for one day, I guess.

"You would tell me if the shop was still in trouble, wouldn't you?"

"Yeah. But I'm not sure if Mom and Dad will tell *me*, at this point. At least not in a straightforward way. I was helping Mom set the table yesterday and out of the blue she told me Dad was looking into getting his certification so he could do substitute teaching next year. I don't even think she meant to tell me. It sort of came out like she couldn't hold it in anymore, and then she tried to downplay it like, *Oh don't mind me, we're fine now*," Ava says, mimicking the voice Mom does when everything is definitely *not* fine. I glance up at her and she looks as unconvinced by it as I felt hearing it.

My shoulders sink. "Both of them have said literally zero to me about any of this."

"You know Mom never wants us to worry about stuff. They both looked on the verge of tears when they told me they needed my college money."

"Maybe that's where we got it from, the keeping all the bad stuff to ourselves thing."

She looks at me like she can't figure out if I'm joking or not, and I'm not really sure how I meant it either.

A wave of exhaustion suddenly rolls over me. Asher, D3, Ava, my parents, and the shop. It's a lot. On top of that, I know that even though I have my phone on silent, the screen is probably full of Instagram notifications from angry D3 followers.

Out of habit, I pick up my phone again and open Instagram to stare at my dwindling follower count. I'm scrolling through my notifications when a reply with my name in it catches my eye.

But my name isn't just in one reply. I keep scrolling. It's in a dozen, fifty, a hundred. And all from handles I don't recognize—

> **S2AIA_girl:** Quinn Calvet posted this.

> **Patriotwitch:** Quinn Calvet is a dangerous liar!

> **Vgood_doggo:** Quinn Calvet must be stopped.

> **Roger_pop:** Quinn Calvet is part of the Cabal!

"What?" Ava says mid-chew, and when I don't respond, "Quinn, what?"

"People are posting my name on The Whine."

"What do you mean?"

"In my replies."

Ava drops her egg roll and leans over my shoulder as I scroll. My hand stops on one comment.

> **AStormIsComing:** The Cabal knows we're coming for them. LMAO if this Quinn Calvet thinks she's gonna stop us from defeating the Cabal. Let's find her and tell her, boys . . .

It's never been a secret that I run The Whine, at least not in Canandaigua. I've never posted my name on the account, but now they know who I am.

"Oh my god, oh my god, oh my god." My hands are shaking as I clutch my phone in my lap. "How does D3 know my name?"

Ava snatches it from me and keeps scrolling, the light from my phone casting a blue hue over her face.

"Cade doxed you!"

"He what?"

"See?" Ava turns the phone to me and shows me his post, his stupid shirtless bathroom selfie profile picture smirking in the corner.

> **TheRealCadeBird:** Quinn Calvet runs this account. She's an enemy of D3!

"I'm going to kill him," Ava hisses. She jumps to her feet like she's about to do just that, but then starts pacing in a small circle around the living room.

"Is it doxing if everyone in Canandaigua already knows I run the account?" I can barely hear my own voice. I'm not even really sure I'm speaking.

Ava spins, nearly tripping to look at me. "Yes! Quinn, he's purposely trying to out you so all the D3 believers will come after you."

Panic claws its way up my throat, and my breath comes out in ragged bursts. "What do I do?"

"We should tell Mom and Dad."

"Then we'll have to tell them everything. Are you really ready to tell them who made the bomb threat?" The edges of my vision swim at the prospect.

Ava bites her bottom lip and goes back to silently pacing. "I just need more time."

I stare at my mostly empty plate, my eyes following the coil of noodles until I can't stand it. I think I got numb at some point along the way. Like, D3 became a thing so fast and I needed more followers, and at first it just seemed so ridiculous and bizarre that I couldn't imagine anyone actually believing it, and then it all suddenly became so obviously horrible that it feels a little bit like whiplash.

But I'm not numb anymore. I'm terrified and I'm ready to end it.

I don't hesitate this time. I do what I should have already done. I deactivate The Whine.

"There. The Whine is gone," I say.

I lean back in my chair and wait for relief to hit me, but it doesn't. And from the looks of it, Ava doesn't feel it either. Because everyone at school knows who I am, and now, thanks to Cade, so do a bunch of D3 believers who could easily spread my name to all their other forums. I might have deleted my account, but if there's anything we've both learned from the last few weeks, Defend Kids isn't going to just go away.

chapter twenty-five

For the first time in months, my brain is . . . quiet.

I still haven't stopped freaking out over Cade's post, but I didn't realize how much hearing the constant ping of new notifications or worrying about what new bizarre claims D3 would make about my posts—like the Cabal is spying on them through their microwaves or something—had been getting to me. How anxious I would get each morning in the seconds between wondering what D3 had been up to during the night and checking my notifications. Or how much of my life it had consumed. Not until waking up this morning without it hanging over my head.

I gave in to curiosity before I went to bed last night and let myself check the subreddit. There was only one post about the Cabal trying to silence D3, but it didn't specifically reference The Whine or me, and the Defender hadn't posted on D3 at all. Maybe the whole thing was like a campfire, and I'd accidentally been pouring lighter fluid on it through The Whine. But now that it's gone, the flames have to die down.

Still, anxiety spikes in my chest after Dad drops Ava and me off at school, because there could be a lot of unhappy club members at school and I still don't know who made the bomb threat. And of course there's Cade, who was pissed enough to dox me. He's definitely not just going to disappear because I nuked my Insta.

"You okay?" Ava asks as if she can read my mind.

"Yeah." The frigid air stings my face and my breaths come out in white puffs.

"Not that I mind, but why didn't you catch a ride with Ximena this morning?"

"She had to go in early." I shrug.

The text I got from her this morning said exactly that with no other explanation, not even when I asked her why, which admittedly is strange. Ximena is *not* a morning person, so if some teacher was hauling her in super early for some reason, I would have gotten a book-length rant about it by now.

Ava and I walk to the back of the school together, a first this year, and cut through the gym. When we move into the hallway, I can't help but glance around, searching for anyone who looks like they might pounce on me for my post. It could be because everyone is bundled in coats and scarves so I can't see them, but it doesn't seem like there are as many students with D3 patches or sweatshirts as usual. Near my locker, Cade's blond head pokes above a crowd of people and I automatically stop. He spots me and glares.

"I'm not a violent person, but I'd really like to go punch him in the face right now for what he did," Ava says.

"You'll have to wait in line."

But Cade passes us wordlessly and I let go of a rattling breath. Cade wouldn't body slam me in a crowded hallway with my sister here. He'll wait until I'm alone.

Ava slowly unclenches the fists that had been hanging at her sides. "I have to go to the front office for a minute, but I can walk you to class first if you want."

"I'll be okay," I reply, trying to give her a reassuring smile before continuing down the hall. Along the way, I spot Mia in the hallway without a coat and no trace of D3 merchandise on her. I may not like that Ximena has football friends, but I can still be happy if Mia's managed to escape the D3 net.

Somehow I make it to my free period before lunch without seeing Cade again or getting confronted by angry D3 members. Ximena's at our table in the library when I get there, writing in a notebook. Normally she pulls the chair out for me in my place if she gets there first, but she must have forgotten this time. Which is fine. I grab it by the back and try to yank it out from the table without the legs squeaking too much on the floor. When I've wrestled it away and slip into my spot, Ximena still hasn't looked up.

"Um, hey," I say, my voice low. "What's up?"

Across from me, Ximena's pencil scratches against her paper, loudly enough that she's probably poking holes through it.

"Not much."

"What'd you have to come in early for?"

She shrugs and flips to a fresh page in her notebook. "Finishing up my final English project with my group."

"Sucks."

Her lips press together.

"Something wrong?"

"Nope," she replies in a tone that is the complete opposite. She's acting like a total zombie.

"Okay. Well, did you see Mr. Schriever's mustache? It basically doubled in size over the weekend," I whisper to her.

She shakes her head, but her dark eyes are fixed on the paper in front of her.

My stomach sloshes uneasily. "Wait until you see it. It's super gross looking. You're not going to be able to pay attention in class."

Ximena doesn't even flinch, which is bonkers because she's fascinated by men who grow sketch facial hair. The final bell rings and the library gets quiet. Ximena's obviously having a day, so I tilt my head down and start working on the French homework I didn't manage to finish last night.

"You see Asher lately?" she asks a few minutes later, still not actually looking at me.

I wince. It's the most she's said, but she picked the absolute most painful topic she could.

"No."

That seems to be all Ximena's going to say, so I pick up my phone, pop my earbuds in, and open my school email. At some point I'm going to have to contact all my sponsors and tell them that I closed The Whine and pay back all the people who have paid in advance. But I can't handle that right now.

I glance up and find Ximena frowning at me. "Seriously. What's with you today?" I ask, pulling one earbud out.

"I guess I'm just sick of your crap, is all, Quinn." She drops her pencil onto the table with a clatter. And then says, more quietly after Ms. Iacopelli shushes us from her desk, "Where have you been this year?"

"What do you mean?" I say once I get over the surprise. Of course I've heard Ximena snap before, but it's never been directed at me.

She taps her chin dramatically. "Well, let me think. Half the time you're keeping things from me and the other half of the time you're flat-out lying to my face. Since *my* best friend would never do things like that, I don't know who *you* are. It's like you were taken over by aliens or something."

My mouth falls open but no sound comes out, like all words have been chased away by her voice. Ximena glares at me expectantly.

"I haven't been lying to you." But I have been selective in what I tell her, my brain unhelpfully reminds me.

"Oh yeah? What really happened with Asher at the dance? Because he wasn't sick. I asked him how he was feeling and he had no idea what I was talking about."

"Well—"

"And why'd you guys break up? And why'd you suddenly deactivate your Insta?"

"Mena, if you'd just let me get a word out." I glance down at my phone, where my email is loading.

Ximena folds her arms over and leans back hard in her chair, waiting. But my breath hitches in my throat and I can't speak as I stare at the screen. My inbox is full of new emails, hundreds of them.

And it doesn't take me more than a second of scanning the subject lines to know who they're from.

Defeat the Cabal!!!

S2AIA!

Anyone protecting kidnappers is going down!

My mind races. Deactivating The Whine didn't stop D3 from finding me. Cade or someone must have posted my school email on the subreddit and blasted it in all the D3 threads. My hand shakes as I open the email with the subject, *This is what's coming for you.* I click on a YouTube link, the only thing in the email, and heavy breathing fills my earbud. It's a video with the title, "LIVE: Infiltrating a Node." The camera view bounces, but I catch a glimpse of a palm tree and a sand-colored building. And then, unmistakably, there's a barrel of a gun.

"Well?"

My head jerks up at Ximena's terse voice.

I swipe out of the video and start packing up my things, my hands slick with sweat. "Look, can we talk about this later, please?" I have to get out of here, find someplace to watch the rest of the video, and figure out what to do.

Ximena practically snarls, and when I head for the door with my backpack on my lap, she follows me. We turn into the main hallway with lockers and both of us stumble to a stop. Except you can't see the lockers because every single one is covered in gold flyers, from the floor to the ceiling on both sides of the hall so it's one solid tunnel of gold. Ximena turns slowly, her eyes taking in the flyers. My hands shake and my unzipped backpack falls to the floor, most of its contents tumbling out in an explosion of noise.

"Q, what is going on?" She kneels down to scoop up a stack of worksheets that flew out of one of my binders.

I don't have to look at the flyers to know they're about D3, but I snatch one from the nearest locker. In black letters across the top it simply reads: *The Cabal is coming for us . . . Learn the truth.* There's a QR code below it, and I fumble for my phone and open the camera app. This time I know it won't take me to the Defend Kids website. I snap the QR code and a new screen pops up. It's a site I know well already.

D3Map.

One person couldn't have papered over the hallway by themselves so quickly without getting caught by Principal Stewart, who is known to roam the halls during classes looking for tardy students. There had to be a whole group of people. And that's how I realize: I've been obsessed with finding one single D3 true believer at school who made the bomb threat. But there's not just one true believer at P. J. Dalton High. The flyers are like a warning that they're not going to stop until they've recruited the entire school.

Posting the fact check about the Turners didn't make them go away and deactivating The Whine entirely didn't either. This hallway and my inbox and whatever is happening in that video are evidence enough.

It feels like the walls are closing in on me, suffocating me. The blood rushes in my ears as Ximena's muffled voice says, "You need to tell me what's happening."

And this time, I want to tell her everything about D3. I'm tired of keeping all this from her.

So I do, there in the middle of the empty hallway. And it isn't easy. I also keep having to pause my story when people come into the hallway clutching their bathroom hall passes, so it takes me twice as long as it should to tell her about D3, Nate Hammer, the dance, those emails. And about Asher. Each time I stop, Ximena stands in complete silence, which scares me even more than confessing everything.

"That's a lot," Ximena finally says. She leans against one of the covered lockers like her feet won't hold her.

Her eyes are unreadable, staring blankly at the other side of the hall.

"I know how ridiculous it sounds, trust me."

The clock in the hallway is the only thing besides the ceiling that isn't covered in the gold flyers, and the second hand sounds like thunder in the sudden silence between us.

"I should have told you what's been going on, but it took me longer than it should have to realize how bad things really were," I say.

"Here I was wondering what was going on with our school and you already knew the answer."

My mouth opens, like the words will definitely come. But how do you explain to your best friend that you liked having something that had absolutely nothing to do with her?

"I thought Cade was just being his tyrant self, but you knew this

292

group or whatever was actually dangerous. Asher then told you he wanted to stop it all and you didn't? Like, I don't even know who that person is," she says, like she's staring at a stranger. "But that's not my best friend."

My shoulders rise a little. "Okay, you haven't been involved, so you don't know what it was like."

"And whose fault is that?" Her eyes narrow. "The Quinn *I* know would own up to what she did, not quietly slink off."

"Would she, though?" Making a joke is so normal, it just comes out. But Ximena doesn't even crack a smile.

Instead, she turns back to the library and my heart sinks.

"Mena, really?"

"What did you expect me to say to all this? Congratulations for finally admitting that you *have* been keeping stuff from me all year?" Ximena says.

"Hold on. Don't pretend you haven't kept stuff from me, too."

"What? What did I keep from you?"

"Oh, I don't know," I reply. "You and I have been planning to go to school in New York together since I can remember and suddenly you announce that Max is coming, too? Without talking to me about it?"

"He may not even get in."

"That's not the point!" And all the anger I've suppressed since Ximena and Max started dating comes rushing out at once. "I've been playing tagalong to you and Max for months and it's sucked, but New York was supposed to be ours! You didn't even think about running the whole life-changing decision past me before you guys went ahead and decided on your own."

Ximena's brown eyes shine with angry tears, and I feel my own filling, too. We have this thing where if one of us cries, so does the other one, like how yawns are contagious.

"So this is what it was all about? You've been mad that I got a boyfriend?"

"No!" I shoot back, but it's getting harder to see what's true anymore. "You could have seen for yourself what was going on. Most of it played out on my Instagram, which you used to pay attention to. But you've been in your own little Max and Ximena world since the summer."

Her nostrils flare. "Did you ever stop to think that maybe *I* could have used *you* this year?"

"Mena, I've been right here."

"Yeah, rolling your eyes at me and Max, and giving me dirty looks when you think I don't see them, and acting like it's a massive pain to hang out with him. I was trying to be there for you after the Asher thing and you were just straight-up rude." Tears slowly roll down her cheeks. "I could have used my best friend because I have my first boyfriend ever and I have wanted somebody to talk to about it. But I've kept everything inside because you've made it pretty clear you're pissed at us being together. I didn't want to hurt your feelings or make you feel left out. So every freaking moment of every freaking day, I've had to walk like I'm on glass so your precious feelings wouldn't get hurt."

My whole body is shaking. This isn't us. This isn't how we talk to each other, but I can't make myself stop. "I'm sorry you feel like I haven't been there for you, but what would I have even said to you? You're basically a pod person now? The girl who became everything you hated about people who date in high school. The codependent barnacle couple you've always made fun of and the rest of us can't even stand. Like, you adopted his personality completely and now everything is about you and Max twenty-four seven."

"Like what?"

"Like making us go to football games!"

"So sue me for wanting my best friend to care about the things I care about."

I shake my head. *"Football?"*

"No, Quinn! *Max!* I want you to care about my relationship with Max because *I* care about Max. You haven't been able to get over your stupid jealousy long enough to actually be a friend."

Her words feel like a slap. Ava had basically said the same thing— that I was too selfish to have noticed our family's financial issues, that I was jealous of the club because she wasn't spending enough time with me. We've made up since, but I haven't been able to forget what she said. Now my best friend is basically saying I've been throwing some kind of childish tantrum, and it makes the anger white hot.

"You don't just care about him, you're obsessed, and I'm sick of constantly being the afterthought to your relationship! When you're not even with him, you're always texting him or talking about him or looking for him. You keep changing all our plans for him and then you get mad because I'm not around when you need me. Is that what you wanted me to tell you?"

"Well, *I'm* sorry you haven't been in a relationship long enough to know how it works and that you feel like you need to punish me for that fact."

Her words hang out there between us. They're everything I've always feared. That I'm a burden. That I'm in the way. That she outgrew me a while ago.

"Well, don't let me hold you back," I say, my voice cracking.

For a minute, we stand on opposite sides of the hallway. A lot like Asher and I did at the dance.

"All I'm saying is that I've tried so hard to make sure you always feel included, Quinn. I wish you had spent as much time worrying about me as I have worrying about you," she says before leaving the hallway.

I don't try to stop the tears from falling now. I'm not sure I could anyway.

For a minute, I stare into the tunnel of flyers until they blur together into one long golden tube, wondering how I got here. A place where I've managed to lose everything, my best friend and The Whine, where angry people are hunting me online and doing who knows what in that video someone sent me.

I wipe at my drenched face and go back to the video on my phone. In the hallway, surrounded by gold flyers, I hit play and the video starts again, opening on the barrel of a gun.

chapter twenty-six

S o, I'm doing this livestream because I'm about to take down a Node," a man's voice says. "The Defender was right when they said Nodes are everywhere. I found one in my own city."

Two hands appear in front of the camera and grip a steering wheel, like he's wearing a GoPro camera. "In the army, I was trained to be a soldier and to fight our enemies." His breath is ragged. "I never thought I'd have to fight those enemies here at home. But someone has to rescue those kids and get proof for the world to see what the Cabal is doing, so I guess it's gonna have to be me."

The camera jostles at the sound of a car door opening. At the bottom of the video, it lists the account name as dhash55 and the number of viewers—22,900 so far.

My heart beats so fast, it feels like it's going to break out of my chest as the realization hits me. I know that username—dhash55. The account had regularly replied to my posts and it was one of the first ones I blocked when I started nuking D3 accounts.

The view turns back toward the car and two hands pick up a long black rifle from the passenger seat. The camera rocks as the person slams the door shut and the person lifts his rifle.

No, no, no. This can't be happening . . . But it is. An invisible vise clamps over my chest. My hands are sweating and I grip my phone tighter to keep it from falling between them.

"Soldiers together, arm in arm!" the voice yells like a battle cry before the camera hurtles toward a sand-colored building, boots slapping against pavement.

A glass door is pushed open before deafening shots rip through the air. The camera blurs and spins with the sound of ear-piercing screams and shattering glass. I can't breathe.

People sob loudly by the time the shooting stops. The camera focuses, revealing several people on the floor, a counter, and a glass partition. It looks like a bank. The camera shifts again, and there's someone a few feet away from the camera, crying. A woman. A man in a white shirt and tie is crouched in a tight ball in front of the counter with his arms over his face.

The shooter charges behind the counter and herds two more people out and yells for them to stay where he can see them. With his rifle pointed at the people on the floor, he spins and heads back to the front door, where he slides all the locks and bolts into place, closing himself in.

I drop my phone in my lap and push blindly down the hall as the video still plays. I don't know where I'm going, but my body screams at me to move. To run. Like I'm right there in the building with those people and the shooter.

"If everyone does exactly as I say, there's no reason anyone has to get hurt," the man shouts from the phone in my lap. "That means no one tries to run, no one even looks at their phone, and no one tries to be a hero. Stay flat on the floor. If anyone so much as pops their head up, I will shoot."

I glance down at my phone just as the camera jerks in time with the tip of the shooter's gun. The man is going around collecting cell phones into a camouflage backpack so no one can call for help.

The door to the newspaper room is open, and I plunge into it. It's dark and empty as I push myself across the room toward a desk at the back. I could stop the video, stuff my phone into my backpack, and end this nightmare. But I can't tear my eyes away.

The shooter turns in a slow circle with his rifle aimed at the people lying on their stomachs around him. "Who's in charge here?"

The only response is the sound of his boots crunching the broken glass and the muffled sobs of faces pressed against the floor. Then silence.

"The manager." His voice goes from zero to murderous instantly. "Which one of you is the manager?"

A noise like choking comes from somewhere and the camera tilts down at a man in a blue polo shirt with his face pressed against the ground. The shooter stalks over to him and a toe of a boot nudges the man.

"You say something?" the shooter growls.

"I-I'm the m-manager," the man stutters, his voice quiet against the thin carpet.

"Get up slowly," the shooter orders, "with your hands up."

Every inch of the manager's body shakes as he slowly rises.

"Show me the basement where the kids are," the shooter tells him.

The man's face scrunches in confusion. "We don't have a—"

"Show me the basement!"

"W-we don't have a basement, sir!" he says. I can't tell if it's the camera jumping or if the man's hands are shaking hard enough for me to see it.

"Then the bank's vault! Where is it?" the shooter yells.

"We only have a safe," the manager says. The camera steadies long enough to show a black tag pinned to the manager's polo shirt that says *Jake*. "It's in the back—"

"Show me!" The nose of the rifle pokes into the manager's chest for emphasis and he stumbles backward.

I hold myself on my elbows on the desk in front of me because my body wants to collapse in on itself.

"Okay, okay. Just, please, don't hurt me."

"Don't do anything stupid and I won't have to."

The manager walks slowly toward a door behind the counter while the shooter warns the people on the floor not to move.

"There's probably some door to the basement where they're keeping the kids," the shooter says to himself.

He has the gun trained at the back of the manager's head, but the manager keeps his hands firmly on either side of his head. I'm barely breathing. What if he shoots him here right on camera?

"I have to enter the code," the manager says once he gets to the door.

"Do it," the shooter replies.

The manager lowers his hands slowly and punches some numbers into a keypad. There's a soft click as the door unlocks. The shooter raises his gun up and the view tilts and whirls again as he pushes through the door. The camera shows a small table, some counters, and a gray metal safe.

The shooter grunts impatiently. "Open the safe," he barks at the manager, who scurries to type the code into the keypad.

The manager swings the door open, revealing several rows of stacked bills.

"There's got to be papers or some kind of evidence or something in here, at least," the shooter says.

A hand springs out—the shooter's—in front of the camera and sweeps the money onto the floor until the safe is bare.

"Where's the rest of it?"

"Th-this is it," the manager says. Dark blue rings of sweat appear under his arms. "We're just a small regional bank. We don't keep a lot of cash here."

The shooter moves in front of a door next to the table.

"What's behind there?"

"Just a break room and another door to the employee bathroom," the manager says.

The shooter raises his gun again and flings open the door. The view swings wildly and my stomach tilts. But when it steadies, there's just a narrow room with a gray couch, four chairs, and a microwave and mini fridge.

The sound of overturning furniture and breaking glass rings out as the shooter crashes around the room, throwing everything onto the floor. I close my eyes until the sounds of destruction stop.

When I open them, the shooter is back in front of the manager, gun raised again. "Show me the other rooms."

"Those are the only other rooms," the manager says.

"That's not possible! They're supposed to be here!" the shooter roars. "I don't know where they are. I don't know where they are! Where are they?" He paces in front of the safe. "What do I do now? They were supposed to be here. It's a Node, I know it is!" The camera angles up, showing fluorescent lights on the ceiling, like he's waiting for god to reply. "They must have moved them! They must have taken them somewhere else. The truck!" the shooter says suddenly. The camera wheels back to the manager. "Where does the truck take them?"

"The truck?"

"The armored truck that comes every Tuesday around the back?"

"W-we have a truck that picks up deposits twice a week," the man says.

"You're lying! I know those trucks take the kids! They must have come early. They must have—"

The shooter freezes at the sound of sirens wailing. Faint at first, but getting louder. But the shooter hurtles toward the manager, pressing his forearm hard into the man's neck and slamming him against a white wall.

"Where'd you take them?!"

"Please!" The manager claws at the hands locked around his throat. I want to scream, watching his face go from red to an unhealthy shade of purple.

"WHERE ARE THE KIDS?!"

The manager chokes and gags until finally the hands release him and the man slips onto the floor, out of the camera's view.

"Please." The manager's voice wheezes. "You can take the money. Just let us go."

"I can't!" he says.

A phone rings in the distance. It's been a persistent sound in the background, I realize, for a while.

"Look, the police are probably calling to negotiate with you or something," the manager says.

"I was just trying to protect them," the shooter says.

Hands motion at the floor, and the manager gets to his feet and crosses the room to open the door back into the main room. When the shooter follows, the camera lands on a woman kneeling in front of the doors to the bank, lifting the last lock that bolted the bottom of the front door shut.

Behind the glass a group of armed police in SWAT gear nears the bottom of the stairs. The woman freezes when she sees the shooter, but not before she slides the lock up the rest of the way with a click even the camera picks up.

The crack of gunshots fills the air and the livestream stops.

First the bomb threat at our school, now this. *This is what's coming for you*, the email that linked to the video had said. Now that I've seen it, there's only one way to interpret the email. It means D3 knows who I am and they could be coming for me next.

My heart races as the screen goes dark and then cues up the

next video. This one is titled: "Investigating the San Diego Zoo as a Possible Node."

My mouth is so dry I can hardly swallow. I jab at my phone to stop it from playing and sit back, my body frozen in terror alone in the dark classroom, wishing I could disappear.

chapter twenty-seven

've only been on a roller coaster once, at Darien Lake for our sixth-grade school trip. Mom was worried I'd get banged up and banned me from "wild rides." But when everyone went on the Tantrum roller coaster, I didn't want to be left out. It wasn't until the car started to fall into the ninety-eight-foot drop and my internal organs felt like they were separating from my body that I realized what a huge mistake I'd made.

And that's what it was like watching the livestream and realizing D3 may have killed people—and I helped them do it.

Asher predicted it—not that he knew there'd be a shooting, exactly, but he was afraid that people who literally think they're soldiers would end up doing something bad. That people would end up getting hurt somehow, and that our posts on The Whine would be a spark.

All the signs were there. In fact, they weren't even signs. D3 flat-out said they were going to do something like this. But I didn't want to believe that their threats, or any of this, was real.

Maybe if I'd shut my account down when I found out about D3 in the beginning, none of this would have happened. And now I will never get the sound of gunshots out of my head.

"Quinn?" I hear Mrs. Newcomb's voice and quickly wipe at my eyes before looking up. She peers at me through the dark newspaper room, takes in my face wet with tears, and quietly shuts the door behind her. She flips on the lights. "Are you okay?"

I let out a shuddering laugh because that's all I can seem to manage. I've been wrong about so much for so long.

Did I honestly think D3 would go away simply because I told the truth about the Turners and deactivated The Whine? Or that Ximena hadn't seen exactly how I feel about her and Max written right across my face?

All year, I thought I was totally in control of everything—school, my friends, Asher, The Whine, the store—and driving along in life just fine. But the reality is, my car went off the road a long time ago. I'm only now realizing that I'm sitting in the rubble of the disaster.

Mrs. Newcomb sets a mug full of coffee and her tote bag onto her desk. I stare at the steam curling and twisting above the mug as she sits down.

"Want to talk about it?"

"I don't even know how to start." My tongue is heavy in my mouth just thinking about trying to find the words.

"We can also just sit here, if it would help to have some company." Mrs. Newcomb picks up her mug and cradles it between her hands, leaning back in her chair like she has all the time in the world.

I rest my forearms against the desk. My old metal one in the back. Without thinking, I guess I went straight to my old desk and tucked myself behind it like it was some kind of bunker.

It's hard not to feel like all of this was for nothing. The Whine is gone, but shutting it down didn't fix anything. And D3 is just as dangerous as Asher worried it was. I didn't realize how tired I am of all the secrets I've been keeping until Mrs. Newcomb gives me the opportunity to spill them all out on the floor in front of her now, like I did with Ximena.

But before I can get the words out, there's a light knock on the classroom door and Asher's face peers in through the narrow window.

I freeze. He opens the door wide enough to poke his head through it. "Hey. I was in class and saw you come in here. Did you see the flyers—" He stops when he spots Mrs. Newcomb. He must not have realized she's here. I almost forgot about her, too, because I was so surprised Asher was actually talking to me of his own free will. "Oh, I'm sorry. I interrupted—"

"Why don't you come in, Asher?" Mrs. Newcomb says, a row of bracelets jingling on her wrist as she waves for Asher to come inside the newsroom. "I'd like to hear about those flyers, actually."

Asher hesitates for a second before coming in and sitting down at one of the other desks.

"You know the Defend Kids club that Cade Bird started this year?" I say after a moment. My voice sounds far away. She nods, eyeing the crumpled flyer on the desk in front of me. "Well, the group isn't quite what it seems to be." It feels like the understatement of the century.

"It's part of a conspiracy group," she says before I can keep going. When my mouth falls open in surprise, Mrs. Newcomb explains, "I started reading up on it when I noticed the students really getting into it. You may have already heard, but I spoke with Principal Stewart and he's suspended the club from school." Mrs. Newcomb picks up the gold flyer and smooths it out on the desk, turning it over in her hand. "I admit I was kind of surprised when I saw your Instagram was part of the Defend Kids movement. I did want to talk to you about it, but since your account isn't connected to the school, Principal Stewart felt like it would be overstepping."

"Oh. *Oh*," I say, finally realizing what she's saying. "No. My account isn't . . . I mean, it was never supposed to be . . . I didn't know what Defend Kids really was until recently. I was never part of the club." I can't stop my face from crinkling in a grimace. Not because one of my teachers follows my Instagram account, but because she thinks I'm a conspiracy theorist. The kind of person who encourages shoot-outs at banks apparently. "You don't have to stay," I say to Asher, who is fidgeting next to me.

He shakes his head. "If you're talking about D3, it involves me, too. I'm the one who asked you to let me join The Whine."

I frown and twist to face him. "But I'm the one who started posting about Defend Kids."

He turns so we're eye level. "Yeah, and I thought it was a great idea—"

"But you said we should stop and I didn't listen, so—"

"And I could have spoken up earlier, or at least not bailed on you and left you to figure it out on your own."

"I'm sorry," we say at the same time, and Asher gives me a tentative smile that I can't quite return.

Mrs. Newcomb raises a hand and we freeze, reminding me how everything else seems to disappear whenever I'm with Asher. Even when we've been fighting.

"How about you both start at the beginning?" Mrs. Newcomb says.

"I'll explain. But first I need to show you something." I unlock my phone, the livestream still open on it.

"I should have shut it all down a while ago." It feels like it's been hours since I showed them the stream. We sat in silence for a while after we watched it, and then I started at the beginning and told Mrs. Newcomb everything that's happened. Or at least, as much as I know about it. I glance at Asher out of the corner of my eye, my cheeks hot. He's been wide-eyed but quiet since the livestream.

"Why didn't you?" Mrs. Newcomb asks in the same steady, understanding voice she's maintained this whole time.

"It'll sound like I'm making excuses for myself," I say. "I didn't want a bunch of internet trolls to take away all my hard work and . . . well, I didn't want to give up my paid sponsors. I kind of need the money right now. My family has been having some money problems lately. When my account started getting more followers, I thought maybe I could help them by getting more sponsors. And honestly, when we first heard what Defend Kids really was, it was hard to accept that anyone actually believed any of it. Especially because my own sister was a part of it." I twist the balled-up D3 flyer in my hands.

Mrs. Newcomb doesn't say anything when I pause. In fact, she hasn't said much beyond asking a few clarifying questions the whole time I've been talking.

"I thought I could fix it without having to nuke everything. When we started thinking something was off with the club, I stopped posting about anything that could possibly be related to D3 or Defend Kids, but they thought my new posts were still coded messages from the Defender. I deleted all my old posts about the club and then started blocking the obvious D3 accounts so they couldn't comment. But that made them think the Cabal was trying to stop the truth from getting out there. Then I posted the fact check about the Turner kids not being real and they thought it meant I was part of the Cabal."

I rub a hand hard across my face. "And now that I've deactivated my account, they probably think that proves I'm part of the Cabal or something." I shake my head, wishing I was joking. "I thought I was doing enough, but everything I did basically fueled them even more, somehow, until"—I gesture at my phone—"this. People could have been killed."

"We don't know anything yet," Mrs. Newcomb says gently. "So let's not go down too dark a path for now. What made you decide to close your account?"

"Cade kind of doxed me in a comment and suddenly everyone was posting about me, saying I was a liar and part of the Cabal." I stuff my hands under my legs to hide the fact that they're shaking. "I got scared, I guess. And then he must have posted my school email or something, because I got all these threatening emails this morning."

"Wait, what?" Asher says. "You didn't tell me about Cade."

"Well, we haven't really been speaking."

Asher's mouth forms a thin line.

"We need to report that to Principal Stewart, Quinn," Mrs. Newcomb says.

I shake my head. "Cade will just make my life worse until I

graduate. Plus, most of the school knows I run the account anyway. But that's one out of the million things that doesn't make sense about the group—"

"There's only a million?" Asher's mouth curls at the edges. It's not a smile; it's barely a smirk.

"Okay, a billion. Like, all the believers, including Nate Hammer, thought my account was run by the Defender, but everyone in D3 at school knows it's me." Dillon had said when I confronted him at the grocery store that it didn't matter to him that I ran The Whine. His brain must be made up of carefully constructed compartments, like Ava's was, reality and facts tucked away and covered up in one compartment and everything D3, wild and spinning, in another. "My sister told me it was like they took true things and twisted them. Like, children really do get kidnapped and trafficked, but it's about three hundred and fifty a year in the United States. Not the one hundred thousand Defend Kids campaigns on."

Asher whistles through his front teeth. "That's a pretty big difference."

Mrs. Newcomb nods. "Right, so they take the true thing, which is that children are abducted, and then they claim this problem is much, much worse. They fabricate some evidence, such as missing police reports or rumors online. And when anyone asks *how* this could happen, they blame it on an evil mastermind or a secret plot, because those things are very hard to disprove."

My body sags against the back of my chair, exhausted. "It seems like if we could figure out who the Defender is, we could stop all this."

There's a lot I don't know about D3, but I'd bet literally everything that the Defender is not some secret government insider. I still haven't ruled out the possibility that it's been Cade this whole time.

"Maybe. But also maybe not." Mrs. Newcomb takes another sip of her coffee. "Conspiracy theorists see patterns that don't exist in disparate pieces of information. They're so desperate for answers to explain the things happening around them. People who believe in conspiracy theories also feel like they can't trust traditional sources of information, like government agencies or the media."

"Okay, but it's a fact that the girl everyone has been calling Annalice Turner doesn't exist. The police even said so." My voice rises on its own. What I really want to do is grab every D3 believer and shake them.

"But these people don't care if they believe the whole system is corrupt—the media, the police, the government, researchers, scientists, and on and on." My heart sinks down lower and lower as she speaks. "Facts cease to exist when people don't believe anyone or anything is telling the truth. They start to think they have to find their own truth."

"Through, say, coded messages left by a secret source that they have to find and translate?"

"Indeed."

I throw up my hands. "But what makes them trust someone they don't even know?"

"Biases are extremely powerful," Mrs. Newcomb says, nodding slowly. "Most people don't realize *how* powerful, or even acknowledge that they have biases in the first place. Our brains are so tricky. They always leap to accept any new information that confirms our personal views, even if doing so contradicts other things we might believe. Humans are so convinced that we're right and we constantly look for evidence to prove it, even if the evidence is made up. So everything that gets put in front of members of D3 by the Defender or others in that group just confirms what they believe."

I feel like turning over every desk in this room because D3 is so infuriating, but Mrs. Newcomb sits there as calm as ever.

"There's also a huge community dynamic to it, too, that plays a big role," she says. "Members feel like insiders to a massive secret. It makes them feel special and important and part of a select group. When that dynamic is at play, the Defender actually almost stops mattering because the community starts to have a life of its own. You probably notice how they use phrases like S2AIA, soldiers together, arm in arm. They create their own language, almost, but only for insiders. And all of that ends up building a community and a unique identity.

"And believing that there's a cabal out there gives them a common enemy, too, gives them someone or something they can blame all their problems on. Bad things they see in the world or happening in their lives are much easier to make sense of when they have someone to blame. It means it's not a random occurrence, bad luck, or their own decisions. Their problems are thanks to a sinister group intentionally working to make their lives miserable. That kind of fear-based narrative can be really unifying, as strange as that sounds. It's something you can build a whole common identity around."

I nod, because I saw parts of that community—the Nate Hammer channel that makes viewers think they're in on some secret, the subreddit and D3Map where the believers talk to one another, even the merch. But I hadn't realized just how much of a, well, culture it is until Mrs. Newcomb explained it now. I sit back in my chair, feeling all the irritation ease out of me, only to be replaced by a giant chasm of overwhelming helplessness.

"There's this guy who really believes in it. Dillon McRae," Asher says, his voice soft and slow like he's carefully picking through a jumble of thoughts.

"I know Dillon." Mrs. Newcomb looks like she has some stories about him. Most of the teachers probably do. She nods for Asher to keep going.

"I've been thinking about him a lot lately and why he would believe something like this," Asher goes on. "His dad died a couple years ago and he became really isolated and withdrawn. I wonder if maybe he was just looking for an explanation, you know? Something that would help him make sense of the world when everything kind of felt like it was falling apart. And a community of people to do it with, like you said?"

"That's very insightful, Asher," Mrs. Newcomb says.

I'd never even thought about what might have led Dillon to the whole D3 world, and what Asher said makes a lot of sense. But what about Mrs. Bird, Mr. Ambrose, Bryce, Ollie, or all the people on the subreddit? What made them fall for D3? Have they all just compartmented their brains like Ava did, or do they actually believe in a Defender and all the conspiracies that go with it?

"Do you know who the Defender is?" Asher asks, and I lean forward eagerly.

"Ah," Mrs. Newcomb says. "That's the million-dollar question. I'm afraid I don't."

"We kind of wondered if it was Nate Hammer," he says.

"From what I've read, he certainly is a huge amplifier of D3 content and messaging, a lot of which he profits from. But most researchers don't think he was the original creator," Mrs. Newcomb says.

"Or maybe Cade?"

"Some researchers think it's bigger—that there could be more than one person acting as the Defender."

I slip down in my chair a little, dizzied by the thought of there being more than one person pretending to be the Defender.

"But that's how these things usually work anyhow," Mrs. Newcomb says. "Someone puts a conspiracy theory out there, and then multiple otherwise unrelated people seize it and take it another couple of steps further."

"But what do people like Cade and Nate Hammer get out of it?" I ask.

Mrs. Newcomb sighs. "Money, fame, influence, attention. I suppose they may actually believe in it, too, but I'm guessing that, at least for Nate Hammer and Cade, that's a secondary motivator."

Anger works its way back up to the top of my head until I feel like I'm going to explode. The fact that they are taking advantage of people who will apparently believe anything to make money is gross.

"So how can I prove to people that none of this is true, besides finding out who the Defender is and telling the whole world?"

"That's the hardest thing about conspiracy theories and the people who believe them," Mrs. Newcomb says. "Any proof you provide, they would likely never believe. If you tell them they are wrong, it often only makes them sure they're right. Conspiracy theories work because they make people distrust everything. And if you distrust everything, you'll believe anything. That's why you've probably noticed the D3 movement has already evolved. It used to just be about the Cabal taking kids. Now it's other theories about the government, the environment, and lots of things."

"How do you know all this?" Asher says, his eyes wide with awe.

A small smile flashes across Mrs. Newcomb's face. "My first job in journalism was as an intern for NBC. I worked on the fact-checking team and then got hired full-time after I graduated."

"Wow," Asher says.

"I'd always dreamed of being a reporter and definitely wanted to be the next Christiane Amanpour or Anderson Cooper. We would work around the clock debunking all the false stuff that would end up going viral online. And it was weird stuff, too. Like, I remember there was this video claiming that bald men could regrow their hair by pouring gasoline on their bald spots."

Asher and I laugh a little because yuck.

"I know, right? But I started seeing how people were actually believing these things. Like, you wouldn't believe how often I had to call the poison control center to get updated numbers because of the number of people who decided that maybe drinking gasoline would make the hair grow faster."

My mouth falls open.

"It wasn't just the gas story either. People were constantly putting themselves in danger or doing violent things all because of false things they read online. So, to make a long story even longer," she says, "I spent a lot of time learning about conspiracies. And over the years, I started realizing the problem was a lot bigger than I'd ever really known."

No wonder Mrs. Newcomb always had this look like she didn't quite fit anywhere. She probably lived all over the world as a journalist before coming to Canandaigua.

"And then you became a teacher?" I say.

She nods. "Almost three years ago. I felt like maybe I could do more good by helping students learn about the news and how to think critically. That maybe it'd have a ripple effect somehow." My face looks as skeptical as I feel because Mrs. Newcomb chuckles. "I know, it's a lot to hope for. But look at how just one conspiracy theory transformed this town."

I shudder thinking about Mrs. Bird talking about "evil forces" from the gazebo, about Mr. Ambrose yelling from the stands at the football game, and about Dillon, who'd genuinely believed I was the Defender's partner.

"It's not just our town," Asher says. "There were palm trees in that livestream."

"You're probably right," Mrs. Newcomb says. "But I have to think that teaching solutions one person at a time can help us fight back. Studies have shown that lies spread at least six time faster than truth online. But we still have to try to give truth a fighting chance."

"There's got to be something I can do to help stop this, then," I say.

"The reality is, D3 existed long before they turned their attention to your account. And they'll be around even with your account gone," Mrs. Newcomb says sadly. "But you could always write about your experience and what you've learned. If anything, this whole thing should show you that words have serious power. I know you're not on staff anymore, but if you ever decide you want to try to put any of this into words, there will be a space for it in the *Daily Stripe*. I think you'll find it's a different paper than when you last left it, with editorial freedom to write what needs to be said."

"Thank you," I reply. It doesn't feel like quite enough for what our conversation has done.

I've felt for so many weeks like I'm groping around in the dark, until talking to Mrs. Newcomb. I haven't fixed it yet, and there's still so much I don't understand about conspiracy theories and D3, but for the first time in a long time, it feels like someone finally turned on a light. Even if it's just a beam the size of a flashlight.

chapter twenty-eight

I jump when the bell rings, signaling the five minutes before the start of last period, and soon, the hallway fills with muffled noise. That means the three of us have been talking for almost two hours, missing both lunch and fourth period.

"Unfortunately, I have to run to a teachers' meeting," Mrs. Newcomb says, glancing at her watch and standing. "But if you two want to stay in here for the rest of the day, I can write you passes. You've been through a lot." Asher and I nod wordlessly. "Come see me anytime, both of you, okay? I'm going to talk to Principal Stewart about the video, and I'm afraid I can't ignore Cade's actions. They don't just know your name," she says. "They know where you go to school."

I nod numbly. Mrs. Newcomb heads for the door, but Asher doesn't move.

"I should have never left you at the dance." He looks down at his hands. "I was afraid and angry. But that still doesn't make it right."

"You definitely shouldn't have. But I should have told you right away when I found out about the Turners. I wasn't trying to lie; I was just worried you'd get freaked and want to bail."

He nods. "You could have told me about your family's money issues, too, you know? It would have made a lot more sense for why you were holding on to the account so bad. I hope you know I wouldn't have judged you for it."

"The money stuff was new to me and I've been trying to figure it out. And I don't know. It's hard to talk about that stuff. Especially when you're . . . a King," I reply.

For a minute, we look at each other in silence, the weight of our problems too heavy for words.

"We could FaceTime tonight and try to figure out what to do about all this," he says after a while. "Because I don't know . . . maybe there's a way to try again?"

"Okay," I say tentatively. I still feel hurt about everything that happened, but Asher is here, apologizing. Maybe we both just got lost in everything else and there's still something between us.

"Uh, I finally finished building that ramp with my dad. The one for my house. So, you know, if you wanted to see it sometime . . ." The corner of his mouth curves in another shy smile.

It's enough to chip away at some of the numbness that had swallowed me.

The first person I want to tell about it is Ximena, but I can't.

I text my dad to ask him to come pick me up after school since Ximena definitely isn't going to drive me and Ava stayed behind. I'm beyond exhausted by the time we get home, my body aching and weak as I drag myself over the threshold. My finger joints creak as I fumble with the zipper on my coat. I'm like the Tin Man in need of some oil, especially after the day I've had.

"No restocking today?" I ask when Dad heads for the couch instead of going straight upstairs.

"We didn't order as much for this week, so we finished before I came to get you," Dad replies. "Everything is fine with the store," he adds.

"Oh, okay," I reply, feeling a little guilty because I wasn't thinking about the store at all.

"So, what's up with Ximena these days, Q-tee-Q?" He hasn't called me by that nickname since I was a kid. I must look as miserable on the outside as I feel on the inside. "Not that I mind picking you up, of course, but I can't remember the last time she wasn't around for so long."

I feign a smile. "Can't a daughter just want to spend some time with her dad?" My voice sounds hollow, even to me. I hug my backpack like a pillow as images from the shooter's livestream play back in my mind, and then drop it onto the floor next to me.

"Well, of course she can, duh." But then he pauses, waiting for the real answer.

I spent most of last period hiding in Mrs. Newcomb's room, trying to find news about the bank, but the only thing I could find was a mention of an ongoing hostage situation somewhere in Georgia, which could be something completely different.

I could come up with an excuse for Dad—Ximena's out sick, Bula's broken, she's busy—something that wouldn't prompt any more probing questions from him. But even the idea of formulating the lie makes me dizzy.

"We got into a big fight." My tongue feels like paper.

"Oh." He says it like I'm speaking a foreign language and he needs a minute to decipher it. Ximena and me fighting is as alien to him as it is to me. "What about?"

"I kept something from her."

"How come?"

His question is two words long, but the answer is so much more complicated.

"I don't know. She's changed so much this year. She has a bunch of new football friends now because of Max and she's basically obsessed with him. And she acts like having a boyfriend makes her so much more mature than me." All the anger that had spurred me on in our fight comes surging back and I take a deep breath.

"Max seems like a good guy, though."

"He is. Ximena would never date a jerk." And it's true. The fact is, if Ximena was going to become a codependent barnacle, she couldn't have found a nicer guy. But that's not the point. She didn't have to go and start wrecking all our plans because of him.

"It's so hard, but sometimes friendships grow apart, especially at your age," Dad says.

"That's not what's happening." It comes out quickly because that's basically my nightmare scenario.

But that's the feeling that's been nagging at me ever since Ximena and Max got together—that she thinks I'm stuck in junior high when it comes to the relationship department and she's moving ahead without me. Ximena basically said so this afternoon when she said she's had to tiptoe around my feelings all year.

She wouldn't end our best friendship over all this, would she? Not after so many years. It's not my fault that she did a complete one-eighty on dating last year. But a small voice in the back of my head is getting louder, the one that says maybe Ximena's sick of waiting for me to catch up. That she wants something else, that we're too different for there to be an "us" anymore.

"She's changed because of him now and it's ruining everything. She wants Max to come to New York with us—that's if she even still wants to go."

"That's the thing: If you love someone and you want to keep loving them, then you have to find a way to love who they're becoming, too," Dad says. "Hey, that's pretty good. I should use that in a book someday." He smiles. "Have you apologized yet?"

"No." I look down at my lap.

I can't pretend like I didn't love having something completely to myself without Ximena this year or that I haven't been jealous of her and Max, but I also can't ignore that she was 100 percent right when she said I've been so focused on how their being together has made me feel that I didn't even think about the fact that maybe *she* needed *me* this year. Or the fact that I might have changed, too. Maybe I shouldn't have been so harsh on her.

"Well," he says. "I'm sure you two will sort things out."

I nod like my life depends on it, because as mad as I got at her, I'm not ready to accept that Ximena is moving on without me. If the livestream showed me one thing, it's that I need my best friend right now.

I could tell Dad everything—what's one more confession

323

today?—and the thought makes me realize I actually *want* to, even if I get grounded for life. I'm still in way over my head, despite sharing everything with Mrs. Newcomb. I wonder how many weekends in a row my parents will make me work once they know the truth.

"And I really don't want you to worry about the store either. It's going to be fine," he says, his forehead creased with deep lines. He looks exhausted as soon as he's said it. And that's how I know the store is not at all fine and the stuff I'm going through is the last thing my parents need right now. "Things will pick up again once the season starts. Even with all those weird one-star reviews we got today." He laughs, but my whole body ices over.

"What?"

He shrugs. "Oh, it's silly. Mom got a notification that we got a bunch of spammy one-star reviews on our Google business page this morning. She said they didn't make much sense."

Panic claws its way up my stomach until it becomes a lump in my throat. What if the reviews are from D3? What if D3 hasn't just hunted me down? What if they found my family, too?

I'm still spiraling with what to do when Ava opens the front door.

"Hey, honey," Dad says to her with a thin smile.

She looks as bone-tired as I feel.

"Hi," she replies, setting down her backpack and peeling off her coat. It takes me a minute to see that her hands are shaking. "Dad, Quinn and I need to talk to you and Mom about something." She looks up at me. "Did you see the livestream?"

I nod. She doesn't even know yet about the emails I've gotten or the one-star reviews on the shop's Google listing.

Ava sits down heavily on the couch beside Dad, folding herself under his outstretched arm. "I spent the last hour in Principal Stewart's office. He wants to see me again tomorrow morning, with you and Mom there, too. But first, I need to tell you about something that's been going on for a while." She looks at me. "We should get Mom."

Maybe confessions, like bad things, come in threes.

NBC WSAV

"Missing Kids" Conspiracy Cited by Gunman Holding Hostages in Savannah, Police Say by Jayce Ferguson

Posted 1 day ago

SAVANNAH, GA—Yesterday morning, a recently opened branch of the Greater Savannah Bank on Broughton Street in downtown became the scene of a shooting and a subsequent standoff with the police. The Savannah Police Department said a heavily armed white man entered the building at approximately 9:30 a.m. and held the twelve people inside hostage at gunpoint, including eight customers and four employees.

The gunman livestreamed the entirety of his attack on YouTube from a camera that he appeared to have mounted on his chest. The platform has since taken down the video, but it can still be found online.

Savannah police have not yet released the name of the suspect, although they have told us that they have identified him and they are expected to release his name in a statement later today. Witnesses we spoke to described the assailant as a white, middle-aged male wearing a bulletproof vest and carrying a semiautomatic weapon. Police said they do not believe this was an armed robbery, but instead the act of a member of a fringe conspiracy group known as D3. The gunman himself claimed affiliation with the group during the livestream and police confirmed that they believe the gunman thought the bank was harboring kidnapped children, a view promoted by the conspiracy group.

According to the National Center for Online Hate, "D3" is a wide-reaching conspiracy theory that has gained popularity within the extreme political fringes in the US in the last year. They say members of the group have been charged with at least four violent crimes across several states in the last six months, including destruction of property, aggravated assault, and at least one violent attack that's being investigated as a possible hate crime.

Savannah Police Chief Dana Ward stated that no children were being held captive in the bank. As the video shows and Savannah PD later confirmed to us, they were finally able to enter the bank after a woman police are describing as a hero unlocked the doors when the alleged shooter was in the back room of the bank. The gunman was the only one to suffer injury—a wound to the leg that the police say "could have been much worse." They have yet to label this an act of domestic terrorism, but police are continuing to investigate.

Domestic extremist experts we interviewed said that the group D3 has all the hallmarks of a growing violent group, and, worryingly, that their popularity is on the rise. This story will be updated as more information emerges.

chapter twenty-nine

Never leave my bed. That's the lesson I took away after everything that happened yesterday, and it pings in my tired brain the next afternoon as I take the long route from the lunch line to my table with my tray balanced on my legs. The route that will keep me out of the direct line of sight of Cade and all his club members, if I'm lucky.

I'd been hoping I wouldn't even have to come to school today. Mom and Dad had been confused, angry, and worried when Ava and I told them about everything. But after they'd cycled through those emotions a couple of dozen times and called the school to confirm the meeting first thing this morning for them and Ava with Principal Stewart, they said I had to come. I'm supposed to wait for them to call me down once they're done meeting with him so I can tell him about Cade doxing me, but so far I haven't heard anything and it's making me nervous.

I weave through the tables and take a deep breath when I realize Cade isn't at his table. But the sight still makes my heart sink because there are as many kids as ever. Even after I posted the fact check about the Turners and then deactivated The Whine, and even after an armed man ran into a bank thinking he'd find kidnapped kids and instead found nothing—things I thought would prove to them that Defend Kids is garbage. I was obviously wrong.

I push against my wheels a little harder, anxious to get away. This is what it's going to be like until I graduate. Running for it when I see Cade, taking the long way whenever he's nearby even if my hands and arms ache. Always looking over my shoulder, anxiety permanently lodged in the center of my chest over the fact that someday someone from D3, like that gunman in Georgia, will decide to come after me. Even though I guess it turned out okay—the news said no one was injured at the bank and they arrested the shooter—it's hard not to feel like nothing will ever be the same again. I can't even bring myself to check my school email again.

The thought makes my stomach twist when I look down at my taco salad on my tray. I don't feel like eating, but when I got to the cafeteria, my brain automatically directed me to the lunch line. Maybe my subconscious was trying to protect me from having to confront Ximena at our lunch table.

We haven't texted since our fight and she wasn't in the parking lot behind my house this morning with Bula, not that I actually expected her to be. But it still stings when I spot her, not in her usual seat next to me on the end of the long table. Right in the middle. There's only one way to interpret the deliberate decision to sit where I can't.

Max is next to her and then Sulome, like she's trying to keep a barrier of our friends between us. On the other side of the table, Adrian sits with two empty spots on each side of him, looking like he's lost on an island, especially since Renata isn't here yet.

Max and Sulome give me weak and wordless smiles when they see me, but Ximena doesn't look up from her food.

Renata comes up behind me as I hover awkwardly at the end of

329

the table and sees the open seat on my left where Ximena and then Max usually sit. "Um?" She glances down at me.

For a second, I think about coming up with some excuse to go eat in the newsroom or something. Mrs. Newcomb would surely take me in again. But this is my table, too, and these are *our* friends. So I drop my tray onto the table with a deliberate *thwap*, slip into my place, and give everyone an overly cheery "Hey."

Renata sits next to me and motions for Adrian to move down to fill the empty seat. Max sits in silence, too, like he can't speak if Ximena won't.

"Okay, can we talk about the massive freaking elephant in the room, please?" Renata snorts impatiently, her head swiveling between Ximena and me. "For some reason you guys have decided to throw our monthslong unofficial seating arrangement out the window. What's with the anarchy?"

"You should ask Q," Ximena says flatly, not looking up from her bag of tortilla chips.

Renata turns to me again, waiting for an answer, but I shrug.

"Well, it's throwing off our lunch dynamic, so you guys better sort out whatever it is now." Renata squirms in her new seat, which used to be Ximena's, like it's covered in ants.

"Plus one. It's far too late in the year for me to find a new friend group, so do whatever you guys need to do to make it right," Sulome says.

"At least fill us in so we can choose our respective battle sides."

Sulome is the only one who laughs at Renata's joke, but we can all hear how uncomfortable it is.

We survive lunch in a half-silence so awkward I'm almost hoping to hear my name over the loudspeaker, summoning me to the front office. Renata and Sulome try to fill the silence by talking to each other in a forced conversation about winter break plans, until they can't stand it anymore and both leave with Adrian in tow. Max watches them go, frowning like he wishes he were with them.

"Mena, can we please talk?" I ask when they're gone. "This ignoring each other when we're sitting like two feet away is ridiculous."

"Okay, yeah, I'm outta here." Max snatches up his tray and uses all his height and muscle to get across the cafeteria and out the door as fast as possible.

Ximena's mouth falls open in betrayal, watching Max ditch her. For a second, I can tell she's debating running away with him, too, but she doesn't move. It feels like an opening.

Before I can think about it, I angle my chair around the table and head for the middle because I won't be able to think straight enough about stopping D3 without her on my side. And more importantly, nothing in my world will ever be right again if Ximena is not in it.

"Look, I'm so sorry for not telling you what was happening with me. I'll never keep anything from you again." I make an X over my heart. "I'll tell you every single second of my day and every single thought I have from now on, if you want to know about it."

I crack a hopeful smile. But Ximena shakes her head, the corners of her mouth crinkling as she purses her lips. I used to be able to read Ximena's face, but I don't know what this look means.

I take a deep breath. "And I'm also sorry for what I said about you and Max. You're right. I've been jealous and I'm sorry I wasn't here for you." I feel a little embarrassed saying it out loud.

"Did I really turn into a codependent barnacle?" she asks in a small voice. It's not the reaction I was expecting.

"Oh. Um—"

"Oh my god, I did!" Ximena covers her face with her hands. "I'm so sorry I've made you feel like a third wheel. That's the last thing I ever wanted."

Her hands fall to her sides, and she sucks her bottom lip in between her teeth. It's the telltale sign that she's trying to keep herself from crying, and it makes my eyes sting.

I push myself closer until our knees touch. "I know. Really, I do. I guess I just felt like I'm so far behind you."

Ximena's forehead turns into lines. "What do you mean?"

I stare down at my hands. It's one of those things I've never tried to put into words before, like when I tried to explain to her why I wouldn't let myself get excited about guys, because I don't know if it's something that anyone but another disabled person would understand.

"Remember when I got so sick that I was out for most of seventh grade?" I had so much time on my hands with nothing to do but think about how much pain I was in just lying in my bed that I ended up creating The Whine.

Ximena nods vigorously. "I'll never forget. I've never been so scared in my life."

I look up. "Really?"

"Are you kidding? You were *so* sick I was afraid that every time I saw you was going to be the last time." Her voice cracks halfway through.

Once I was well enough to come back to school, we slipped back into our old routines. We never really talked about it. I desperately needed everything to go back to the way it had been so that I could concentrate on figuring out my new normal. But Ava wasn't the only one there with me; Ximena was, too, and she watched it all happen.

"I just feel like I had to spend so much of my life focused on health stuff that I didn't get to do all the normal stuff for a long time, like boys and parties and school things, and now I'll just endlessly be in catch-up mode with everyone else." I blink hard and look away to stop the tears.

"It's not a race, Quinnifred," she says gently, the sound of her using my nickname making me smile a little. "And honestly, the relationship thing all feels like too much for me sometimes. Like, I know. Woe is me, I have the kindest, sweetest, hottest boyfriend ever." She holds her hand up against her forehead like she's about to faint. "But Max is the first guy I've ever really liked, and dating doesn't exactly come with a manual. Sometimes the whole thing feels so overwhelming. I don't want to be the person who misses out on all the high school and college things for whoever they're dating. I want to do all the things we've ever said we're going to do."

I'd only ever noticed how completely submerged she was in all things Max. I hadn't seen any sign that she's been nervous about it or that it overwhelmed her, until now. Guilt settles itself in my gut because all of this is totally new information, and as Ximena's best friend, it absolutely shouldn't be.

"I'm so sorry, Mena. For everything. For the terrible friend I've been to you this year, for everything I kept from you and how much I let you down." The words come pouring out of me like a hose on full blast. "You always see the very best version of me. I want to be her, the Quinn you think I am."

"Everything's been . . . I don't know. Weird." Ximena shrugs. "I'm ready for it not to be that anymore."

"Oh my god, me too!" My face is probably going to split in half from the massive grin spread across it.

"I know it's always been me and you—"

"Yeah, it has. But there can be room for other people, too."

Ximena squeals and rushes to swallow me in a giant hug, and I squeeze her back, burying my face in her thick curls. Even though it's probably never going to be easy sharing Ximena with all the people who will come into our lives, it was silly to think we would stay the same forever. Ximena's changed this year, but so have I, and maybe that's okay.

"Speaking of others," Ximena murmurs against my ear before we separate.

"Hey. Everything okay?" Asher suddenly slips into the seat next to me. I shrug because it's hard to put into words that I feel like a wet towel wrung out too many times, or that I'm still surprised we're speaking again. "I tried FaceTiming you last night."

"Sorry. Ava and I told our parents everything, so I was kind of busy."

Asher leans back in his chair, letting out a long, low whistle. "How'd they take it?"

I purse my lips. "Pretty much how I thought they would. They were supposed to be with Ava meeting with Principal Stewart this morning, but I haven't seen or heard from any of them."

"Actually, I saw two police officers with Bryce Marks in the front office just now."

"Um. What?" Ximena says.

It's like the floor has been pulled out from under me, because instantly I understand.

The signs were there all along. How committed she was to finding the Turners. Desperate, even. How she dropped Model UN and didn't seem at all fazed when that customer started ranting about government conspiracies. And how Ava was so desperate to protect the identity of the caller, even when our parents pressed her on it last night.

Bryce was the one who made the bomb threat.

The two have been inseparable this year, and Ava obviously didn't want to tell anyone it was Bryce because she knew this was how it would end if she did.

"Okay, what is happening right now, Q?" Ximena says, waving a hand in front of my face and making me jump.

"Bryce is the one who made the bomb threat the night of the Sadie Hawkins." Just saying the words out loud makes me want to vomit.

"That makes no sense." Ximena looks at me and frowns. "I thought it was a prank."

"Unless"—Asher takes a shuddering breath—"it has something to do with Defend Kids?"

A grim silence settles over us as it sinks in.

"I have to find Ava," I say. She must be in the front office with Mom and Dad, watching all of this unfold right in front of her.

"I'll come with you," Ximena says, already on her feet.

"Me too," Asher says.

News must have spread quickly because half the school is milling outside the front office by the time we make it there. I scan the crowd for any sign of my sister, her purple hair or her backpack, but I don't see her anywhere. I grit my teeth and push headfirst into the sea of butts and crotches.

"Excuse me, sorry, excuse me, can I squeeze by, please?" I keep my eyes trained on the floor until I reach the front, where Mrs. Mendez, the secretary, pleads with everyone to leave. But Ava and my parents aren't there either.

"Everyone needs to go back to class, please," Mrs. Mendez says loudly, her voice straining over the noise in the hallway. "Fourth period starts in ten minutes!" Eventually she throws her hands up and retreats back into the office, securing the door shut with a purposeful *click*.

A few people drift away, but a second later, Principal Stewart's office door opens and he steps out with Bryce sandwiched between two police officers. They move to the main office door, Principal Stewart at the front, and the crowd moves back to make room for them.

"I want everyone out of here right now or else it's an automatic detention," Principal Stewart barks as soon as he opens the door and students scatter.

The officers lead Bryce out through the door. Her hands are cuffed behind her back and a female officer has a hand on her arm. Bryce's head is ducked low, but I can still see tears streaming down her face behind the curtain of her blond curls. As they lead her out the door, I catch a glimpse of her T-shirt, which reads *Model UN: Football for Smart People.*

She looks afraid, small. Like she's not quite sure how she ended up here. I don't know what her story is or how she got caught in the darkness of D3, but I know Bryce isn't a bad person. And Dillon probably isn't either, despite all the things people say about him.

"Quinn." Principal Stewart's voice makes me jump. When I turn, he's wearing a weary frown. "Your parents took your sister home, but they'll be back to talk about that other matter. Come to my office at the end of fourth period."

"Okay."

He nods and pushes through the remaining group of kids back to his office.

I turn to Asher and Ximena. "I need your help with something. Both of you."

"Anything," Ximena says, and Asher nods.

"I think we need to do one last post for The Whine."

"What about?"

"About this, all of it," I say, gesturing to Bryce, the crowd, and the couple of people in it still wearing D3 sweatshirts. "I might not be able to stop people from believing in D3. But I can tell them everything I know about the lies they've been fed and about the people doing it. It's like Mrs. Newcomb said. We have to try to give truth a fighting chance. Can you meet me in the gym after school?"

There's got to be a way to pull people like Bryce and Dillon back into the light.

After school, Ximena, Asher, and I head outside near the ramp. My teeth knock together, and I swallow back the lump in my throat while my hands clench into fists in my lap. I should feel at least a little better after my meeting with Principal Stewart. After I explained how Cade doxed me, he said he would give me a new school email address so D3 can't reach me there anymore and promised there would be consequences for Cade.

But I'm about to show myself on The Whine for the first time ever, and suddenly I'm terrified. Asher hovers in front of me with my phone pointed at me and nods to say he's recording. I hesitate. My brain warns me that D3 members think I, at best, lied about the Turner kids being fake or, at worst, am a member of the Cabal. If a member of D3 was willing to go hold a whole bank hostage, I'm not particularly safe. But Ximena smiles at me encouragingly from behind Asher, and it's enough. This is something I need to do. I take a deep breath and start talking.

TheWhine:

"Um. Hi. My name is Quinn. I'm a junior in high school and I run The Whine.

"A few months ago, some people started a hoax about kids they claimed were missing. For a long time, I believed it and I even posted about them here. But the whole thing was totally made up. The kids didn't even exist.

"The same people who started this hoax have also been falsely claiming that my Instagram account and all my posts were coded messages that were evidence of a big conspiracy that some anonymous person has been posting about. They call that person the Defender.

"But it's all a lie. I started my account a few years ago to try to promote the awesome part of New York that I'm from. And that's all it's ever been.

"Until a few weeks ago, I had never even heard of the Defender or the group that calls themselves D3. The real truth is that the people promoting it are just trying to take advantage of you. Most of them know none of what they're saying is true.

"I've seen this conspiracy hurt actual people I care

about and I just want it to stop.

"I never meant to amplify something that wasn't true and I'm very sorry that I did. I—I . . . I just wanted you all to know the truth."

chapter thirty

The whispers start when I get to school the next day and follow me down the hall to my locker, but they crescendo as I'm reaching for my French workbook on the bottom shelf. I don't think I'm imagining them. Usually the hall is almost deafeningly loud between periods, but all I can hear is a quiet hum of murmuring behind me.

I shift a little in my chair to glance around and find two pairs of eyes watching me.

"Um, hey," I say to Sasha Millburn, one of the sets of eyes. She doesn't reply, but cups a hand around her mouth to whisper something to Kiran Castiglione, like her hand is a magic cloak of invisibility that will hide the fact that she's obviously talking about me. Kiran's blond eyebrows lift in response to whatever Sasha said, and she shakes her head at me.

I know it's because of the video I made about D3 and posted after I reactivated The Whine yesterday. After I posted it, I gave my phone to Ximena and had her change the password to my account so I wouldn't be tempted to look at my notifications. But before I did, the video had already gotten more than a thousand views. I can't even imagine how many people have watched it since. All the attention on me right now suggests it's a lot.

I turn back and grope around for my other books, plunging my face into the dark safety of my locker. Maybe I'll skip the next time I need to change out my books because, somehow, the whispers are getting worse.

Behind me, the hallway has filled a little more, and I can feel dozens of eyes on the back of my head. What did I expect was going to happen after blowing up the conspiracy so many people in my town fell for? My bangs are going to have to do some serious magic blinder work today. At least there's one person I don't have to worry about—Cade. Principal Stewart called Mom and Dad last night to let them know that he had suspended Cade for doxing me. And it might be worse for Cade than that because after Bryce was arrested, Phoenix came forward and admitted to Principal Stewart that his and Lily's kidnapping was fake and that Cade was behind it all, according to a text he sent Ximena. Doxing isn't illegal, but faking a kidnapping definitely is.

When I drop my workbook into my lap and close my locker, Dillon McRae's on the other side of it.

"Why'd you do it?" he barks, his camouflage coat zipped up to his throat even though we're inside. "Why did you post that video?"

I swallow hard. "I told you I didn't know anything about D3 and I wasn't some secret translator. I thought everyone else deserved to know that, too."

He furrows his brow. "So this whole time you really were just posting about normal stuff. The wolf picture and the bank picture and all of it?"

"Yes. They weren't some secret code or whatever," I say.

"And what you said about the Turner kids—"

"I meant it, too. They don't exist. And Cade made up Phoenix and Lily's entire disappearance. I overheard Phoenix and Cade talking about how it was all fake."

"But that means . . ." He trails off, like the words are just too painful.

I finish the sentence for him. "The whole conspiracy was made up, Dillon." His lips press together so firmly, all the blood drains from them and they almost disappear. "None of what D3 says is true. Not the stuff about the Nodes, or about the missing kids. People are just seeing what they want to see, making claims about things that actually mean nothing. Someone faked the Turners, just like Cade faked Lily and Phoenix's disappearance. It means that the Defender is a liar."

I probably shouldn't be so blunt with Dillon, but he needs to know the truth. Dillon's eyes flick to the D3 patch still on his coat and in that second, his face shifts through about twenty different emotions—confusion, betrayal, anger, panic, disorientation—as he realizes that if I didn't know anything about D3, that my posts couldn't be the evidence the Defender says they are, and that maybe everything he believes about the Defender is wrong, too.

But accepting what I'm saying means Dillon will be rejecting probably the one community he feels like he fits in. If Asher was right, and Dillon turned to D3 because of losing his dad, cutting off that community won't be easy to do.

"There are a bunch of articles about how conspiracy theories work," I say carefully. "I think it'd help you understand how D3 tricks people. I can text you the links if you want to read them."

"Like, give you my phone number?"

"Yeah," I say, hoping I won't regret it.

Dillon chews on his bottom lip, his hands curling into fists. "Okay," he finally says.

He recites his phone number before heading down the hall, and I take the first proper breath I've managed since he cornered me. Maybe none of it will change his mind at all. But maybe it will. Either way, he's questioning things now, and that seems like something.

"New friend?" I hear Ximena's voice behind me.

"Hardly. Though I guess stranger things have happened, as we found out this year. Actually, I kind of just blew up his whole worldview. He's a D3 believer."

"Figures. He's always been creepy."

"Trust me, there's a lot that's creepy about D3. But I think Dillon is more . . . lost than creepy? He was just looking for answers, like the rest of us, and found all the wrong ones in all the wrong places."

"I can get that." She pushes a chunk of curls behind her shoulder. "Doing the video was very brave of you, if I haven't said it yet."

"You've said it about fifty times since yesterday. But it wasn't brave," I say, because with all the whispers and stares, I wish I could crawl into a hole and hibernate for however long it takes for people to forget what I did. "It was literally the least I could do. Just setting the record straight and making sure that they can't use The Whine for their conspiracy anymore."

"Still. I'm proud of you, and I can tell Asher is, too."

I can feel my cheeks warm a little. "Maybe. He did ask if I wanted to hang out at his house this weekend. He and his dad built a ramp for me."

Ximena swallows back the squeal I can tell she wants to release and nods thoughtfully instead. "Cool, cool."

I laugh.

Two tenth-grade boys are staring at me and whispering from across the hall, so Ximena screws up her face and sticks out her tongue at them. They jump. "Yeah, maybe go whisper about the girl who got arrested yesterday for making a fake bomb threat. Or about the kid who just got suspended for the rest of the year for doxing their classmate and making up a whole conspiracy. Or about the two people who faked their own kidnapping. Or *maybe* just mind your own business!" They shrug and wander away. Ximena sighs long and low before turning back to me. "Honestly, out of all of them, you're the least interesting to gossip about. No offense," she says as loudly as she can. "Did Ava come to school today?"

I shake my head.

"That was probably a good idea."

"Apparently Bryce's dad got her out on bail. It's not like Ava thought she would be at school or something, but I think she just can't deal right now."

Ava said Bryce called her and asked her to come over right after she'd made the bomb threat, when Ava had been driving around to clear her head. Bryce told Ava she did it because people weren't taking the threat from the Cabal seriously enough and she thought she had to do something to wake people up. But a few minutes after she'd done it, Ava said, Bryce started freaking out about it. That's why Ava thought she might be able to pull Bryce back out from the darkness of D3. She realized she couldn't once she saw the tunnel of flyers at school. Ava dissolved into tears again from her bed where she was telling me the story yesterday, and I could feel my heart snap just watching her.

I almost chickened out from posting the video on The Whine after Asher, Ximena, and I were done recording. But I couldn't get the image of Bryce being led away by the police or Ava's words out of my head. If D3 has messed up someone like Bryce and that gunman in Georgia so much, I had to do whatever I could to stop the group.

"Do I even want to know how bad it is?" I eye Ximena's phone hanging in her hand at her side.

"No," she says. "You definitely don't. It turns out lots of conspiracy theorists are also misogynists and ableist. Lots of angry people live on the internet. Who knew?"

Besides locking me out of it, Ximena's also keeping an eye on the notifications in case people started making threats, and I had her delete every single post I ever made, except for the video. I want to leave it up for as long as possible so people will see it. You would think I'd be sad about losing all the years of my posts and my sponsors, but mostly I just want it to actually work this time.

"People have got to see the truth about D3 now," Ximena says, as if reading my thoughts.

"I hope so. The Defender hasn't posted since my post about the

Turners, so maybe my video will be the end of it." There's almost nothing I want more.

"Totally. Remember when Harper Gianotta did that TikTok video of her piercing her nose when we were freshmen and a week later, half the school was doing it, too? I had to stop, like, four girls from stabbing their noses with safety pins in between classes in the bathroom. But then Harper's got infected and suddenly nose rings were over. I bet it'll be like that."

I nod, but I wonder if that's true just as a senior girl I've never spoken to says not so quietly to her friend as she passes us, "*I think she just wanted attention.*"

For a second, I tilt my head down, letting my bangs do their work. But the truth is, they can't hide me from the whole school or whatever the internet is saying about me. At least next week is Thanksgiving break and then it'll be winter break in a few weeks, so I'll be able to hide out for a while and hope people move on to something else.

"Ignore them. They can think what they want to think. And hey, at least we won't have to deal with Cade anymore. They'll arrest him as soon as they can prove he planned the whole Phoenix and Lily thing." Ximena holds out her hand and I smile up at her before lacing my fingers in hers. She starts walking down the hall, towing me along with her while I steer with my other hand on my wheel. It's something we haven't done since we were in middle school—her idea to save my shoulders from getting shredded from long distances. I let the cold metal slide against the skin of my palm with my other hand.

"I was thinking," I say. "Maybe I'll rejoin the newspaper staff next semester. I'm going to have some free time without The Whine, and Mrs. Newcomb said the paper has editorial freedom now. And maybe she's right about it helping educate people about the truth and stuff."

Ximena smiles down at me, the kind that makes me feel warm even on the coldest New York day. "I think they'd be lucky to have you, Quinnifred."

I squeeze her hand and she squeezes back, and together, we block out all the whispers.

D3Map

I have been silent these last few months, but that's because I've been working. Don't give up, D3f3nd3rs. A well-placed source tells me the Cabal moved the WOLVES before our loyal soldier could get to them. Stay vigilant. There are NODES everywhere, always on the MOVE. We've been planning, and now we're READY. Our work isn't done. #S2AIA

Posted by D3F3ND3R
March 17

Author's Note

As a former CIA officer and an expert on disinformation threat analysis, I have spent years studying the governments, groups, and people who intentionally create and spread lies online—what is called disinformation. I've always wanted to understand why anyone would knowingly lie and why people would believe lies and, as a proud tech nerd, how they spread those lies. But I'm most interested in the impact of falsehoods and conspiracy theories: how people fall for wild claims without evidence as a way of bringing a kind of order to what they otherwise see as chaos around them, how conspiracies can change people and whole communities, and how steadily consuming false and misleading content can influence a person's decisions and their beliefs. This is one of the reasons I wrote my first book, *True or False: A CIA Analyst's Guide to Spotting Fake News*, a nonfiction exploration of how lies have been used throughout history.

Conspiracy theories have always been a thing. In 1954, a fringe religious group called the Seekers in Illinois believed that the earth was going to be destroyed in a massive flood, but that everyone who believed in the group would be saved by extraterrestrial beings the group called the Guardians. The head of the Seekers even picked a date on which the event was supposed to occur and dutiful believers showed up to her house on that day to wait for something that never occurred. Each time neither the Guardians nor the flood arrived, the Seekers came up with different excuses and picked another date for the events to occur. Eventually the group gave up, but not because they stopped believing in what they thought was a prophecy—because they had convinced themselves that they had been righteous enough that they had spared the earth from the flood. Three social psychologists studied this group and through it coined the term *cognitive dissonance*. That is, a phenomenon where people will dig in their heels when presented with evidence and facts that contradict their personal beliefs. In other words, people don't like to be wrong.

The Seekers were not the first conspiracy theory, nor were they the last. History is filled with them: Bigfoot, Area 51, flat Earth, and chemtrails, among many, many others. The difference between early conspiracy theories and today is that people who believe in conspiracy theories now have social media. I can't help but wonder if the Seekers would have been a much larger group if social media existed back then and they could have broadcast their beliefs to the whole world, because similar groups have become very popular through the internet and social media.

In *At the Speed of Lies*, I wanted to explore the dangerous impact on just one small town in America in which people got steadily sucked into a conspiracy theory, propelled by fear and worry into no longer believing the facts and evidence in front of them, and who make terrible, life-changing choices as a result. Using fictional characters (who I hope you loved!) was a way to show how easy it is to be pulled in without realizing it, and how what happens in one place can easily affect what's happening elsewhere, simply because we're all so interconnected online. It can often seem impossible that anyone would believe in conspiracies, like the Seekers, but the reality is, it's a slippery slope. A claim can start off as something that sounds logical, maybe with even a kernel of truth in it, like the fact that kids do go missing. And then it slowly twists people into believing increasingly extreme and false conspiratorial ideas.

Though fictional, this story is based on actual events and conspiratorial beliefs that are still spreading all over the world. In 2016, anonymous and fake social media accounts started falsely claiming that high-profile Democratic politicians were operating a global child trafficking ring. As the conspiracy theory spread online, some people claimed the proof was in a batch of hacked emails they believed contained coded messages. The belief spread so quickly that that same year, an armed man drove from North Carolina to a pizza parlor in Washington, DC, where he believed that kidnapped children were being held. He livestreamed his attempt to storm the restaurant, but when he and his viewers did not find any children being held there, it did not stop the conspiracy from continuing to spread all over the world, eventually leading to the formation of a conspiracy movement called QAnon whose adherents believe, like D3 did, in prophecies left by an anonymous person they call Q. Child rights organizations, antitrafficking nonprofits, and police departments have all said that the growth of the group has led to so many false reports about supposed missing kids that their resources are being stretched to the max and they are distracted from finding real missing children. This is just one of the dangers of spreading falsehoods online.

When I was a kid, conspiracy theories were considered fringe beliefs, ideas you'd maybe heard of but no one you actually knew believed. As they are becoming increasingly mainstream, it is important to understand how they work, and especially how dangerous they can be. For additional reading and resources, check out cindyotis.com/resources.

Acknowledgments

I've been writing stories since I learned how to hold a pencil, so publishing this—my debut novel—was quite a journey, and I received so much help, support, and encouragement along the way.

First, thank you to every disabled reader and creator. When I was a kid, I desperately searched for novels with main characters doing interesting or exciting things while also being disabled, and I came up mostly empty-handed. So I wrote my own. This novel isn't about disability—rather, it's about a girl in the crosshairs of a quickly shifting world and she's disabled. Our stories don't start and stop with disability, and disability representation in literature is starting to recognize that. This evolution would not be possible without people like you writing and supporting our stories. Our experiences as disabled people in a very abled world are not all the same, but I hope you saw something of yourself in Quinn and felt proud of our wonderfully diverse community.

Thank you to Caryn Wiseman, my agent and champion, for believing in me and my words.

To my whole team at Scholastic: It takes a village to produce a book, and I'm so grateful for mine. To Jody Corbett, my incredible and thoughtful editor: It's not an exaggeration to say you made my actual dreams come true. Thank you for being my partner in this and for loving Quinn as much as I do. I'm endlessly grateful.

Thank you to David Levithan; to production editor Janell Harris, designer Cassy Price, and editorial assistant Kassy Lopez; to the extraordinary publicity team of Erin Berger, Seale Ballenger, and Aleah Gornbein; to the wonderful Lizette Serrano, Emily Heddleson, Sabrina Montenigro, Maisha Johnson, and Meredith Wardell of library marketing; to Rachel Feld and Avery Silverberg of marketing; and to the sales team: Kelsey Albertson, Holly Alexander, Julie Beckman, Tracy Bozentka, Savannah D'Amico, Barbara Holloway, Sarah Herbik, Roz Hilden, Brigid Martin, Liz Morici, Dan Moser, Nikki Mutch, Sydney Niegos, Caroline Noll, Debby Owusu-Appiah, Bob Pape, Jacqueline Perumal, Betsy Politi, Jackie Rubin, Chris Satterlund, Terribeth Smith, Jody Stigliano, Sarah Sullivan, Melanie Wann, Jarad Waxman, and Elizabeth Whiting.

I am so lucky to have had the support and friendship of several talented authors and creators who have inspired me with their own work. My deepest thanks to Sarah Darer Littman, my friend and fellow Writer of Seriously Tough Stories; to Becky Albertalli, whose sincere kindness and talent continues to make the world a better place; to Nadine van der Velde: Honestly? Still not sure what I did to deserve your friendship; and to my book bestie, Jennifer Iacopelli, for telling me to add the *At* in *At the Speed of Lies* and for so much more. Thanks also to Kiersten White, Gloria Chao, Natalie C. Parker, Adib Khorram, Emily Lloyd-Jones, Cindy Pon, Liz Lawson, Jennifer Moffet, Courtney Summers, and Lillie Lainoff for their support. My deepest appreciation to the talented authors of the Roaring 20s debut group, whose mid-pandemic start may have been rocky but whose future is only bright.

Thank you to my dear friends who have listened to me talk about this book for literally years, read so many of my trunked manuscripts, and sometimes had more faith in me than I had in myself. Kelly, Sheryl, Kim, Kathy, Elizabeth, David, Siobhan, Nina, Peg, Arielle, and the many Ryans I'm lucky to know: You truly are a squad of some of the best cheerleaders a girl could ask for.

When I was a sick kid trying to figure out life, I was lucky enough to have a Ximena of my own. Megs, your friendship was one of the brightest spots of my childhood, and I'm so grateful.

For Wade Jacoby, who is so missed by everyone who knew him. I've wondered so many times what you would think of this book—I hope you'd be proud.

Thank you to the beautiful and inspiring small towns, landscapes, small businesses, and people who make up my home area of Western and Central New York, especially the Finger Lakes, where this novel takes place.

To my family: the siblings and the kiddos; my nephews, nieces, and niblings; my aunt and uncle; and my cousins, for cheering me on.

And especially to my parents: When it comes down to it, each book I am lucky enough to write will always be because of—and for—you.

About the Author

Cindy L. Otis is a former CIA officer, a national security expert, and the author of the nonfiction book for young readers *True or False: A CIA Analyst's Guide to Spotting Fake News*. In addition, she is a frequent media commentator and writes regularly about national security issues, often cited by the *Washington Post*, the *New York Times*, the BBC, NPR, and CNN. You can visit her online at cindyotis.com.